WHERE THERE'S A WILL

C STREET MYSTERY
BOOK 3

RICK ROTHERMEL

ROUGH
EDGES
PRESS

Rough Edges Press
An Imprint of Wolfpack Publishing
9850 S. Maryland Parkway, Suite A-5 #323
Las Vegas, Nevada 89183

roughedgespress.com

Paperback ISBN 978-1-68549-235-9
eBook ISBN 978-1-68549-234-2
LCCN 2023941183

This book, its story, and characters are dedicated to the memory of the late great David Janssen. He could become anyone, and his "Richard" and "Harry" were great inspirations to this and many other storytellers.

Thanks to my friends, confidants, and legal advisers, David Beuoy and Bill Barrett.

WHERE THERE'S A WILL

1

Beverly Hills, California — April 26, 2002

A well-polished bright-red Ford F-450 truck—with an aluminum "rollback" vehicle deck—idled slowly past the circular driveway of an upscale midcentury home on the hillside a half-mile west of the iconic HOLLYWOOD sign. Atop the deck, behind the truck cab, sat a pristine, restored, bright-red 1968 Shelby Mustang GT500KR fastback. The driver stopped, checked the address on his clipboard, and steered the truck onto the polished paving stone surface of the driveway. As he stopped in front of the stylish home, an attractive, well-dressed blonde woman in her thirties walked from the front landing and stood smiling as the driver—a rotund Black man wearing tailored overalls—opened his door. His white cloth oval name tag read "Philip."

She smiled at the driver and said, "It's even more stunning out in the sun. He's gonna love it!"

The driver smiled as he greeted her. "Hello, Miss Tate! Yes ma'am. I got plenty of admirers an' lots of 'thumbs up' on the freeway up from La Jolla." He offered his hand. "I'm Phillip Atkins, and this is your new, or rather new, classic, Mustang Shelby

GT500KR. Give me a few minutes to get it off the truck, we'll do a delivery inspection, and I'll wipe it down for you. I don't think we'll find any flaws, but you have to be the judge of that. Your word rules. After we look it over, I'll get your signature and get out of your way."

He turned to the levers at the side of the truck and set the motions to lower the deck to the driveway. The last step was to back the car from the deck and park it beside the truck in front of the house.

Philip Atkins hesitated, then started, "Ma'am, I know we're not supposed to fawn over our customers, but I have to say my wife is one of your biggest fans. We both love that *Trauma Center Hospital* series you star in. Our oldest daughter loves it too. She's in school now to become an EMT. Your work in that show has had a great impact on a lot of people."

Sylvia Tate smiled and reached out to touch his right arm. "Oh, Philip, thank you so much. That's always so good to hear. As actors, we sometimes wonder if anyone is paying attention. That's a great ensemble cast and crew, and I'm proud to be a small part of it."

"Yes, ma'am. Well, here's your car. Now if you see any flaws that weren't there last Thursday when you signed the papers, you point 'em out to me."

With that, Philip started walking around the car, examining the surfaces, his digital camera at the ready, waiting for her to point out flaws. There were none, but he would occasionally flick away tiny pieces of road dirt and dust with a microfiber cloth that he was using to wipe dust off the car's flanks.

Sylvia Tate followed him around the car, caressing the lustrous scarlet sheet metal with her fingers. "Now, Phillip, you just call me Sylvia. Thank you for the compliments. That has been a great run for the entire cast, and we'll be on it for two more years at least." Their small talk continued as they completed the exam of the car. "It's absolutely beautiful, Phillip. My fiancé is going to love it."

"You're getting married? Congratulations! He is a lucky man."

He proffered a stainless-steel ballpoint pen and an inspection approval form on the clear Lucite clipboard for her signature.

"Oh, we've been together for years. It's just time, ya know?" She put pen to paper, then turned to him and smiled. "Hold on, let me get something from the house."

As she stepped back, he asked, "Where can I park the car for you, ma'am?"

"Phillip, it's *Sylvia*! Just back it into the farthest garage stall if you would; I'll be right back." She trotted toward the open front door.

Moments later, as Philip finished restoring the truck bed to its travel position, Sylvia Tate returned, holding two photos and a Sharpie felt-tip marker. Smiling, she laid the photos on the deck of his truck and asked, "What's your wife's name, hon?"

"She's Marilyn."

The first photo was a publicity shot of the *Trauma Center Hospital* cast. With a flourish, Sylvia Tate signed, 'To Marilyn, Phil's a HUNK! Best wishes always, Sylvia Tate.' She handed the photo to Philip, saying, "Wave it back and forth so it'll dry quicker." With a sly smile, she went to the second photo, a photo of a slightly younger Sylvia in a demure one-piece swimsuit wearing a come-hither stare. She signed, 'Phil: Love ya! We'll always have SHELBY! Syl...' She waved the photo as he had done, then handed it to him and smiled.

"Well, thank you so much, ma'am...I mean, Sylvia. It's been so nice to meet you."

She moved to stand beside him, taking his small camera from his hand and pointing it at them, selfie-style. As she pressed the button to take the image, she planted a kiss on his cheek, leaving him with a shocked expression. Then, giggling like a schoolgirl, she placed a crisp hundred-dollar bill in the upper chest pocket of his uniform.

"You stop on the way back south, Philip, and get a nice lunch, my treat."

"Well, I don't know what to say. Thank you so much, ma...er,

Sylvia." He gathered his photos and regained his truck. "You have a wonderful day."

With that, Philip started the big truck and slowly rolled toward the street. Sylvia Tate watched and waved, then sprinted toward the house, pushing the front door closed with her elbow as she passed. Finally in the bathroom, she leaned over the toilet and puked for thirty seconds, which seemed more like a half-hour.

She'd been warned. This first trimester was gonna be a solid bitch.

2

It was a few minutes after one o'clock on that warm, breezy September afternoon. My ankle was hurting. It itched under the cast. The cast would come off that next Saturday, and I'd already decided that I'd probably spend half of that day scratching the itch. I was home that day, walking my corner property, clearing stray fallen palm fronds as I waited for my latest referral client. Wade Hawkins was a businessman from somewhere in the Deep South. My attorney referral had said that Hawkins was in Southern California to settle his parents' estate with his sister.

My job would be locating his estranged sister, reputed to be an actress. They'd had no contact in almost twenty years, and it seemed he would prefer to continue that tradition while granting her half of their parents' sizable estate.

A few minutes after one that afternoon, I heard the strained tones of a small white import sedan as it pulled into my driveway, coming to a stop behind my Trailblazer. The door opened, and a middle-aged Caucasian male, one Wade Hawkins, stepped out. He was dressed in a gray suit that had been well-tailored for his slightly thick frame. He stood a bit less than six feet and wore a crisp white shirt that was unbuttoned at the neck. He had a receding hairline and graying temples. Frowning, he closed his car door. He wasn't smiling. I speculated that he rarely did so.

He walked toward me as I approached his car. I extended my hand, he shook with me. His grip was unimpressive. "I'm Street. Thanks for driving out. I apologize for the imposition." I motioned toward my foot. "How was your trip out?"

He looked across at me with a sour expression. "Oh, it was hideous, as I have come to expect in this city. I've been out here a few times on business, traveling to and from has always been a nightmare. That said, I suppose LAX isn't all that much worse than the Atlanta airport. That one is a genuine bear to navigate."

"Having experienced both venues, I think I'll vote for Atlanta airport almost any time over that other place. I'll toss in a negative vote for DFW in Dallas as well. LAX just needs a new home, away from the rest of LA." I looked at him and saw a bead of sweat and a torrent of dissatisfaction. "Follow me. Let's get out of this heat." I turned and walked with him toward the double doors that opened into my office/den combination. I'd been in the house for almost two years by then and had made strides toward renovating the more oft-visited areas of the house. Guy's gotta keep up appearances. The new HVAC system hummed softly, and the ceiling fan stirred the cooler interior atmosphere.

I walked to my desk and offered him the leather guest chair opposite my position. "So, tell me how I can help you, Mr. Hawkins. Ms. Noel told me you are looking for your younger sister and that you've been out of touch for a while."

He looked across at me and spoke with a weary tone and a moderate southern accent. "Yes, Ann left home the week after she graduated high school. Some guy from out of town told her she was pretty, and she bought his whole line. Her departure just crushed our mother's spirit for years. She came to LA to get discovered, ended up doing God knows what with God knows who, just to survive."

He coughed, then cleared his throat and continued. "My daddy was the biggest fish in a very small pond, Mr. Street. He built a very successful group of businesses as he worked very hard and very smart for decades. Our mother passed almost a year ago, and he just recently followed. Their wills both stipulated that upon their passing, their proceeds be distributed equally between their living heirs. Since our two younger siblings are predeceased, Ann and I are the recipients. My local counsel recommended that I employ assistance out here to settle the matter. I am hoping to expedite the solution. That's the sole reason for my trip."

"That all aligns with what Lynn has mentioned. First, I'm sorry for your loss. Now, let's see what I can do to locate your sister. I've done a lot of work along those lines for Ms. Noel, and I should be able to wrap this up in a brief period. She tells me that you have some pictures of your sister? Some letters from her? Some past addresses?"

"Yes, sir, I do." He opened his briefcase, withdrew a short stack of papers, and laid them in front of me. "Look at these and see if there's anything of value."

I looked at the stack and then at him and said, "I'll check these out and return them to Ms. Noel. If I may ask, where are you staying while you're in town?"

"We're at the Embassy Suites South, next to the airport. My wife has never been out here. We're taking a few days' vacation while this is being dealt with. They stuck us in a room in the front, there's a lot of airport noise. I'm not sleeping all that well there."

I grinned. "I know the place quite well. I stayed there when I was moving here a couple of years ago." I smiled at the memory. "It can get noisy at times. I was in room 218 for five weeks straight while I waited for my house to close and transfer. The noise didn't bother me all that much, but I knew it was there. When you get back this afternoon, just ask the front desk to move you to a different room. The ones on the south side of the hotel, toward the west end, near the pool, are usually the last to fill on the weekends. They're much quieter. There's no noise from the Cantina on the first floor in the evenings either."

He frowned, pursed his lips, and said, "That's a good idea. I'll ask about that when I get back down there."

"And I have another idea. If you wish, I can help with a better car while you're out here. A friend in the South Bay area handles executive car rentals. He services accounts for the movie studios and aerospace firms in the South Bay. His cars usually go to the executive producers and studio types, so they're Cadillacs and Lincolns, some Lexus sedans and the like. What do you drive at home?"

"I have a white Escalade. My wife has a new CTS."

I smiled. "Ah. I had you pegged as a Cadillac guy. Nice cars. What franchises did your family have?"

"Oh, we had a few. Pontiac, Cadillac, Saturn, GMC trucks, Massey Ferguson, John Deere, several others. When Daddy passed, I closed them down, sold the farm implement operations to a long-time rival nearby. The land is worth a lot now, and GM is going nowhere fast, so it's a pre-emptive move on our part. Time to move on."

I nodded. "That's interesting. So...let me get in touch with my friend. You can call your rental agency and have them pick up your renter from the Embassy Suites. I'll call Louie. He'll bring you a replacement this afternoon. He owes me a favor or six. We'll count it as part of our service. How long will you be out here?"

"I figure ten days or so. I want to take the wife to San Diego, maybe take a day trip up the coast. I hear Santa Barbara is quite nice this time of year."

"Santa Barbara is always beautiful. I can recommend a hotel there if you need a place."

"That sounds good, Mr. Street." He rose from his chair. "You can text me with that if you wish. You have my number. I will await your further developments."

I stood, walked around the desk, and followed him to the door to the patio, then to his car. He turned to me as he opened the driver's door.

"How long do you think your end in this matter will all take?"

"I'll start this afternoon. The material you left may give me some leads. Ms. Noel's office will keep you apprised." He opened the driver's door and took his seat in the car.

"Thanks again for coming out."

"No problem. Good luck with the ankle." He started his car, a Nissan something from the grille emblem, backed from the driveway, and again, stopping short of saying "Thanks."

As soon as Mr. Warmth left, I clomped back to my office and called Lynn Noel. She answered on the second ring, as usual. Her voice was bright and cheery, as always. Lynn was the most consistently cheerful and optimistic woman I had ever encountered.

"Hey, Street! How was your meeting with the grieving brother?"

"It went okay. He's a real bundle of warmth and passion, isn't he?"

"Seems so. He loses his dad and closes the businesses a few days after the funeral? Think of all the people he put out of work."

"What did he tell you about the sister?"

I could tell Lynn was smiling. "Oh, she's the root of all evil. She left the shelter and security of her family's home to come to tawdry Hollywood so she could become a world-class slut or something. Happens all the time. Did you see her pictures?"

"I'm looking at them now. She's a total babe, much like yourself. These pictures are from a while back, but I sort of recognize the face. I may have some of her work in my collection somewhere. Two hundred TV series DVDs on the shelf, she might be in there somewhere. How's hubby?"

I could hear her smile. She was married to one of my best friends. "He's borderline wondrous as usual. Thanks for asking." She paused. "Oh, and you are required to attend a cookout at our house on Sunday afternoon after five. He wants to show off his new barbecue grill. The thing is as big as a house."

"So I've heard. The new 'cue unit goes with the new patio, the new garage, and the two new cars, right?"

"Just one new car so far. Mine isn't here yet. Maybe next week or so, I'm told."

I chuckled. "Oh, the crosses we bear."

"Yeah, I know. I lucked out. I married a jeweler."

"One of the best."

"I'll tell him you said that."

I smiled. "He already knows, trust me."

3

I went to work immediately, partly to take my mind off my ankle. The materials that Wade Hawkins had left me were sketchy at best. There were a half dozen letters to her mother, each a youthful, excited pronouncement telling of some celebrity she'd met or a big part in a TV series that she had landed. She'd been in a few episodes of *Beverly Hills 90210*, cast in the early seasons of that decade-long ordeal as an attractive student—were there ever any others—in the background or eventually a less young, still very attractive teacher with a few spoken lines? A check on the IMDB website would help, but the names on the photos were obsolete, so I needed more current references.

Also included were a few headshots. These are the eight-by-ten-inch glossy photos that will introduce the subject in their most glamorous and hopeful form to potential agents and, hopefully later, casting staff, directors, and producers. The fondest hopes and dreams of all those potential De Niros and Streeps were represented in those photos. The names at the base of each picture varied. These pics displayed two pseudonyms used at early points in her career. The individual envelopes displayed three different addresses. I went to the map function on my computer to establish the locations and printed that image for future reference. I would soon learn much more.

Like any other element of the entertainment industry, the head-shot photography business is nothing if not self-promoting. Each of the pictures displayed a foil-stamped name label behind it, one Kiefer Silver-Graves. After I checked my copy of the *Production Industry Handbook* to ascertain Kiefer's current address, I called to set an appointment for two hours later.

Being an avid student of Hollywood history, I had traversed the avenues of the city in search of the city's rich media industry history. Early in my residence, especially when I was searching for a place to live, I had driven well over a thousand miles searching the LA Metro area looking for DVD stores, old movie theaters, and historic landmarks that could hold my interest for a few minutes. This particular area of East Hollywood was pretty cool on its own.

A few miles east of Hollywood proper—if there really is such a thing anymore—Griffith Park Boulevard winds through the older suburbs a half-dozen miles north of downtown LA. Many of the homes, singles and duplexes, dating back to one of the numerous boom times of the aircraft industries across the hills in the San Fernando Valley and the earliest periods of cinema and TV. The valley was ringed with more affluent homes and populated with the technical staff of the studios found on either side of the foothills.

Most of the exteriors for the classic *Three Stooges* and the *Our Gang* shorts from the thirties and forties were filmed in this area, and I knew that at least one of the historic soundstages still survived. Paramount Studios had used the close proximity to the area in the sixties and seventies for mysterious rendezvous in *Mission Impossible*. Joe Mannix had jumped off a quaint local bridge to escape assassins in one memorable episode. If you looked to the north, you could see the iconic Griffith Park Observatory perched atop the foothills like an oddly shaped marshmallow atop a really lumpy chocolate cake.

The tree-lined boulevard, three lanes wide with parking on the south side, was packed solid. I found an empty slot a block away from the photo studio on my third pass. I walked back toward the three-story 'stacker' condo on the south side of the street, the formal location for KSG Photography. The entrance was an open two-slot garage door, vehicle entry impeded by a pair of traffic cones. A standup sign carrying an enlarged photo of a ridiculously handsome, smiling young Caucasian male on one side and his ideal genetic female match on the other. A well-rendered metallic silver Porsche Speedster replica sat in the center of the double garage stall, and the walls were lined with prior client's photos, each of them thumbtacked to the wood paneling.

Sitting sentry to the garage/waiting area was a rotund middle-aged mixed-race woman wearing an orange smock. As I approached, she stubbed out one cigarette, something very long and very thin, and lit the next. Eventually, as she exhaled, she looked up from the fifty-inch computer monitor and greeted me, providing with the greeting a strong whiff of the stale nicotine funk.

"How may I help you?" Her voice seemed smaller than the rest of her carriage.

I passed her my card. "I have an appointment with Kiefer."

She talked past her cigarette. "Yes, of course, you're Mr. Street. Please take a seat. He's wrapping up with his earlier client. He'll be with you momentarily."

I looked around and found a white plastic chair on the other side of the Porsche and took the perch for fifteen minutes until the photographer emerged from his inner sanctum. He followed a lithe young brunette woman and stared at her lovely rear visage as she walked. I'd have happily stared at any portion of her. The girl walked to the entry desk as Kiefer called out numbers to his sister. The girl turned, stepped back toward him, whispered something to him, kissed his cheek, then walked out of the studio.

With her departure, Kiefer stepped toward me and extended his hand. "Mr. Street! Thanks for coming in. We don't get many PIs here. Let's go back to the studio and you can tell me how I can assist you."

He led me through a labyrinth of small well-lit rooms and past a trio of sliding glass doors to his private office. He took a seat across from me behind a clear Lucite desktop. The small room was walled with headshots, some framed and autographed. I recognized a few of the faces and a couple of names. The variety and number of subjects were impressive. I opened my folder, laid the pictures I had in front of him, and explained, "I'm trying to locate one of your former clients for an attorney friend of mine. You shot these images of her before she changed her professional name at least once. It's a family matter and we're on the clock. Any assistance you can provide would be greatly appreciated."

He smiled a slightly crooked smile. "Ah! Anniegirl! Major babe when she hit the scene, and she's become one hell of a great actress." He looked from the photo to me. "We hooked up when we were both starting up." He looked back at the photo. "And my god, what a body that girl has! She was...is...amazing. I gotta tell you, brother, I have access to some of the most beautiful women in the friggin' *universe*, and I remember many of them. Annie is one of my all-time favorites."

"I see. So you did more than these, um...photo sessions with her."

He smiled. "Yeah. You know it. We were living together for a little over a year, and I am fully aware that we were using each other to our individual benefit. When she started getting better gigs she left, amicably, and we have remained friends. I did a set of pics with her a year ago. Her series work had given way to long-form TV movies and cable projects, and she wanted to create a new approach. She still looks amazing. We all get older, if we're lucky, but she has aged far better than most."

I knew what the photog was doing, telegraphing his success with women. Fine. More power to him. "That's great. So would you have any current contact information for her?"

"Certainly. You say this is a family matter?"

I explained, "Yes, the parents have passed, there is an estate to be settled. There are considerable assets that are subject to dispersal. Her brother is in town to deal with the matter, and he'd like to wrap this up as early as possible. I'm told that the brother and sister haven't spoken in years."

"Very well. Sounds good. I remember that she had issues with her family." He pulled out his well-traveled Rolodex and thumbed through the cards for thirty seconds. He withdrew one card, wrote the information on a file card, and then he hesitated. "But if you don't mind, I'd like to call her to get her okay before giving out her digits and address. She's a prominent figure now, and security for celebrities is always an issue. As a friend, that's the least I can do."

I concurred. "Please...be my guest."

He turned his chair from me, dialed his cell, and had a brief conversation. He read my business card to her and explained the situation momentarily. He looked over his shoulder, smiled, and winked at me as he ended his call. Then he swiveled back around toward me and passed me the information he had written on a sticky note.

"Here you go, buddy."

I looked at the file card, then back at Kiefer. I copied the information onto my own file card, then I passed his note back to him. "Well, thank you for your help, Keifer. I'm sure my attorney friend will appreciate the assistance. I'll pass the word about your work. She is far more photogenic than I will ever be, and I'd imagine that she or perhaps some of her clientele may have use for your talents."

Kiefer sorted a short stack of his business cards and handed them across the desk to me as he rose from his chair. "You run in a different crowd than I do, Street. Any referrals will certainly be rewarded." He reached across the desk, and we shook hands. "Now, if you'll excuse me, I have another new client waiting. It was great meeting you. Feel free to contact me any time." He walked around the desk and followed me past the camera post. "Let's have a beer sometime. I love cop stories."

"I have a few, but most of the time, it's just paperwork and following up on trivial information. Hardly any fistfights and no car chases lately at all. It gets boring at times."

"Ah. LA...another myth dissolved. Dammitall!" He put his hand on my shoulder and gave it a squeeze. "Thanks for coming by. Stay in touch, and good luck with the foot!"

————

After I regained my car, I checked the big Thomas Guide map book for the address the photographer had provided. A half-hour later, I drove past the house in advance of my phone contact—I'm big on recon.

The south-facing hillside a half-mile west of, and slightly below, the iconic HOLLYWOOD sign had been built up as a residential development in recent decades, with a labyrinth of streets lined with upscale homes, mostly builds from the 1970s-on. It's no Holmby Hills, but it's not bad. The subject house was a two-story hybrid, a modified A-frame built on a double grade, back from the street and concealed by thick shrubbery. A circular driveway with a polished paving stone surface served as most of the front yard. To the side of the wide, bright-red front door, small white neon digits called out the street number. A three-stall garage with red doors made up the rest of the street side. One garage was open, and a late-model black Infiniti sedan filled the space, license number SYLTATE.

This must be the place. I drove past, looped around the next block, and drove back past. Nothing had changed.

4

Now I had a familiarity with the goal address for the next day. After I spoke with the actress, now using the name Sylvia Tate, and set an appointment for the next day, I called Lynn and brought her up to date. With the day's work completed, I had the rest of the afternoon to myself, so I hit the 101 freeway southbound from home and spent the next forty-five minutes in traffic driving to the Golden West exit off the 405 in Orange County, on my way to visit my car. There's a story there.

I'm a lifelong car guy. When I was born, I was brought home from the hospital in my dad's college car, a bright-red 1969 Pontiac GTO. It was dead sharp, a Ram Air III with a four-speed stick. The Beach Boys played from the under-dash Sony 8-track over a bank of decent 6-by-9" speakers. It was a few years old by then, and still his pride and joy. I've been told that a ride in Dad's GTO would calm me down and/or put me to sleep at any time until my second birthday. The Goat gave way to a minivan when I was four years old and starting to gain siblings, but I still had vague memories of it. I had been a lifelong devotee of those cars, their era, and the genre.

In my second year as a cop with Atlantic City PD, I had been assigned to a support role in the raid of a large chop shop operated by a car theft ring. There were twenty of us working that day, and it made the local TV news that evening. As a lesser-ranked officer, I was tasked with a position in the inventory team. The job isn't over till the paperwork is done. Two days in, out at the back of the barn that served as headquarters for this crew of Toby Halicki-wannabes, were a half-acre variety of cars, most of them engine-less, windowless hulks. Each had to be recorded and documented as fully as possible to determine their origin. Among them was an old GTO.

Primer spotted, a little rough around the edges, missing its wheels, engine, transmission, and most of the interior. It had seen better decades but was still less molested than its abandoned brethren. I chronicled its VIN like all the others, and though I probably lingered a bit examining it, I put its record in the stack of file folders with the others. It may have been older and, in my mind, a little cooler than the other hulks we chronicled that day, but it was still ancient, tired, *beat*, and *used up*.

As part of the investigative procedure for the chop shop bust, we had to run the ownership records on every car we dealt with. After forty-one vehicles, the slog was almost over when I got the folder on the old GTO. Turned out it was my dad's old car, a half dozen owners, and three decades later. I was hooked by then. When the seizure auction took place three months later, I was one of three bidders. The car was ugly and useless unless you *really* knew what you were looking at. I had convinced myself that I did. I won it at auction with a final sealed bid of $280.10.

In the carport of my condo in AC, I spent the next year putting the car back in working order. With the strong muscle car after-market from the nineties on, anyone can build, or at least finish, one of these mid-sized 1960s General Motors A-body cars from a stack of catalogs. All it takes is money. I spent a good share of my savings on the project.

I first sourced a date-coded Pontiac 428 engine block and went a little overboard having it rebuilt at a shop out-of-state, ending three months later with a 462-cubic inch *stroker* unit that had mountains of torque. When complete, it would create a shade over 400 horsepower at the rear wheels but would still run happily on premium pump gas. That was backed with a T-56 6-speed manual and a Hurst shifter that I chose after driving a coworker's late-90s Camaro SS. A bulletproof Ford 9-inch differential with a 3.90 gear ratio from another Southern California vendor brought up the rear. Tubular exhaust headers, an aluminum driveshaft, a stainless-steel exhaust system, and a fresh reproduction gas tank finished that spend, creating a fast, solid drivetrain sitting in a seriously mismatched physical package.

The car lived in my carport while I waited for budget, parts, pieces, and simply the time to take it farther toward being roadworthy and a little less ugly. That project taught me many things, including basic welding skills and a strong dose of *how stuff works*.

The day after the shipper delivered the big wooden crate holding the newly-rebuilt engine was my last duty day before my annual vacation. Two weeks away from wearing a starchy uniform, sitting for hours in a tired Crown Victoria, either dealing with odorous miscreants or facing daily stacks of paperwork, sounded great. I was also planning an overdue weekend with my long-suffering fiancée.

Ange and I had met during my senior year in college and had dated off-and-on for five years as she finished school and began her own career. She had stood by while I began and became established in my career with the PD. We were a great match. Her family was blue-collar middle class, five kids, close-knit, just the way I'd always seen as ideal. She and I had gotten along beautifully, and her energy was incredible. That afternoon, she met me in the lobby of the massive casino/resort in Atlantic City an hour after my shift ended, and we began an idyllic weekend that would eventually change my life completely.

After a brief amorous session upstairs in a small suite that overlooked nothing in particular, we came back downstairs, had dinner, and wandered into the casino. Turned out there was a well-promoted citywide slot tournament running that weekend. Feeling adventurous, my fiancée signed me up for it. Long story short, by Sunday, my sessions put me in the top three finalists, and after a final bout late Sunday afternoon, I was deemed the lucky winner, to the tune of a shade over four million dollars.

I spent the next four hours in the administrative wing of the casino, walking away with a nine-figure certified check—two decimal points. Taxes from the state of New Jersey, the city's special gift to itself, and the IRS withholding for federal taxes whittled the net down to just under two million bucks. As a bonus, we were treated to a week free of charge, with all the trimmings, in the presidential suite of the major casino property. The local media had a few sessions with us as well. TV and the local papers portrayed me as a worthy public servant who just happened to have lucked out big-time. That publicity caused the only real problem.

I had been having a great time after the check cleared, going on a spending spree—a new wardrobe and a new little red Miata that my fiancée'd had her eye on for a while. Being a really generous guy, I also did a bit of detective work, made a couple of calls, and paid off her parents' mortgage, a small one but something that I knew had been worrisome for them. Her dad, a great friend of mine, was not a healthy man. Helping him out felt really good to me.

That following Thursday, I was asked to lunch by my ACPD supervisor and my duty sergeant. Therein lay the rub. Turned out the department had an obscure rule that barred officers from entering casinos on duty days, in uniform, for personal or non-official purposes. Since I had been recorded arriving at the location a half hour after my shift ended, still wearing my uniform, they took *offense,* and I was subject to *official* discipline that would slow my progress toward an upcoming, well-earned promotion. They didn't budge, neither would I. *Click.* Done.

To be honest, the end of my ACPD career really didn't bother me all that much. I was overqualified for street duty due to my master's degree in criminology. My unaccredited assistance in solving a few knotty unsolved criminal cases had gone unrewarded. I dunno, maybe they thought the degree made me *uppity* or something, but good work is good work. I tendered my resignation from the Atlantic City Police Department in person that afternoon as my bosses and I sat in the restaurant that afternoon, just before dessert was served.

I now had options. In discussions with my fiancée, I had voiced my favorite of the possibilities. I'd had a lifelong fascination with Southern California, and now that I had resources, I saw relocation as a workable option. We'd get married, move west, buy a house, and start our family. I'd get a cop job or maybe a PI license and make like my old heroes from afternoon TV reruns of classic '60s and '70s cop and detective shows.

Voicing that wish prompted the first argument my fiancée and I had ever had, and the last. It lasted almost a whole day. She steadfastly refused to leave her parents or her birthplace behind, even for a short time. I tried everything I knew to convince her, but after a day of strained conversation and more than a few tears on both sides of the question, we went our separate ways. It wasn't my choice. That night was the first I'd spent alone in over a year, and I didn't like it at all.

Now bereft of a mate and a job, I decided early that next sleepless morning to face my realities and go for it. I wasn't happy about either situation, but the sudden availability of funding started to ease my angst quite a bit. I did some online research regarding how things were done *out west* and started planning the move. I really got into it over the next week after I returned home, finishing the mechanical assembly on the Goat, making it roadworthy, selling my daily driver compact pickup, putting my condo on the market, holding a garage sale to offload assorted household junk, shipping some random household materials to a storage facility in Downey, California, opening an account and transferring funds to a new credit union in LA, and getting mentally prepared to make the long, solo cross-country trip. Fortunately, the condo sold in three days. By late that next week, I was completely stoked and ready for the changes at hand.

Eight days and a meandering 3200 miles later, I pulled to the Ocean Avenue overlook in Santa Monica at dusk. I took a series of images of the beach, the ocean, and that magnificent sunset as I leaned on the front of the car and basked in the warmth of the moment. I had a lot of work ahead of me, but at that moment, I knew I was *home*.

———

With this day's sleuthing tasks completed and the next day's agenda set, I stopped for lunch at the Hollywood Tommy's drive-thru—chili burgers are good for the soul. Then I hit the 101 south toward the One-Ten, then the 405. The drive brought me to the Golden West exit to Westminster in Orange County. I needed to visit my GTO for the first time in a week and a half.

My friend Pete was the expert—he contends *legendary*—custom painter chosen to work his magic on the old girl. A heavy coat of filler-primer that had been laid over the massaged body a week prior needed to be knocked down using a labor-intensive method called stick sanding. We used foot-long plastic, hard-foam blocks wrapped with fine- and finer-grit sandpaper to rid the body's gently contoured surfaces of unwanted ripples and voids. The goal was utter perfection, and that takes work.

The labor was simple, long vertical strokes with a hard foam sanding block followed by lengthwise strokes over the same area. Each session was repeated by another using a finer-grit sandpaper. It was a great upper-body workout, but the finished product was deemed sufficient to help the end result. Pete was pleased and stopped just short of offering me a job.

I left the shop an hour after his *official* closing time and hit the Imperial Highway location of 'The HAT' to get a beautiful pastrami sandwich for dinner. A pair of Tylenol eased the ankle throb a bit. I returned home that night covered head-to-toe with gray dust, tired but sated and happy.

I fell asleep in the recliner, then finally went to bed—the real one this time—at two that morning. The next week would be less idyllic than the one that just ended.

5

After learning her official stage name, I did a quick IMDB search for *Sylvia Tate*, finding an impressive roster of work going back over fifteen years. Her most familiar product had been a decade as fourth credit in a successful major-network medical drama. The lady was a star. I was impressed.

My tactics when dealing with the rich and powerful in LA had developed over my time working with West LA super-hero-attorney Lynn Noel. Her clients were often the ridiculously wealthy denizens of West LA, Holmby and Beverly Hills, and Westwood. She had done a real estate closing for one of Neil Diamond's neighbors once. I'd asked for her client's autograph after I heard that. She'd declined the request.

My task today was multifaceted. I would go visit the actress/heiress and determine her concerns in advance of taking her to Lynn's office for the signings and the settlement of the estate in the coming days. If she didn't want to have contact with her brother, that request would be honored.

A half-hour later, I left for my appointment at Ms. Tate's hillside abode in Hollywood. She met me at the front door, a very attractive blonde woman who looked a bit younger than her forty-ish vintage. She was taller than I had imagined her to be.

"Please come in, Mr. Street." She stepped aside, closed the front door, and led me to the large sunken living room at the far end of the foyer walkway. She gestured toward a comfortable-looking leather armchair. She took her place on an overstuffed sofa next to a lighted end table. An opened Sue Grafton novel, *S is for Silence*, lay on its pages on the arm of the sofa.

The room was a two-story affair with an elegant wood plank-paneled cathedral ceiling and a graceful, curving stairway leading to a perimeter walkway that would lead to the upstairs bedrooms. The house looked a lot bigger and more impressive on the interior than it did from the outside.

Sylvia Tate spoke clearly, and I noticed the precision in her words. "Thank you so much, Mr. Street, for coming to the house. I know it may seem overly dramatic, but there is no love lost between my brother and me. He is openly hostile, to the extent that I would feel threatened were I in his presence."

"I met your brother earlier this week. Not to brag, but I doubt he could violate your safe space with me in attendance."

She smiled. "You do look as though you could take care of yourself. Were you ever a policeman?"

I responded, "Five years in Atlantic City. I came west to see the sun."

"Ah! I thought I detected a hint of an Eastern accent. I'm big on people's dialects. They say everyone in LA is from somewhere else. That may be true. How long have you been out here?"

I shifted a bit in my chair. "A little over two years. I got lucky at a citywide slot tournament in Atlantic City, won some money, and made my break. I'm a lifelong fan of the classic LA vibe. I was brought home from the hospital in a red '69 GTO with the Beach Boys playing on the 8-track. That stuck. My kid hood heroes were the classic TV detectives from the seventies and later. They were all in good ol' Los Angeles. When the door opened for me, I just had to make the move. It's been great so far."

One eyebrow lifted as she asked, "You're good at your work?"

"I'm told that I am. It's poor form to question honest praise. And along that line, I've seen *your* work. You're a very talented, very transparent actor."

She smiled again. It was a great smile for which she was famous. "Thank you. That's always good to hear. Mr. Street, would you like a glass of iced tea? I may be the only person in the industry who doesn't drink hard liquor."

"That sounds good. It's a warm afternoon, and I spent a lot of time in traffic."

"Join me at the counter. I'll have that in just a minute." She rose and walked across the room. She was a very attractive woman. I'm careful to notice such things. She asked, "What is your plan for the meeting tomorrow?"

"It shouldn't be much of a problem. Lynn is aware of the issues between you and your brother, so the signatures can be obtained in separate rooms if that is your wish. The procedure shouldn't take more than a half hour at Lynn's office. I'll take you there and bring you back home. You'll end the afternoon a good bit wealthier."

She looked at me as she poured the iced tea into tall frosted glasses, then added some round ice cubes that weren't cubes. "I have to tell you, Mr. Street, that money doesn't mean a lot to me. I wish my parents had spent more of it on themselves. I've been blessed with talent and an excellent, active, and quite lucrative career. I've made my own money...lots of it." She slid the glass across the counter to me with a round metal coaster with a pad on the bottom. "I'd gladly exchange whatever I'm inheriting for a warmer home life when I was a kid, with parents and a family who were supportive, capable of sentiment and communication. My dad was a workaholic, my mother was eventually bitter and unappreciative of the family she had raised and the life she'd been provided. They didn't have much time for what I was doing out here. When I got my starring role in a network prime-time TV series, I don't think there was anyone back there who gave a shit. Pardon my French."

I put my iced tea glass on its metal coaster on the counter. "We don't get to choose our families. I saw plenty of bad ones when I was a cop. Just be glad that you came out of it all in good shape. What about your other siblings? Wade mentioned that they had passed, and I see no mention of them in the papers that Lynn is dealing with. I believe there were two besides you and your brother?"

"That's right. My brother and I are the sole survivors. Our brother was killed in a freak car wreck. Our sister was in the same crash. She lingered a while before she succumbed."

"And this brother is the only one who worked with your dad in his business? That was most of what we talked about. He seemed to take great pride in that."

"You would think so, wouldn't you? My younger brother, Jack, and a couple of our cousins worked for Dad as well, just not in an executive position. Wade always made *certain* that he brokered the power among the offspring."

"He sounds like quite the power-tripper. I detected a bit of that in his attitude."

"Oh, that's not half of it. I had ways of keeping track of what was happening back there. I knew of the friction between the siblings, just as I expected that Dad would pass shortly after Mom died. Most of their families had passed in that manner, one mate soon after the other."

"Those traditions carry on in some families."

"You know what made me mad? Before my dad's body was even in the *ground,* my brother had canceled the car dealer franchises and let the contracts to have all eight of the company's buildings razed. That was *after* he let all the employees go. There were people in that town who had worked for Dad for thirty years. My dad *loved* his employees. They were as close as his family. They deserved better. Wade couldn't have cared less."

What could I say? "I'm sorry to hear that. I suppose the estate settlement will be a load off your mind. After tomorrow you'll be free of that connection."

"I suppose. I have a couple of auditions later this week. That'll take my mind off it. I need that."

I frowned, doubtful. "Wait. They still make you audition? I would think you'd be a *go-to* for a series lead."

She chuckled. "That, my dear Mr. Street, is the life of a working actor. A year or so after a series goes away, sometimes even before the syndication kicks in, the fame and the *pay-only* status for the casting process wears off. Agents, producers, and casting execs seem to forget the recent past. It almost seems that you have to start over again. I take acting classes over in NoHo once a week too. Acting, my friend, is *work*. Never doubt it."

"That's good to know. You wear it well. I'm a pretty serious TV buff. I have a decent tape and DVD collection. I've seen some of your work. You're quite good."

"Thank you. Let me guess—you're a mystery buff. Any favorites?"

"Mostly the classics, if the seventies created any. James Garner, David Janssen, and Mike Connors were the best. Rockford, Orwell, and Mannix were my heroes coming up. SoCal from back then just looked *amazing* on the small screen. The streets were wide and smooth, the skies were blue, the women were wealthy and gorgeous, all the guys had cool cars and great hair. And guns! Lotsa guns. No convertibles for me just yet, but I still have decent hair."

She laughed. "Yes, you do. So, you have an eye for drama."

"I think so. There are some other favorites that are just haunting. *Naked City* is a favorite. It was done a couple of decades before I was born. It was unique in that it was often just pure human drama. The cops in the series sometimes just seemed like an afterthought. 'Route 66' was done by the same production company, and had many of the same traits."

Sylvia smiled her great smile. "Those were classics, and a great training ground for actors who became legends in the industry. Are there any that you disliked? You sound as if you're really discerning where tv is concerned. Early in my career, I worked in a few series."

I was on a roll... "Well, okay, since you asked, I never had any respect for the elderly hero types back in the nineties. *Murder She Wrote* just got on my nerves. Small, peaceful town where everyone knows each other, they all get along, until right in the middle of it, here's this nosy old lady poking her nose in everyone's business, then the town folks are dropping dead everywhere. I always suspected that she was at the bottom of all the carnage and her books were just a cover. That *Dick Van Dyke* series about the doctor got on my nerves as well. Hey, pops, you're a doctor. Stay in your lane, save some lives. No disrespect to the actors, but those shows did nothing for me."

She lifted her glass and pointed a polished index finger toward me. "Just a thought, Mr. Street, you should try a screenwriting course. I'd bet you'd be good at it. God knows we could use some fresh eyes. Your police career and now your investigator work would be great tools."

I said, "Thanks for that. Joseph Wambaugh was one of the first to make that work. I've heard that in recent times, writers have no right to expect to recognize their original work once the studio types get through with it. That would be tough to take."

"Sad to say, that's true as often as not. You learn to take the check and move on. There is little originality left in that area of the arts."

"Do you think the developing cable and internet channels will create a lot of new markets?"

"Eventually, certainly. There will be a lot of failures, and regular network ratings will sink like a stone. A lot of good talent may go by the wayside, and a lot of mediocre work will end up on screen. There will be lots of opportunity, regardless. It doesn't help that the program executives are all about twelve years old now. There will be a lot more of them desperate for decent product." She grinned. "Sorry for the rant, Mr. Street. I'm starting to sound like a bitter old actor."

"I don't think so at all. You're an industry pro. You've proven your worth many times over. Those three Emmys on the mantel are ample evidence of that."

After she drained her glass of tea, she raised her chin slightly and showed a confident smile. "Yes, they are."

I finished my tea and pushed the glass toward her. Taking that as a signal, I moved the conversation toward a wrap. "So, barring any changes, I will pick you up at nine-thirty tomorrow morning. The appointment is at eleven, so we can take our time getting to West LA. Afterward, I'll deliver you back here, a very wealthy young woman."

"And you don't think I'll have to confront my brother?"

"If you wish, and as you've requested, no contact will be necessary. Lynn and I have made similar arrangements numerous times. This'll be a piece of cake. If your brother attempts to cause any issues, I will protect you."

"And perhaps pummel him?"

I played it straight. "Only if absolutely necessary. He is a client of my boss, just as you are. Pummeling would probably be considered poor form."

Sylvia smiled. We rose from our respective seats, and she led me toward the front foyer. "I will buy you lunch tomorrow after the meeting. Have you ever been to The Daily Grille on Ventura?"

"It's one of my favorites. I look forward to it!"

She smiled thinly. "Thank you for this, Mr. Street. I appreciate the special attention." We walked to the front door, bade our goodbyes, and I walked to the Tahoe. As I drove away, I had many questions about the actress, her brother, and their respective situations —shared and separate. Most of the answers to many of the questions were really none of my business, but when had that ever stopped me?

———

With the week's work determined, I decided to call the doctor's office and get the foot cast removed a few days early so that I could be at full speed on the job at hand. After a bit of discussion, the clinic finally invited me to come in for a late appointment at five that afternoon so that I could wait another hour for a male nurse practitioner to take a jigsaw-looking thing and saw the plaster cast off my foot and ankle.

I was eventually impressed that the guy had the presence of mind to wet the cast to cut down on the dust that the dried plaster would normally create. Gee, maybe he'd done this before. Two minutes with the Sawzall thing finally loosed from five weeks with a caged foot, and I was finally able to scratch the itch that had been hounding me for weeks. It would be sore but bearable for the next week before I forgot about it altogether.

6

At nine o'clock that next morning, my friend Louie delivered my ride for the day, an upgraded and very shiny late-model black Chevy Tahoe. Louie was one of those unique LA "characters," but better than that, he was also a savvy entrepreneur. A retired Secret Service agent, his South Bay specialty vehicle provider service had somehow acquired a stock of former FBI and Homeland Security Agency SUVs, low mile, late models, mostly solid black, some with ballistic panels within the doors and polycarbonate side windows instead of glass. Cosmetically perfect but stealthy, they seemed the perfect security tool for potential light-jeopardy events. I doubted that this estranged brother would start lobbing hand grenades in our direction, but this *appearance* of security was a visual and psychological advantage, if only as a marketing tool. Making the client feel better is always a good thing.

I gave Louie a ride back home and then solidified plans for the non-meeting of the hostile siblings. Sylvia Tate and I arrived at Lynn Noel's law office in West LA a few minutes before eleven that morning, ready for the rapid conclusion to the clients' family dealings. Her brother had arrived before us and was exiting the pearl white Escalade that I had arranged for him as we arrived. With

Sylvia's request in mind, I parked at an outlying slot until I was certain that Wade had been sequestered in *his* meeting room. When Lynn called me to announce the positioning, I pulled to the rear entrance of the building, parked, and escorted Sylvia Tate into the building and then to *her* meeting room.

Lynn made quick work of the signature procedure, but there was a hitch with Sylvia's side of the dispersal process.

"No, Ms. Noel, I need that to go to my Las Vegas address. All of my business dealings go through that entity and address. California taxes the absolute hell out of real money. Nevada is far easier to work around."

Lynn responded, "All right, I will make that alteration. I'll need to verify your tax ID number and any other pertinent documents."

Sylvia Tate looked at Lynn, then at me. "Of course. I have that right here." She went to her purse and withdrew a coil of paper. She unrolled the papers and chose one pale yellow sheet, which she slid across to Lynn. "There you go. I've done this before with my studio contracts."

Lynn smiled and asked, "Do you have property over there?"

"Yes, I do. I bought five acres in Henderson and had a home built there a decade ago. Developers and realtors are always hounding me to sell off a portion of the property, but I like it there. Let them wait."

Lynn asked, "Are there any other changes necessary?"

She laid her copies of the papers on the table in front of her. "Just one more. We decided early on that Ann Hawkins had no marquee pull. My legal name is now Sylvia Tate, and all of my business is done through that name and my SylTate LLC business entity, through the Nevada address. Just adjust the name and the business address, if you would."

Lynn left the room and returned a few minutes later with a freshly corrected set of documents. Sylvia looked them over, initialed and signed the requisite spots, then signed for the final check. Sylvia silently laid it on the table in front of her and stared at it for a minute. She looked at me once, making no comment, signaling no emotion. I saw the face of the check and the amount, $8,736,318.64. I was impressed. Them that has gets more. After two minutes of silence in the room, she cleared her throat and looked at me again, then at Lynn. Her face was slightly flushed. Fat money will do that to you.

Sylvia asked, "So, are we done here?" She shifted her chair backward a few inches. "Ms. Noel, what is your fee?"

"That was handled from the gross amount by the Georgia Law Firm." Lynn looked at me and made a curious tilt of her head, her silent signal that we would talk later. She extended her hand toward Sylvia as she rose from her chair. "Ms. Tate, our part is done. It's been an honor meeting you. I like your work. The *Trauma Center Hospital* series was appointment television for my husband and me. If you have any further concerns, don't hesitate to contact me." She slid across a business card, one of her cool etched aluminum ones. "We recently added an exceptional entertainment attorney to our staff, in the event you ever have need. If I may ask, who is your agent?"

"I was a client of Silver Associates on Wilshire. Arnie Lankershim was my primary."

"I remember Arnie. It was sad that he passed. When you have need again, please consider calling us. My staff is one of the best in town for that work, and I can promise that you'll never get lost in the crowd."

Sylvia had seemed to tense up at the mention of the talent agent. "Yes, of course. Thank you. Mr. Street? Can we go?"

We rose from our seats. Sylvia shook Lynn's offered hand, then turned toward the door. I stepped ahead, opened the door, then stood aside for them to pass. We passed the short hallway to the rear door of the office. I opened that as well, but I hadn't looked past the opening. My mistake. I'd momentarily relaxed my usual *head on a swivel* tactic, and in stress situations, that's almost never the right move.

Wade Hawkins stood twenty feet from the rear door, beside his idling borrowed Cadillac. As Sylvia walked from the exit, he stood there and glared at her. I stepped in front of her and asked, in a firm voice, "Are we going to have an issue here, Wade?" I was five inches taller than he was, a decade younger, and in far better physical shape. I could've pressed the issue, but we had already established that pummeling the client's brother would have been poor form.

Wade looked at me, eyes narrowed and face flushed, and said, "I'd like a word with my sister."

I looked at Sylvia as she shook her head to the negative. "That is not gonna happen, Wade." I stepped in front of her and stared at Wade straight-on. "Some other time. Sylvia is in my care, just as you were the day before yesterday. Call me, and I'll see what I can arrange. You have my number." I used my right hand on his upper arm to gently but firmly move him to the side as Sylvia passed to our left toward the Tahoe.

Wade glared at me as I elbowed him to the side. "We'll see about that, Street." His frown and the cold tone of his voice spoke volumes.

I stepped back, turned to Sylvia, and led her to the Tahoe. As I opened the door and helped her inside, I looked back at her brother, still standing and staring at us. I considered at that moment that he could be a genuine threat.

Moments later, as we pulled to a stoplight on Wilshire Boulevard, I turned to Sylvia. "We need to talk about your brother."

Quietly, she said, "Yes, Mr. Street, we do."

7

Sylvia Tate and I were seated in a booth at the Ventura and Laurel Canyon location of The Daily Grille, near the rear of the room. I had taken my usual *visibility* position, a holdover from my days as a cop in AC. Sylvia had ordered a very nice bottle of wine, and we were debating the menu for our—what—late lunch? Early dinner? It was two-thirty in the afternoon.

I offered, "I'm fond of the crab cakes myself. That's not the most decadent of the offerings here, certainly, but they've always been good. What are you having?" I asked Sylvia as the waiter approached.

"My recent favorite is the blackened salmon. But..." She paused for a few seconds, then, "But I'm getting a Filet Mignon, medium, with *all* the trimmings. I am *hungry*. Please don't tell the industry-wide vegetarian mafia. I may never work in this town again."

I feigned shock. "Oh, dear. There goes your Hollywood Liberal Co-Existence Permit! What will Rona Barrett say?"

She looked at me and frowned, "Not a hell of a lot, Street. Is she even still alive? In any event, I think she retired quite a while back."

"Hey, how could that be? I watched her in an episode of Mannix just the other night. She looked perfectly healthy."

I relayed the orders to the waiter, and he poured the wine into her proffered glass, then my own.

Sylvia responded, "*Mannix?* My God, Street, that has to be from before you were born!"

"That it was. I love the classics." I took a sip of the wine, a great hearty red that would go better with her filet than my crab cakes. I'll never tell. "So, tell me about your brother. The relationship seemed *strained*, to say the least."

"Oh, it is. He and my dad went into a blue-nosed rage when I left home to come out here. My mom was cooler than they were with it. She had read the situation better than anyone else there. I had been tapped for a scholarship to the University of Georgia, probably headed for a major in Economics. I was a good student, but I couldn't *imagine* working in a cubicle forever. I had done some modeling and worked in a few commercials in Atlanta, and the pay was decent. I took the leap and drove my old Firebird to LA. The rest, eventually, was history."

"It took a while for you to get a break."

"Yeah. It always takes some time to get noticed. I played the game like everyone had to, and I lucked out a time or two. A couple of years in and I was getting auditions and finally a decent agent. He worked his ass off on my behalf...after I moved in with him." She smiled a thin smile. "I probably lucked out there as well, at least for a few years."

"I met your photographer friend."

She laughed. "Kiefer! Oh, man, what a hound that guy is! He'd screw anything that didn't move out of the way fast enough. I think he still does. He and I *worked* one another as we chased our individual goals. It was quite a ride."

I surmised, "The laws of cost/benefit hold true in most industries."

She nodded her agreement. "That's a good way to put it. It seems to be the way it was done out here back then." She looked at me. "It may sound tawdry or whatever, but I didn't get passed around and traded off like some girls do because I had Kief as backup. He was really good for me, and I was for him as well. No regrets there at all. It would be a lot rougher now."

"Good for you. I've heard some stories. I know there are plenty who get used up and tossed aside. I'm glad you persevered and made it through the gauntlet. I like your work."

She sipped her wine and said, "Thank you. It sounds as if you're a serious TV buff."

She had me. "Yeah, I wanted to be a cop when I was a kid, and that was stuck into my adolescence, helped by a steady diet of afternoon reruns on TV. One station ran four episodes of *Adam 12* every day, so Marty Milner was an early hero. There are countless police officers all around the world who had that same early influence. I'm pretty picky though. Your IMDB roster says you did a few shows of that type."

"Yeah. Some of them were good training grounds, though the roles were minor."

"That's how you learn."

Our waiter arrived with our salads and temporarily spared us of further strolls down memory lane. An hour later, after an exceptional meal, we moved to the front of the dining room and listened to the combo that was thrumming away on the outer front deck of the restaurant. After a while, we took the stairs back down to street level and walked—jaywalked, really—across Laurel Canyon Boulevard to the sidewalk newsstand. Sylvia picked up a couple of women's titles and a fresh copy of the daily *Hollywood Reporter*. Heading back to her home, we took the scenic route—Laurel Canyon Boulevard southbound, then a turn to Mulholland Drive, back to the 101, then south to Hollywood Boulevard just in time to catch much of the evening rush hour traffic. Welcome to LA.

The sun was setting over the shiny distant profile of Century Center as I drove up the hill toward Sylvia's street. As we turned the corner, we were surprised at the setting. In front of Sylvia's home, halfway down the block, were a quartet of LAPD black-and-white Crown Vics, all lit, and an alarm company service truck. I pulled the Tahoe to the opposite curb and walked toward the forward of the two black-and-whites. I showed my ID, explained my passenger's identity, and asked the senior patrol officer about the event.

"Yes, Mr. Street, the house was broken into. We don't see any significant signs of theft, but we will have to let your client be the judge of that. We couldn't get in touch with her, so we called the alarm company and closed the house up. If you wish, we can wait until she goes inside to see if anything is missing."

"I appreciate that. I'll bring her from the car, and we'll meet you at the front door."

I walked to the Tahoe and explained the situation to Sylvia. She immediately stepped out of the truck, and we walked to her house. She hesitated as I introduced the Patrol Sergeant. Once inside, we looked around the house, and she didn't immediately recognize any damage or missing items. I walked through the interior rooms, then through the kitchen to the garage as Sylvia spoke with the alarm company rep.

The garage held her black Infiniti sedan, white California plate SYLTATE, in the first of the three stalls. The floor of the garage was attractive in itself, wearing a thick high gloss layer of acrylic with carpeted runners between the parking spaces and in front of the cars, forming an aisle leading to the kitchen door. I ordered a similar treatment during the remodel of the garage/apartment building behind my house a year later. The center space was empty, but the far space held a larger, or at least taller, car under a car cover with a Beverly Hills Car Cover Company logo on the front. I had a similar cover for my GTO. I lifted the side of the cover just aft of the front tire and was surprised to see a white rocker panel stripe on a pristine red front fender with white letters proclaiming GT500KR. Cobwebs fell from the underside of the chassis to the tire.

Wow.

Just then, I heard Sylvia call me from the kitchen door. I dropped the cover and returned to the kitchen just as the alarm company rep left the room. She looked stressed as she stood by me and spoke quietly.

"Mr. Street, may I hire you for personal protection for a few days? This intrusion has..." She paused for a few seconds. "I don't know, I'm just on edge. This has never happened to me before." She stepped closer to me, and I put my arm around her.

"That's just natural, Sylvia. Gather up some clothes, and let's get out of here. Where would you like to go?"

Before she took the stairs, she answered, "Vegas. I have my other home there, it has everything I need, and I know I will feel safe there. It's a fortress. Are you game?"

I remembered something she had mentioned earlier. "That's no problem for me at all. What about your auditions? You said you had two upcoming."

She nodded her head and responded, "Let them wait. I couldn't concentrate now anyway. I'll call them from Vegas and try to re-schedule."

"If you say so. Let's go to Las Vegas."

While Sylvia packed, I stepped to the front of the house to speak with the patrol officers standing on the driveway. I introduced myself, showed my credentials again, and asked, "Are there a lot of daytime robberies in this neighborhood? I'm not up on my crime stats for this area."

The senior officer, a three-striper named Lund, said, "Mr. Street, this is where we come to take a break or do paperwork if we have a slow shift. This is the first break-in on this street since I've been in this division, and that's been five years. There are a few domestics from time to time, mostly spoiled rich kids rebelling against their parents. Last year some guy's new Porsche Cayenne got snatched from a house on the next block up the hill, but he had left it running in his friggin' driveway. Do tell."

I asked, "Any ideas on this one?"

"Who knows? Did she do something to piss someone off recently?"

I scratched my chin and answered, "If it's the most likely suspect, all she did was *exist*. It may just be a long-festering family dispute. If I find anything, I'll let you know."

The officer passed me his business card. "You do that. I have a good clearance rate. I hope you can help me keep it that way."

"I'll do what I can, trust me. I was on the job back east, I know the feeling." The officer grinned and offered a fist bump.

Sylvia appeared at the open door as the officers returned to their cars. "Mr. Street?" I turned to her, and she continued, "Can we talk?"

"Sure. Did you pack?" I stepped inside the front door to see the answer, three large soft-sided bags set next to the front door. "Let me get the car. I'll be right back."

———

A half-hour later, we pulled into my driveway. I parked in the back of the house, checked to see that the house was secure, and waved her in from the patio.

As she walked into the den/office, she stopped, looked around, and said, "Hmmm...just as expected. Very masculine. Very nice."

"Thank you. This was a fixer-upper when I bought it, but I've refinished a lot of it over the last couple of years. Make yourself at home, I'll be right back."

I went to my bedroom, snatched my *go bag* from the closet, unzipped it, and dropped my shoulder holster, cop Glock, and a box of shells into the side compartment, then closed the bag. Unsure of my client's need for formality, I added a garment bag with two sport coats, a trio of dress shirts, a tie, and a couple of pairs of slacks, plus the assorted accouterments, laid them into a vinyl garment bag, then carried it all back to the den.

"Street, this is impressive. I like this." She was standing next to the shelves that held my DVD collection. "You have really good taste in TV." She turned to me. "You even have a few of my old shows on there. I have a DVD setup at the house, can we bring a few of these along?"

"Sure. That would be interesting. Do you like seeing yourself on the small screen? I've always heard that actors hate that. I have heard that Al Pacino has never watched any of the Godfather films."

"Yeah, some do. I don't. Most often, when I watch myself, I just feel like I could have done better work."

"You're your own worst critic? I like that. Gotta keep the upward performance spiral alive. One of my Crim professors back east was big on that." I took a seat behind my desk and picked up the phone. "Let me make a couple of calls, and we'll leave."

Sylvia selected a few DVDs as I called Lynn and brought her up to date on the situation, then called my car provider and arranged for a few more days use of the up-armored Tahoe. After ending the phone work, I loaded my bags into the Tahoe, and we left for a quick trip to Sin City. It wasn't how I'd expected to spend the next few days, but it would turn into a productive and profitable journey.

8

Wade Hawkins had been in Los Angeles for three days when he visited this Detective Street that Monday. He had left his wife Lucy at the hotel for two days that previous weekend as he went out looking for his sister. There had been all of the addresses that had been taken from the mail that had been gathered from their mother's belongings, and he had suffered driving that shitbox rental car as he tried to find each and every one of them. His back was killing him.

From seedy shared apartments in Hollywood proper to a small condo in Studio City, he'd drawn blanks at every stop, and on both days, he had lost track not of only time but his sense of direction. Getting lost in Los Angeles had been a nightmare. He had driven through some genuinely scary neighborhoods and had been the subject of a few hostile stares along the way. It all made him miss home, the modest burg of Fairwater, Georgia, even more.

After the meeting at the attorney's office, he now had a *current* address for her, and he lost no time going there after the detective got in his face in the parking lot. He had bought one of those big map books and figured out the proper route through the tacky hell-hole that was daytime Hollywood to the hillside abode that was his sister's *official* California address.

Wade was surprised at the home he found in the hillside neighborhood. While it was a little too gaudy for his taste with its red doors and the like, and certainly wasn't something that he'd want to live in, it was definitely a nice house. He parked a couple of houses away until he saw one of the neighbors standing on her driveway, watching him and talking on her cell phone. Afraid of having the police called on him, he drove away, but then he came back fifteen minutes later and parked on his sister's driveway.

———

After the meeting at the attorney's office, Wade was more angry than he had been. Expecting her to return home promptly, he found the house yet again and parked on the driveway. He went to that gaudy red door and checked it, trying to get in, but the motion detector on the front landing lit the porch lights and spooked him. He returned to the Escalade and left quickly.

9

Beverly Hills, California — 2002

The stunning young Lizzie Totts walked into the office of Silver Associates Talent Management on the eighth floor of the shiny metal tower at the corner of LaCienega Avenue and Wilshire Boulevard, and heads turned. The lobby of the agency was a busy place, but that day, a small group of pre-teen female casting hopefuls and their mothers were cooling their heels on the sofa next to the front window. The girls stared in awe as Lizzie walked past them in her long strides. She removed her large dark sunglasses and studiously ignored them as she walked.

The receptionist, a veteran of the post—and occasional celebrity rudeness—for well over a decade, smiled up at the young blonde.

Lizzie Totts smiled thinly and softly said, "I have a two o'clock with Arnie Lankershim."

Suzanne Brick, recognizing the face and the carriage, smiled back and said, "Yes, Miss Totts." She lifted the phone and pressed one button. After a beep, she said quietly, "Arnie, your two o'clock is here." She paused for a few seconds. "Yes, sir." She lowered the handset as the door to the office past her shoulder opened.

Arnie Lankershim stepped from his office's open door and greeted his guest. Dressed to the nines, he had shed his suit coat and rolled up his sleeves in order to look *busy* for his potential client. "Lizzzeee! You look amazing! Welcome! Come right in! Wow!" He stepped aside and smiled as the young woman passed, then said over his shoulders to his assistant in the foyer of his office, "Laura? Hold my calls?" as he closed his office door. He walked to his Lucite desk, took his chair, and looked across his desk at the young woman.

She spoke in a soft young voice that somehow also sounded smoky. Her perfume was subtle but definite. "Thank you again for seeing me, Arnie. I liked what I heard after you spoke with my assistant. As you know, my goal is to continue and expand my career and, of course, obtain more mature roles. I've reached the point at which I need to leave the kid stuff behind. I would like to re-invent the career of Lizzie Totts so that my former work is all but forgotten. You seemed to grasp that concept. Tell me what you have in mind for me and what you can do on my behalf."

Arnie looked across at the young woman and tried to concentrate. She practically defined hot. Petite, perfectly sculpted, and braless, she wore a short, low-cut, shape-defining white sheath thing that left little to the imagination. Her long, streaked blonde hair fell past her shoulders in a stylish disarray. Her piercing blue eyes shone with a youthful energy. Her scarlet lower lip displayed just the right amount of *puff*.

As she took her seat in front of his desk, Arnie spoke in a definitive manner...his turf, his rules. "Miss Totts...Lizzie...here's how I work. First, I need to know your perceptions and your intentions. Let's do this. Tell me about your work to this point. I know you started very young. Tell me about your career so far."

Lizzie Totts tilted her head slightly. Arnie saw even that half-inch movement as sexy. "Well, I lucked out. My dad, as you are aware, is famous in his own right, and that name recognition opened a lot of doors for me. No shock there. The Burbank crew crafted two consecutive series around me and, again, my dad's last name. I think I started getting bored about a month in. The scripts were geared for nine-year-old girls from Topeka or somewhere, and every other sentence had a pause for a laugh line. I was over it pretty quickly." She smiled thinly now. "By the time I was twelve, I was demanding onstage rewrites and causing delays in shooting because the material was insulting to me as well as my audience. Forty-year-old studio execs are convinced that they communicate with pre-teen girls. They are mistaken. Seven years later, I'm ready for a real career, and I know I'm worthy of vastly better material. I have the talent, I have the name, I have the physicality. My Q rating is at Kardashian level most of the time. I'm ready to spread my wings and leave all the kiddie crap behind. I want to be a real stand-alone personality known for my work, and I want it to happen quickly. I want Emmys and Oscars in my near future. Can you help me make that happen?"

Arnie smiled at her. "Sure. I believe we can. Your confidence is inspiring. We have a great team here in LA and exceptional connections nationwide. One of my other clients just scored a co-star role on a Law and Order spinoff. Frankly, I see you more as a stand-alone, perhaps even above-the-title in TV movies and series pilots." He folded his hands for a moment in front of his chin, then asked, "Do you see yourself as a comedic or a dramatic actor?"

"My comic timing is good, according to my reviews, but I prefer serious dramatic roles. I want to grow as an actor. *Funny* doesn't always enable or promote that growth very well."

"There have been some great dramatic actresses who started with comedy. One classic example is Elizabeth Montgomery. She was best known for Bewitched, but she absolutely killed it in her later dramatic work. I could see you as a latter-day Tuesday Weld as well. She started in her teens, had a great variety of dramatic roles. I'm certain that we'd soon be fielding numerous offers from varied genres if that's the direction that you select."

"That is what I want."

Arnie had to ask. "Are you taking any acting lessons? There are some exceptional groups out in the valley. Several of my clients, some prominent and popular actors, have benefited greatly from them."

"I'm open to almost anything, Arnie. Are you willing to take an aggressive leadership role in my career? Can you make me a bankable star by the time I'm twenty-five? That's what I want, more than anything." She stood from her chair, walked to the tall window overlooking Wilshire, and looked out, fully aware that the shape of her body shone clearly through the thin fabric of her dress. "Can you help make that happen?"

He had seen this ploy from others, but he was still impressed. "It will take work from us and discipline from all involved, Lizzie. The discipline part is vital. You know all about that potential trap from the gossip that followed you during your previous career. I have searched your internet sites, I have to congratulate you on controlling those. You have to keep that area as clean as possible. Bad news there can become an issue very quickly if you're not careful. Producers, directors, and studios are tiring of adult actors who don't act like adults."

"I have staff that handles exposures like that for me."

"Are you dating anyone?"

"I have a very small social circle, some are friends from my former career, but I have certainly outgrown many of them. I'm flexible. I actually prefer slightly older men."

As he looked at her standing next to the window, he thought, *Oh, I can imagine.* Gathering his thoughts, he said, "You were said to have been involved at an early age with your co-star in your second series. That's the most negative press you've ever received." He had heard the stories from the set of the comedy telling of the delays in production on the sitcom because, at age fifteen, she and her handsome, Italian twenty-something co-star were *busy* in one of the StarWaggon mobile dressing rooms an aisle away from the soundstage door.

She turned from the window, looked at him, then stepped

closer. "Wow. You've done some homework." She smiled coyly. "As for Adam, I was coming of age, I was maturing physically, and I needed a stable, discreet teacher for adult endeavors. He was a very good teacher." She smiled knowingly as she cooed, "I learned quite a lot."

"You were a public figure from what, age nine? That's a tough role for anyone. Your rift from your parents was difficult as well, I'm sure."

"My father is a good person. He has his own career, as do I. I'm on the way up, he peaked well over a decade ago with help from my career exposure. Our differences in recent years mostly have to do with his insistence that I remain *his little girl*." She stood in front of his desk, inhaled, and smiled as she tilted her head a couple of degrees to the right. "Arnie, do I look like a child?"

Arnie smiled, and his eyebrows lifted. "No child I've ever seen, Lizzie. You are physically stunning, and we will certainly use that in our marketing." He took a breath and gathered his thoughts, then asked, "Do you have a favorite photographer?"

"I know someone who does headshots. Do you want full-figure as well? He has offered to do those."

He thought, *Oh, I'll bet...* but he said, "Give me that name, we will definitely need a new session. We have a studio set up just for that, two floors up. The full-figure work may be down the road a bit. We have time for that."

"Playboy has made offers since last year. I could probably get the cover." She smiled.

"That figures, but you don't want that. That skews far too old. You don't need to bang Hef, and you don't need forty-year-olds all over the world licking your centerfold. Let's keep your work and your target market as young as possible while concentrating on serious roles. Let's *up your game* a lot in the next few years. Broaden your horizons. Do some traveling. Continue your education. What are you doing in your private time? Are you taking any college courses? Do you have any interest there?"

Her nose wrinkled in distaste. "I haven't seen the need. Look,

Arnie...I'm famous, and I'm financially secure. At nineteen, I own a two-million-dollar home in Nichols Canyon, free-and-clear, and I even have an offer of a free loaner car from the Lamborghini dealer on Ventura. Sitting in some airless classroom in the valley is just not at the top of my go-to list."

Arnie Lankershim shifted in his chair and spoke firmly. "Lizzie, listen to me. If we do business together—and yes, at this point, that is an if—I will make many requests of you. Each of them will be in the interest of creating a well-rounded adult actor in great demand industry-wide. You will make an impressive amount of money per year and per project. If that's not what you want, if you just want to play a series of trivial celebrity games, please let me know right now. I have other clients who demand their share of my time. It's your choice."

Lizzie frowned for a moment—people didn't talk to her that way—then she looked squarely at Arnie Lankershim. She hesitated for a few seconds, pursed her full, scarlet lips for a few seconds, squinted her piercing, bright eyes a little, then smiled quickly. "Arnie, get the contracts together. Let's do this."

"You're sure?"

"I am. Make it happen." She did not smile.

The discussion continued for another hour. Signatures were given, witnesses were consulted, numbers were discussed and settled upon before a photo session with the agency shooter took the images that would accompany the news release that would make the next morning's edition of The Hollywood Reporter and the other *trades*. Lizzie Totts departed the Silver Associates Talent Management agency that afternoon with official legal and professional representation, leaving Arnie Lankershim an agency hero.

10

As a traveling companion, Sylvia Tate was quite charming and entertaining. I was surprised when she changed the radio from a music channel to KFI, Los Angeles's major talk radio station. We discussed the upcoming presidential election, and I was impressed that she wasn't a typical show-biz leftist.

"Oh, I'm mostly a loyal southern Republican, but I can't tell that to anyone I work with at the studios. You have to abide by the approved mantra and political party alignment. Oh, and I'm not gay either. Sorry!" She threw up her hands. "At the end of the day, after being absorbed in the approved mantras for ten or eleven hours, I'm hungry to take in some Rush Limbaugh or maybe catch John and Ken on KFI." She mock-whispered, "Don't tell anyone! My career would be toast!"

I chuckled. "Your secrets are safe with me. I'm a live-and-let-live kinda guy, and we may agree on a few points. I'm securely non-committal in public settings."

I had chosen the indirect route to Nevada, north on I-5 to State Highway 14 to Palmdale, then across the high desert on the Pear Blossom Highway to Lancaster to connect with the 15 freeway north to Nevada. The route was a few miles longer but a little more relaxed than taking the late-afternoon I-10 to the I-15 freeway exchange at Ontario. The weather was warm, and the sky was clear —when is it not in SoCal—and the trip was pleasant.

As we passed Victorville on the I-15, Sylvia asked, "Can you believe that Roy Rogers and Dale Evans owned thousands of acres of land in the desert along through there? I've heard lots of stories over the years."

I looked across the cab of the truck at her. "Oh yeah? Anything juicy?"

"Well...in his later years, Ol' Mister Singing Cowboy from all those sappy westerns would bring his friends—lots of stuntman buddies and cowboy actors—to one of the old filming sets he had built out here. He called those his *drinkin' ranches*. When Dale was out of town, he'd call his friends, and they'd get blind-ass drunk and fall off horses all weekend. I'd pay a thousand bucks to watch that."

I surmised, "The keywords there have to be 'When Dale was out of town.'"

"Yep! Typical male."

"Except for all those fringy outfits."

"True enough. That was a real fashion statement back then. I was raised on his movies. I met him a few years before he passed away. It was interesting. He was like a shell of the guy we'd seen on screen, he was practically skin and bones, but there was still a little sparkle in his eye."

I responded, "Well, he lived a long life, made a pile of money, and had a big family. Good man...given all of that, I think I can probably excuse his drinkin' ranches."

"Yeah. Men of that strength and integrity are few and far between now. So, Street...are you married? Involved?"

I answered, "Right now, it seems like I'm married to my work. I'm hoping that changes sometime in the near future. Lynn tries to set me up with her friends on occasion, but nothing has taken hold as of yet."

"What do you think of the women you've encountered here in

California? C'mon, you're young, handsome, ambulatory, and solvent. What's not to love? Surely you've dated since you've been here."

"It's a mixed bag. I have met some beautiful women in the last two years, and I was quite interested in one in particular. She came from a relatively wealthy West LA family. Her retired firefighter dad owned a couple of blocks of Santa Monica apartment buildings. Thing is, she had been adopted as a baby, and she'd been dumped by some of the assholes she dated and lived with. She hinted that her dad may have made a move on her once when she was a teenager as well. She had major abandonment issues, and that, with everything else, led to her alcoholism, something that she very craftily concealed. It got to where she couldn't keep her stories straight. This was a beautiful woman, Sylvia, but so wounded and damaged that I had to take a hike. I hated to do so, but the situation was just hopeless."

"That's really sad, Street."

"Well, after the engagement in Jersey went away, I think I was adrift with regard to women and relationships. That last one may have knocked me back some. I'm concentrating on work until something worthwhile comes along. And I'm always looking. I see lots of fine women, but there's a lot of damage among them as well." I looked across at her. "How about you? I'm surprised that there's not a Mr. Tate somewhere."

"There would have been. My agent and I lived together for a few years. I thought we were great together, I thought we could work out whatever differences we had, but he had other ideas. I'd waited for him for a while, I was set to propose to *him*, had a big weekend planned around his birthday. He blew the absolute shit out of that, spent that weekend with a cute new client at our cabin at Big Bear instead of with me. I saw the writing on the wall. I ended it."

"Oh, I'll bet." I smiled. It was funny to me, seeing and hearing this wealthy, beautiful, accomplished, dignified, and somewhat formal woman become less tense as the miles passed. I had started to wonder about her brother's possible involvement in the break-in at her house, so I opened that area of discussion. "Sylvia, did you and your brother have any contact before this visit? Would he have had your address from your contacts with your mom or your sister?"

She looked across at me. "I suppose it's possible. I've had that home address for well over a decade, and I did use it when I would send anything back there. He and I never really had any contact other than maybe one phone call in twenty years, and then he just called me a whore and hung up."

"Yeah, he does seem a tad starchy."

"I use the word *brittle* myself. He's about as flexible as a potato chip. And he'd be the cheap thin Dollar Store off-brand kind, not the good ones with the ripples."

I left the Interstate in Barstow to gas up and visit the men's room at a busy station a half-mile west of the off-ramp. Sylvia stayed in the car while I pumped ARCO premium. I also made a call to Lynn's cell to ask a question and make a suggestion. After I hung the nozzle back onto the pump, I went inside the convenience store, did my private business, and snagged a couple of bottles of water to take to the car. I could see through the store window that Sylvia was on her cell as well. It's the California way.

Back in the truck, I passed the water to Sylvia, who looked at me and asked, "Have you ever explored Barstow? Let's take a few minutes. I did exteriors on a location shoot for a TV movie here a few years ago. Parts of it look like the town where I grew up."

As I keyed the ignition, I answered, "My friend Zig says Barstow is 'a wide spot in the road, then they moved the road.' I drove out through town once, it's nothing special." I pulled out onto Main Street and turned right to go west, uphill. The area near the freeway was dotted with antiquated motels, a towing yard, a Dodge dealer that seemed to stock only trucks, a few fast-food spots, and signs suggesting local LEO and California Highway Patrol outposts. At the crest of a hill a mile further, the downtown area began.

Facades of former franchise department stores, probably closed for decades, now offered lines of thrift shops and antique stores, all lacking any semblance of activity, charm, or ambition. A half-mile further, another pathetic used car lot and a lone, desperate-looking Pontiac GMC dealer with a half-dozen used cars on display led to more long-abandoned, or perhaps just vacant, storefronts and ancient motor court motels.

Sylvia watched the scenery pass for five minutes and finally said, "This is depressing. It looks a lot worse than back home. Let's turn back." After a local police car passed at the next intersection, I made a U-turn and started back east.

"Hey," I offered. "Time marches on. Nothing stays the same. Think of the history under us right now. Think of all the people who came to California through the decades, right here on this road before the freeway was built. This is *Route 66* for God's sake! It's pure Americana! It's Marty Milner in a '62 Corvette." I tried to inject a little levity into the atmosphere. "In a few years, I don't doubt that Barstow will regenerate. It happens everywhere! Hell, I'd bet that someday all those old motor courts will be rebuilt in some boutique-y, trendy style. This entire town will regenerate, and maybe even get its own Walmart! Think of *THAT!*" I looked across at her as we slowly traveled toward the on-ramp. "And then all those thrift stores we passed will sell all that used clothing to the locals so they can look like authentic Walmart shoppers! Dammit, Sylvia, it's nature at work in the twenty-first century!"

Sylvia laughed. I did too. Mission accomplished.

––––––

We returned to the northbound I-15 accompanied only by engine and road noise. There was more traffic now, more than a few work-trucks and semis. I stayed in the fast lane, and we passed quite a few. Sylvia and I chatted for a while, but she eventually reclined her seat and *rested her eyes* for a while. I decided to forgo my usual stopover at the Greek drive-thru in Baker for fried zucchini. I suffer for my profession. Soon we were entering the infamous *Baker Grade*, a steep stretch of road that climbs thousands of feet in elevation. The truck traffic stayed to the right, and we made good time, climbing toward the next bottleneck, the heavy road construction through the mountains that, when completed, would widen and re-route the freeway. The resulting traffic clot extended the trip ninety minutes into the early evening.

After the final downslope out of California, heading past the State line settlement of Primm, we cruised toward Las Vegas. I'm always surprised at the optical illusion that the lights of the city provide after you make that last sloping turn. The sheer size of the structures lets you think that the Strip is five, maybe ten miles out, but the time to travel is triple that. It feels like it'll take forever to get there. After a few laps, you get used to the grind. The incredible growth of the Las Vegas metropolis over the next decade would fill in all of the gaps in the scenery. I was pleased that evening that the state troopers weren't out plying their trade. The Tahoe was perfectly happy to cruise at eighty-five miles per hour on cruise control.

We took the appropriate off-ramp from the 15 and found Sylvia's home a half-hour later. It was a nice place, five sculpted acres, as she'd described, with a large ranch-style home perched at the far end of a winding driveway. A half-acre of fine white gravel, dotted with cacti of various shapes and sizes, pretended to be the front yard. A three-space carport established the west side of the 'L' shaped structure, and a wide red door similar to her other home centered the front elevation.

"Park under the carport, and let's go in." Sylvia led me to the front door after I pulled her bags from the back of the truck. As we entered the front foyer, she said, "Thanks for bringing those in. Just put them on the table in the hall. Would you like something to drink? Maybe a sandwich? The kitchen's in here." I followed dutifully.

The kitchen showed much more of a feminine touch than the hillside home in LA. The colors were bright, and there were new stainless-steel major-brand appliances throughout. The sink had a cool double-lever faucet that I knew to be top-of-the-line. I was impressed. As Sylvia closed the fridge door, I told her so.

She responded, "Well, thank you, Street. I can tell from your home that you know quality when you see it." She stepped to the counter and set the tray on top, the makings of submarine sandwiches. "I like it here. The desert suits me."

"It does me too, except for the heat. Do you spend much time here?"

She started assembling her sandwich as I watched. "Oh, maybe a week each month. If I have advance notice of auditions and if the material is good, I'll drive over here for a few days' preparation." She lifted a fresh gherkin and bit half of it. "Oh, I love these! A friend here in town prepares them and the rest of my produce. She is an absolute artist." She folded her bun over the impressive fillings. "Dig in! This is good stuff. Want a beer? Sam Adams okay?"

"That'll work. So, this is where you unwind...I can already see the difference in your demeanor." I built the sub on a six-inch roll, with thin-sliced pastrami, baby Swiss cheese, and a hearty-looking dark mustard, then added thin-sliced tomatoes and a couple of the recommended length-cut pickle slices. Sylvia motioned that I join her at the other end of the counter where a place mat and a fresh, still-sweaty Sam Adams beckoned. I took the seat.

"So, Street...you need to tell me your daily rates. I know this is a spur-of-the-moment job, but I pay quite well, and I can tell you're a pro at your work. Name your price."

I did so.

"That's no problem. I'll handle any expenses while we're here as well, of course. I hired a retired pro football player a couple of years ago at the behest of the studio, he charged a bit more than you." She grinned and lifted her eyebrows while she chewed. "Steroids are expensive." She worked on her sandwich as she watched me dig into mine. The next five minutes were silent. The travel had made us hungry.

Sylvia opened the next conversation as she put our plates into the dishwasher.

"You asked me about my brother. His presence has renewed some really bad memories. My biggest issue with him, and my dad as well, is the way I was treated before I left home. My dad ruled the roost for most of my youth. He was strict. Even in his own adolescence, Wade took my dad's side in everything I did. When I went on my first date, just shy of my seventeenth birthday, I lingered a little too long in the boy's car. It was my *brother*, not my dad, who came out of the house with a fucking shotgun. Mind you, the boy and I were just sitting in his car talking about school, but Wade's filthy fantasies ruled the day. Needless to say, word got out at school by the *next day*, and I couldn't *buy* a date for my entire senior year. Fortunately, I had started going out of town for modeling gigs, and I was able to cast a wider net. That worked, and by my eighteenth birthday, I had offers for modeling and commercial work."

"You took the best route. More power to you. It worked." I lifted my bottle to offer a cheer. We clinked, and I sipped. Sylvia smiled.

"It was tough for a while, early on." She sipped from her beer. "How about you?"

"College and Army Reserve for a short stretch for four years, Atlantic City cop for five starting a few weeks before 9/11, night school masters in criminology. When I won a bunch of money at a casino slot tournament in AC, lots of things changed there, so I pulled up stakes to come to LA. Got my PI ticket earlier this year after serving my apprenticeship with the attorney you met earlier today. I have a pretty decent house and a little money in the bank. I love my work, and I'm told I'm pretty good at it. To quote Michelti Williamson from a TV show that I liked, 'I'm livin' the dream in Boomtown'."

"I can tell. I like a man who's satisfied with his position in life. Confidence is really, really sexy. You wear it well."

I finished my beer. "Thank you, ma'am." I smiled and squinted my eyes at her. "Wanna elope?"

She laughed and smiled back. "We'll talk later."

11

I slept a bit too well that night in Sylvia's plushly-appointed guest room after downing a couple more Sam Adams. I had checked the grounds and established a perimeter for observation from the house itself. We had set a three-day stay, trusting that brother-dearest would be headed back home by the end of the week. The property was beautiful in the morning light, an expansive five acres with a large retractable screen-covered pool, manicured grounds, and lots of those shaped cacti that I've only seen in Nevada. The house security system was adequate for an un-threatened suburban entity.

I'd always been surprised at the many 'anonymous' celebrity residences in Las Vegas, except that many locals credited Wayne Newton with having lived at about a hundred different addresses. In truth, he'd only had a half dozen or so and had settled on one permanent abode some years before.

The garage held a well-maintained burgundy '93 Corvette coupe, one of the 40th Anniversary models. The license was current, and the key was laying on the console. Sylvia said she had bought the car for her boyfriend/talent agent after he arranged a serious pay raise for her when the *Trauma Center Hospital* series went into one of its earlier seasons. She asked if I thought it would be okay to use the car for our local travels. I negotiated a compromise: we'd use the secured truck for the legal stuff during the day and keep the 'Vette in the garage until we went to dinner. Guys gotta eat...and look good driving to the restaurant.

At nine that morning, I was awakened by the aroma of bacon. Having probably overslept, I showered quickly, dressed, and went to the kitchen. Sylvia was there in a dressing gown and matching robe. Aside the double-door refrigerator stood a plump Hispanic lady with dark hair...what, an attendant? The cook? The maid? The caretaker of the property? Sylvia greeted me.

"Mr. Street? This is my friend Alma. She and her husband, Billy, live in the guest house out beside the garage. She's a wonderful cook, and she'll prepare anything you ask for."

What could I say? "Good morning, Alma. Nice to meet you. I'm a pretty basic guy when it comes to food. Let's see...could I perhaps get three eggs, scrambled in butter, some crispy bacon, and some wheat toast? And let's see, some of that orange juice in that carafe on the counter?"

With her thick Hispanic accent, she answered, "Certainly, Mr. Street."

As I waited for the plate, I took a stool next to Sylvia. "So, what is our agenda today? I know we have to get your paperwork delivered for your banking. Is there anything else on the schedule?"

Sylvia sipped her coffee, then lowered her cup and said, "Accountant at eleven, second accountant at two. Lunch in between. Sound good?"

"Certainly. Any word from LA?"

"I got an email from my insurance agent, looks as if everything passed inspection. My security tech is putting an electronic lock package on the doors. That has needed updating for a while."

"You might consider an update for this property as well. Any word from your brother? I halfway hoped he'd try to get in touch."

"No, I doubt he'd try that."

My breakfast platter appeared in front of me as requested, a wondrous thing indeed. As I ate, Sylvia and I talked about a little of everything. At one point, I asked her about her deceased brother and sister. It turned out to be a sore subject.

"See, Beth and I got along *great*! She even came out to visit a couple of times after I got my series. She loved the busy nature of my work, and we had a great time together. I think she talked my mom out of hating my very existence. Beth was just a sweet spirit, very religious, so I put her up at the Beverly Garland Hotel so none of the effects of my *sinful cohabitation* would rub off on her. I let her use the 'Vette, we had it in LA back then, I hadn't bought this property yet—and it had a gate pass, so she had no issues with studio entry."

"Did she and Arnie get along?"

"He treated her like visiting royalty. He said she could've been a star. He'd have loved to take his shot at her as well, I'm sure. She was just a beautiful girl, very natural...and what...maybe *unspoiled* is a good word."

"She sounds great. How did she die?"

"Oh, it was a freak thing. She and my younger brother were coming back from a car dealer auction in an Atlanta suburb one evening, and some kids were dropping rocks and stuff off an overhead pedestrian crosswalk out south of town. A chunk of a cinder block came through the windshield and practically decapitated my brother. Jack lost control of the car, and it went off the road. It rolled over, and Beth was trapped inside for almost an hour. By the time they cut her out and sent her to Atlanta by Life Flight copter, she had practically bled out. There were a lot of fractures and massive internal injuries as well. She hung on for almost two weeks before she died. Those ICU doctors and their staff fought like hell for her."

"Aw, Syl...I'm so sorry to hear that."

"Thanks. It was just one of those freak things, ya know? Their deaths put our mom on the downhill slide. My brother being killed in a car crash was one thing. He worked with vehicles every day. He was a short-track race car driver for a decade. He probably drove a hundred thousand miles a year between his work and touring as a racer in a regional tour. He was also a few years older than she was. She was the surprise baby just after Mom turned forty. She was the baby of the family and always treasured for that. That accident caught Mom totally by surprise. She was gone less than a year later, and my dad died shortly after that."

"Sounds as if your family was closer than my conversation with Wade would suggest. He never even mentioned your brother and sister."

"That sounds like *Wade's World*, all right. No pun intended."

I tried to not laugh. "Ah, but a world-class pun it is."

"Why thank you, Mr. Street. I try to be at least as good as my material. That works sometimes."

"I do have questions though. I was a cop in Atlantic City for five years, I saw a few instances where kids would drop rocks and stuff off overpasses. I could see the hazard, but if no one was hurt, we usually caught up with them and yelled at 'em. More often than not, *that* scared the crap out of 'em, and I hope it did some good. There weren't any injuries, just some broken windshields and, at worst, some minor sheet metal damage. I don't know that I ever heard of anything as big as a cinder block being used as artillery."

"Like I said, it was a freak thing. They grow some of those rural Georgia boys big and dumb. Maybe the sense of scale was off a bit."

"Was anyone ever captured for the crime? That would be second-degree murder or first-degree manslaughter, two counts, at least. Were any arrests ever made?"

"Not a one. The concrete shattered on impact, kinda like Jack's cranium. So no prints there. And no witnesses ever came forward, so it goes in the cold case file eventually and forever."

"So your sister lived for a while before she passed."

"Oh yes. One and a half weeks after Jack. Mom was just sick with grief. I think the trip I made back for the funerals was the closest she and I had been in decades. Dad was busy with work, but I could tell that he was sad too. He was a quiet, stoic man. He didn't display his emotions much at all. He and Mom actually *hugged* me at the end of the service. Trust me, Street, that just never happened in my family. There was just no *touching*. Wade attended too, with his wife. My last surviving sibling just walked past and, under his breath, called me a slut." She took a breath. "Nothing new there."

"Well, I'm sorry. No one deserves that treatment." I stood, walked to the dishwasher, opened it, and put my plate inside. "Let me get dressed, and we'll start our travels. That sound good to you?"

As she stood from her chair, she smiled a sad smile and said, "Sure."

———

The day went smoothly, with less than zero friction between Sylvia and anyone else. Bringing lots of money to an entity usually cools even the most pretentious attitudes. I cooled my heels in the outer offices of each of her contacts. Sylvia was the very picture of professionalism and politeness, but then again, she was gaining an upper seven-figure windfall with no decimal points. Who could be irate over that? We returned to her desert oasis at half-past four, and she asked that I join her for an evening out. The caretakers of her property had taken the burgundy Corvette from its resting place in the garage, washed it, and positioned it nose-out in the carport.

About five o'clock, Sylvia called from the living room as she hung up her phone. "Street! Dress up for tonight. We're going to a concert after dinner. I just landed a pair of tickets from my agent here in Vegas."

"Not a problem. Whose concert?"

"Barry Manilow!" As she rounded the corner into the room, she looked at me. "You like him, don't you?"

I demurred. "He's had an incredibly long, successful career, and he's a great talent. Man's a legend!" Then I smiled.

"Yes, Street, but do you *LIKE* him? I can turn down the tickets." Her facial expression made it clear that there would be a preferred answer.

"No, no, don't do that. It'll be a great show. Where will we have dinner?"

"There's a great Oriental place at the Wynn. They know me there. It'll be fun."

"Excellent! I'll practice my *Copacabana* and *Mandy* lyric memory. It all sounds great."

She laughed, and her expression made it clear that she didn't believe a word I'd said. "We'll have fun, Street! I guarantee it."

And we did. The dinner was great, and the Manilow concert was actually a lot of fun. Sylvia was called out from the stage as a special guest, a favorite *agent stunt*, as I learned later, and she was happy. We ended the evening with her Las Vegas agent and his wife for drinks, and I liked the guy, even though I'll never be a Hollywood-type, show biz kind o' guy. I promise.

————

The rest of the trip developed nicely. Sylvia visited her cosmetologist the next morning, then spent the rest of the afternoon on her phone in the shade of the pergola by the pool. There were a few guests, including local friends, one of her TV series co-stars, and that same agent from the previous evening. Everyone got along famously, and we had zero issues with hostile intruders. My ankle had even stopped aching.

12

By Friday afternoon, all the errands had been run, and all the tasks completed. We left the house a bit after one pm, after we packed the Tahoe and hit the 15 southbound. It wasn't a quick trip, again, due to the delays from the I-15 construction zones through the mountains south of the State line. I took the truck route for the first twenty miles of the detour, and that helped speed the travel a bit. My usual stop at the little Greek drive-thru café in Baker was the only diversion from rapid forward momentum. Sylvia had never made that stop before and seemed entertained by the shockingly low-end practices of her employee, me. On the other hand, she did like the fried zucchini. I was making progress.

Sated, I resumed the interstate and made great time back to her hillside Hollywood home. Along the way, we had a couple of hours of casual conversation, and once I did attempt to open the topic of Arnie Lankershim.

I asked her, "At the end of the day, what do you think happened to him?"

"Street, I wish I knew. His disappearance broke my heart. We had great plans. I wanted to start a family. I wanted to spend the rest of my *life* with him. He had given me a great career, and I *loved* him. I wish he was still here."

"I get that, Syl. How long did it take for him to be declared dead?"

"That took a while. That was actually the last time I had any legal work done. The *Trauma Center Hospital* series lasted two more years, and our contract work was already settled, so there really wasn't any professional impact from his absence. I hired another agent from Silver, and after a while, we meshed fairly well." She paused and gave a sigh. "I have to say, though, he was no Arnie Lankershim."

"Were you in his will?"

"Yes. Like I said, we'd been together for a while. He had been married before, but he and his *ex* hadn't spoken in five years."

"Where had he gone to law school?"

"He was a USC graduate. He'd moved here when he was twenty-two. He was from Chicago originally."

"I have Lynn in my life, so I know about the bond that can be formed with attorneys. It sounds like he was a good guy."

Quietly, she said, "Sure, mostly. We all have our strengths and weaknesses." She reclined her seat a couple of notches and leaned back. We continued the trip in silence except for the seventies oldies playing on the radio.

———

I dropped Sylvia at her home, and I did a security check of the property before I left. Sylvia handed me a check as I stood in the foyer. She gave me a light hug, kissed my cheek, and thanked me for my help. I drove away and made it home by eight that evening.

Back home, I unpacked the Tahoe and rinsed it off in the driveway in preparation for returning it the next morning. I checked my messages and found one from Louie, the source of the Escalade that I'd arranged for Wade.

"Hey, Street, Louie. Hey, man, when do you think this guy will bring the Escalade back? Call me, babe."

Instead of calling him immediately, I lit the desktop and checked for messages. Finding none from Wade, I called Louie and apologized. Louie was understanding to a degree. "Hey Street, you didn't take the car, your man Wade did. It's insured, and I know shit happens. You have a way of finding this guy, I wouldn't mind getting my car back. Let's talk in the morning."

––––––––

I caught up on my sleep after the road trip, but the next morning, it was time to do little detecting. I called the Embassy Suites, where Wade had said he and his wife Lucy were staying. The front desk clerk answered and promptly searched the registry.

"Mr. Street, this guest checked in a week ago, checked out yesterday. I spoke with him, he said he was going home to Georgia. He acted as if he couldn't stand it out here. Candidly, I think we liked him as much as he liked us. He was really overbearing. Please don't tell my boss I said that."

The check in date was when? Wade had insinuated that he'd arrived on the weekend previous, not seven or eight days before. "Your secret is safe with me. Tell you what, John...I'm going to drive down, and I'd like to take a look at the registry. Can you let me do that?"

"Sure thing, Mr. Street."

13

Wade Hawkins returned to the Embassy Suites south of LAX and parked his shitbox renter across the street from the front entrance of the hotel. He was tired from the traffic and the strain of dealing with all this estate business, and more than that, he was tired of LA itself: the noise, the traffic, and perhaps more so, the lack of power that he felt here.

He entered the hotel at the center set of front doors, then took the curved, tile-layered stairway to the front set of rooms on the second floor. Halfway along the row of doors, he used his key card to enter the small suite that he had reserved. His wife was seated on the couch, watching Oprah or some such drivel on the big screen TV. He leaned down and kissed her on top of her head, maybe the most physical contact they'd had on this trip.

She asked, "How was your day, Wade? Did you get everything handled like you wanted?"

"I made a little progress. The attorney was cooperative and put one of her staffers on finding Ann. Hopefully, we'll know something in a day or so."

The phone by the side of the sofa rang. She looked at it before Wade reached across her and answered it. "Mr. Hawkins, this is

Jimmy at the front desk. Your rental car has been delivered. I have the keys here at the desk, or I can send them to your room."

Wade knew that delivery would entail a tip. Everyone here had their hand out. "I'll be down in a few minutes to pick them up. I have another rental from National at the Airport, can I leave those keys with you and have that car picked up here?"

"Yessir. We do that all the time. Ask for me when you come down."

"I'll do that."

As he hung up, his wife asked, "What was that about?"

"Well, maybe the one piece of good news I had today. The detective I talked to offered to have a friend of his loan us a better car to use while we're out here. He was pretty nice about it, I guess, but I'm still not a fan. He was kinda cocky. We'll see if he followed through on his promise. I'll be back in a few minutes." He rose and walked to the door.

———

Wade returned to the suite in a better mood than he'd been in when he left. He actually smiled when he came through the door. "Hey, Luce, looks like we lucked out for once. That detective fella came through for us, got us a decent car to use. Let's get dressed and find somewhere to get a good dinner."

"Can we go find a shopping mall? I need some flat shoes and some suntan lotion. Do they have Walgreens here?"

"I think I saw one near here. Maybe there's one up by the airport. We'll find one somewhere."

Lucy continued before he had finished his answer. "Are you sure? You know I hate those off-brand places. I don't want any of that Dollar Store crap. That stuff never works worth nothin'."

Wade looked around the room until he found the TV remote, then he hit the button and turned off the noise, or at least the electronically generated portion of it. He had long since tuned her out.

14

Beverly Hills, California—2002

Arnie Lankershim watched as the photographer manipulated Lizzie Totts into position for her headshot photographs. The man was said to be an artist of sorts, but he'd been insistent on the conditions for doing the session. This KSG studio, such as it was, seemed to have turned out some excellent work through the years judging from the multiple rows of photos layered around the walls of the tiny outer office. One set of images that he recognized instantly was a half-dozen images of a younger Sylvia Tate. Arnie smiled as he recalled the earliest meetings as she was establishing her presence in the business. He also recalled that she had moved on from Kiefer Silver-Graves to Arnie soon after they'd met.

Through the sliding glass doors that established the boundaries of the impromptu studio, he could see and hear the shooter placing Lizzie as he wished. The big black camera clicked a dozen times in rapid succession and would stop as the photographer changed the lenses or settings. Wardrobe changes were frequent, and it was easy to discern that the photographer had his own vantage point for the process taking place behind the folding screen. He wondered how many other young women this guy had watched during his career. Nice job if you can get it.

Lizzie Totts seemed to be enjoying herself as well, energetically flirting with the older man. As the end of the two-hour session neared, the giggling started, and the whole ordeal went south. The photographer looked at Arnie a time or two before the agent lifted his arm and tapped his wristwatch. Let him flirt on his own time. After Lizzie emerged from the studio, she rushed to him and gave him a hug. Moments later, in the car, she said, "Thanks for this, Arnie, this was fun! Can we go over to Ventura Boulevard? That car dealer wants to talk to me about giving me a Lamborghini."

"Lizzie, you don't want that. He's not *giving* you anything. He's involving you in an unpaid promotional contract that causes you massive tax problems and makes your car insurance rates go through the roof. We can work on it, maybe get you a deal on something better suited to your driving abilities. Crash one of those damn Italian cars, and you'll be paying for it the next five years."

Lizzie pouted. That was her main tool of communication when she didn't get her way.

15

Beverly Hills, California—2002

Sylvia Tate had arranged for a day off from work that Friday and had planned the event that she hoped would change her life and define her future. She spent most of the morning at the spa over on Ventura Boulevard, then picked up her order from the boutique in Beverly Center. Her morning sickness had subsided for the moment with the assistance of a recommendation from her OB/GYN. She and Arnie had been quite amorous the night before, and she was glad for the assist. For whatever reason, he had been more *active* lately, something she welcomed even though she occasionally wondered why.

Her next stop was the hair salon at Paramount Studios, one of the locales that she considered an undiscovered treasure. Her favorite stylist from the early days of her series now worked there. Beverly had become a friend early on but had tired of the long hours of series work after she had remarried. When she landed at the salon at Par a week later, she had called Sylvia in an effort to build a solid, loyal customer base. Sylvia had renewed the friendship and had become a regular client during the off-season and studio hiatus periods. Two hours later that day, she emerged onto the side street a block off Melrose, visually perfect, in preparation for Arnie's arrival at home that evening.

Why was she nervous? She hadn't exactly planned the pregnancy, though they had certainly talked about such a situation. The idea of starting a family seemed natural once they had become successful. At thirty-four, she was starting to feel that she was on borrowed time, and dammit, this was what she wanted. Her producers had already been advised and had seemed delighted at the news. The series was a hit. It was in its eighth season, with two more penciled in by the network, with commensurate S8 salary increases for all involved. Syndication was already a lock, so there seemed no end in sight for secure income.

As Sylvia returned home that afternoon, she caught her image in the full-length mirror in the entry hall. She stopped and examined the image and was struck with the thought that this—this place and this moment—was what she had always imagined when she dreamed of herself as a success.

She unloaded her stuff from the car and then went into the guest room to rest for a short nap. This would be the nursery in a while. Her favorite recliner was in there, a big cushy cloth one, and this had been a full day, so she sat back, put her feet up, and closed her eyes for a few minutes.

At a little past five-thirty, she started from her nap. Looking up from her perch, she saw Arnie hurry past the doorway.

She called out to him, "Arnie! I'm glad you're home! You're early!"

He looked a bit more flurried than usual. "Yeah, babe. Um...I'm also out the door in a minute or two. Anything happening? How was work?" He leaned over to kiss her on the forehead.

"Well, sure...I have plans, with you. Did you forget? Your birthday?"

"Aw, man...it completely slipped my mind. I have a strategy meeting with the staff for a couple of my clients. I'll get back just as soon as I can. You know how it is this time of the year." He pulled her close and kissed her on the forehead. "I'll be on my cell if you really need me. Gotta run!"

Sylvia followed him to the front door, her stomach suddenly in knots. "But Arnie, we had plans! We have to talk. It's important!"

He stopped and turned as he stepped onto the front landing. More adamant now, he said, "Syl...honey...I'll be back as soon as I can get back. I'll call you when I get some time." Then he hurried to his Lexus.

Past the car's open doorframe and limousine window tint, Sylvia Tate spied a smiling young face piled with light-blonde hair...Lizzie Totts. As Arnie slammed his car door and hurried off the circular driveway, Sylvia's vision cleared, then she puked into the shrubbery next to the front door. It was gonna be a long weekend.

16

Back at home, I tried to catch up on phone calls, correspondence, and my own inner thoughts. The phone calls took fifteen minutes, just two from Lynn, asking for progress on the matter at hand, and one from a different potential client. I called Lynn to verify that the cookout at their home was still on for that Saturday evening. The correspondence included a half-dozen bills—welcome to LA, Street —and two aptly-titled samples of junk mail.

My inner thoughts were quite something else. I'd spent my solitary part of the trip back to LA from Sin City concentrating on the stories I'd been told about Arnie Lankershim and attempting to sort out my feelings, opinions, and suspicions gathered from the most recent days with my client. I was knee-deep in my personal iceberg, with far more intrigue and mystery beneath the surface than above it. My client, Sylvia Tate, was a charming and successful woman who was well on the way to becoming a friend. I wanted to trust her, but there was something—a subtly mysterious quality— that I couldn't quite get a handle on. I don't expect to unearth every secret personality element of every friend I have, but when questions linger, I tend to pay attention.

The knottiest questions that I had centered on Sylvia's former agent, Arnie Lankershim. She had claimed that Arnie had been consistently and famously unfaithful to her. Yet when she called him out for the one specific dalliance that killed a greatly important planned weekend, he got all depressed, headed for the coast, and pole-vaulted into the surf, ending his life as well as any chance for reconciliation. Really? That didn't make any sense. Sylvia could be very convincing, but this was a stretch.

Okay, so what had happened to Arnie Lankershim? Where was the body? Had Sylvia murdered him in a rage and done away with the corpse out of revenge or in an effort to take over his possessions and wealth? She had her own *wealth*, probably more than he had, really, but that rarely stopped anyone from wanting more. What about the covered Shelby Mustang in the garage of her LA home? There had to be a story behind that, too. Sylvia had mentioned that she'd bought it for agent/paramour Lankershim at a great cost. Judging from our conversations, I knew that she liked fancy, expensive cars, but this one, worth more than her others combined, had sat long enough that there were cobwebs hanging from the chassis. I needed specific information, and that wouldn't be available out in the open. I decided to continue to play the game as it had been established, apply what I had learned, and work toward the proper eventual conclusion from there.

I needed to do some research on Lankershim's professional turf, the agency for which he'd worked, Silver Associates. An internet search established the ownership structure, mostly veteran talent agents. Most of them had started out as young attorneys specializing in entertainment. That's fine, but I was looking for other qualifications. As with most businesses, if you want to learn the ins and outs, the details of who's doing what to whom, you need to find a long-tenured secretary.

Suzanne Brick was the go-to for every aspect of work done at Silver Associates. Her longevity in her job was practically legend in the industry as well as within her company. She had endured at S/A through twenty-one years, three owners, two name changes, five promotions, nine pay raises, and two of her own marriages. Suzanne Brick had it goin' on.

————

Suzanne met me at a nice restaurant on Wilshire Boulevard, two blocks east of the agency facility. We took a table on the border of the sidewalk next to the front wall of the restaurant, her choice in the interest of lessening the risk of random eavesdroppers at nearby tables inside the restaurant. No one else wanted to dine in the midst of exhaust fumes and traffic noise, so we had the outer deck to ourselves. Fans and misters overhead kept the atmosphere fairly pleasant. For this initial visit, I didn't mind.

A stout, dark-haired, well-dressed woman in her forties, Suzanne would have looked the part of a strong administrative authority in practically any business anywhere in the LA basin. I could tell as she approached me that she could take charge of any setting and was not someone with whom to be trifled. We made our greetings and exchanged business cards before the management seated us.

As we took our seats, she looked at my card and said, "Thank you, Mr. Street, for being honest about who you are and what business you're in. I work with agents and actors, and, on occasion, they can be tawdry people whose behavior can attract attention from detectives. They have come to me on occasion, usually with some bullshit cover story that is obviously weak. Much like actors, detectives really need good material before they can be successful. I'm much more open and amenable to an honest approach...and, of course, a nice free lunch." She smiled at the last.

"I try to be straightforward as often as possible, and I need lunch too. We'll get along fine."

Our officious waiter appeared. Suzanne ordered a small Caesar salad and an iced tea. I went for the chicken chili and iced tea, then we resumed our conversation.

"Thank you for that. I'll be as upfront as I can be, as well. Can you tell me what happened to Arnie Lankershim?"

She looked over her glasses at me. "Right to the point. I like that, Mr. Street. What happened to him? There was plenty of speculation and many doubts regarding the story that was being given most often."

"Okay, but what do *you* think, or perhaps more accurately, what *did* you think at the time?"

"I was curious, but the disappearance also added to my work assignments. In my spare time, I had my doubts. The rest of the executive staff were fighting to take over his accounts, so I was a traffic cop for that situation."

I smiled. "You're not answering my question, are you?"

She reminded me of my grandmother as she lifted her index finger and pointed it at me, suggesting silence. "I'll answer in my own time, Mr. Street."

I nodded in agreement.

"I had known Arnie for about ten years as the agency grew. He was always polite to me, but he was in no way the best agent or career manager at the office. He lucked out considerably when he landed his girlfriend third credit in that primetime, top-rated medical series. She was kind of a user, hanging on to him for dear life as he gained attention for her, little by little. That's not a rare situation in our industry. Everyone uses someone. Lots of people use more than a few."

"How much did you know about Sylvia Tate?"

"I did all the paperwork for every job she was hired for. I met her a few times at company functions. She and Arnie were very friendly with me after she signed with him. Later on, his new favorite client, in fact, his *last* one, Lizzie Totts, was friendly to anyone she thought benefited *her* as well. Sylvia was far more adult, far more professional."

"Okay, I know the image the Totts girl has now, party girl famous mostly for being famous. Might they, Lizzie and Lankershim, have spent time together outside the offices?"

"All things considered, I wouldn't doubt it at all. He was known to play around. Agents and talent have been known to exchange bodily fluids on a regular basis. Some agents even marry their clients. And divorce them. "

"Of course. Welcome to Hollywood. In this case..."

"Lizzie and Arnie? Maybe. Arnie was not monogamous to Sylvia. They had been together for a while, and they had their issues, but I don't think they were any worse than any other relationship."

After a little more informal conversation with Suzanne Brick, I threw in the towel. Her loyalty to her business and her coworkers was impressive. I was not about to obtain specific negative information on her agency or her coworkers. Ya can't win 'em all, Street. I did, however, obtain Lizzie Totts's phone number.

Suzanne smiled when I asked her for the number. "There are plenty of men in this town who have *wanted* that number, Mr. Street. And if you believe the tabloids, plenty of men in this town have had their way with her. For some, as you know, her sexual exploits are a good bit of what she's best known for. If I am right, much of that reputation is fantasy on the part of her publicist, who, at the very least, does nothing to quell the rumors. The gossip makes her a hot, or at least *hotter*, property with a certain demographic. It does not assist her career as an actor. Just my opinion, of course."

"I don't want to ask her to the prom, Suzanne, I just want to see what she knows or speculates about Lankershim. I'm somewhat outside her target demographic."

Suzanne grinned and looked over her glasses again. "Yes, I suppose you are. Then again, maybe not. Give it a shot, ya never know." She chuckled as she consulted her phone and wrote the number on a 3x4 sticky note that she had withdrawn from her purse. We were wrapping up our light lunch, and I figured that my time was short. She put her napkin on the table next to her plate.

"Mr. Street, I have to run an errand on my way back to the office. If you have any questions or if you need any more information on Arnie, please let me know. I'd be interested to know what you find. I liked Arnie a lot. He was good to me, and that's not always the case in my business."

"I appreciate your time. You have my number as well."

We rose from the table, and I watched as she retreated toward the low wrought-iron fence gate and the sidewalk. I sat back down and finished my chicken chili, decent stuff indeed, then ordered dessert before paying the ticket and leaving to walk back to the parking garage beneath the office tower that held Silver Associates and a few dozen other businesses, including a notorious pornographer. Ya can't always pick your neighbors.

With nothing else on the agenda for that afternoon, I went home, changed into a pair of jeans and a relaxed blue Shelby logo T-shirt, and waited for Louie to arrive to pick up his Tahoe.

That happened an hour later. One of his shop trucks, a blue Chevy Colorado, pulled to the rear of my driveway, let Louie out, and backed from the driveway to return to the shop. I opened the door to the den as he was walking across the patio. He had a smile on his face, as usual, because he's a really confident guy. He's especially secure in the operation of his business. We met at the door, shook hands, and warmly greeted one another. He carried his laptop to the leather chair on the other side of my desk and motioned that I take the seat next to him. I knew where we were headed.

"Street, you know there's nothing that goes out of my property without a tracker…"

"Of course. What does the screen tell you? If it's static, let's go get it."

"Okay, Street, let me put this code in. Let's see where that ol' boy went." After fifteen seconds, he looked at me and said, "Got it! Looks like he's, lessee…parked over off Imperial Highway south of LAX near the coast."

I said, "Looks like it's in the parking garage at the hotel. Not bad, Louie. Let's go get it."

I closed the house, and we made the trip west to La Cienega, then south to the 405 for a few miles to the LAX exit, then west again, ending at the front of the block-long hotel. I left the Trailblazer parked across the street from the hotel, and we walked down the ramp to the garage. The pearl white Escalade was parked at one corner at the far end of the garage.

The big white SUV was in a dark corner of the dark garage, parked at an odd angle edging into two spaces. It didn't *look right*, so we made a cautious approach, finding the car empty and locked. The driver's side front tire was flat, that front fender bent outward, and the amber running light lens broken. I motioned to Louie, who pressed the button on his key fob. The security system beeped, the lights blinked, and the horn sounded. Then he opened the driver's door. I looked inside. Across the passenger side of the front seat, I could see a dark red smudge on the opposite door panel and across the base of the seat. I'd seen enough accidents and crime scenes during my cop years to have no doubt as to its source.

Louie spoke first. "Looks like someone's been leakin', Street."

"That it does."

Louie had already tapped the digits on his cell to call the LAPD. As an old hand in law enforcement, he knew the drill that was to come. All we had to do now was wait for the badges to arrive and for their support crews to do their thing. Louie's business location was also a storage lot for vehicles towed by the CHP in this area, so its storage during any investigation process would be maybe a hundred feet from its normal parking space. Hey, we're in LA. It's always wise to diversify.

The patrol officers arrived first, followed by a couple of detectives. Louie and I gave our statements, Louie regarding the assignment of the vehicle to my client and me detailing the recipient of said vehicle and the details of the various dealings I'd had with him. After the detectives and the crime scene techs examined the car and signed the release, Louie called one of his tow trucks to inflate the flat tire, retrieve the Escalade and take it on a flatbed from its current spot to his storage lot.

There was an In-N-Out Burger drive-thru a mile away, and

Louie hadn't eaten lunch. As the detectives finished their duties, I suggested that we take a break.

"Okay, Louie, let me know your rate for the Cadillac. I'll buy you lunch, too."

He nodded his head. "Why yes, you will."

———

Fifteen minutes later, as we took our food to the table, Louie asked me, "So what kind of loon is this *Wade* guy, Street?"

"I can't tell you a lot. Oldest son of a successful rural southern car, truck, and farm implement dealer from a small town north of Atlanta. Hasn't spoken to his sister for years, but he came out here to deliver her half of their parents' sizable estate. He's a piece of work. I'm sorry I involved you in the situation."

"Not your problem, C-man. You did nothing wrong. If this Wade dude is the perp, the cops are on the job looking for him now. Let *them* worry about it. I'll hardly miss one car out of the fifty-seven in our inventory. It'll work out." He paused for a moment, then asked, "What about the sister?"

"She's Sylvia Tate, you've probably seen her on TV. Our man Wade pretty much despises his sister, has for decades, and she doesn't trust him as far as she could throw him either. She even hints, mildly, that she is afraid of him and what he could be capable of."

Louie made a face and said, "Jeez, man. Sounds like a friggin' afternoon melodrama."

"Yes, it does. All it needs is that corny organ music."

"That it does. Well, now that you're a big-time officially licensed PI, are you gonna take a look at who's done what to whom?"

I chewed a few french fries—the crispy ones that I always order at In-N-Out—while I considered my response. "That's a definite maybe. I'll see if Sylvia wants me to take a look. This latest item, the blood in your Caddy, doesn't lessen the possible complications. I'm not a big fan of family drama, but if she wants, I could even go to Georgia and take a look. Time will tell."

Louie started to gather the napkins and assorted debris into the cardboard box that had enclosed his meal. "Well, anything I can do to assist, let me know. My FBI cred could help."

He drained his Coke, and we put our debris in the trash receptacle, then walked back across the parking lot to the car. As we returned to the Embassy Suites, one of Louie's flatbed tow rigs arrived. He signed off on the LAPD impound storage form, gave the patrol officers their freedom, and bade me goodbye. I left a few minutes later, my mind busy with plans and questions.

17

Five Days Earlier...

Wade Hawkins returned in that little shitbox car to the room he shared with his wife at the Embassy Suites LAX South after he survived that gawdawful freeway traffic dealing with that snotty attorney and her PI, whatever the hell he was about. They'd made him traipse all over LA to make arrangements to give that slut sister of his half the family fortune, and he hadn't liked any part of it.

His attorney back home had told him that to avoid a potentially messy estate problem, he had to locate his sister and perform the due diligence to get this crap handled. He and Ann had had almost no contact for years, since she'd chucked everything of value and split for Hollywood. Some guy from Atlanta had told her she was pretty, prob'ly got lucky with her too, for all he knew, and she'd bought it, hook, line, and sinker.

So he flew his wife and himself to Los Angeles all these years later to hire another damn attorney to handle the matter. He probably didn't have to go to all that trouble and expense, but he sure as hell didn't want her coming to town and seeing what he was developing there. The attorney would have someone find his sister and set up meetings for the settlement. He didn't even want to see her again. More expense. More time away from the things he'd put into motion, the things that would really matter in a few years.

He'd brought Lucy this time. She had nagged him endlessly, bleating that he never took her anywhere and that she'd never seen Los Angeles. He'd come here for dealer conventions, franchise expansion and corporation and credit establishment conferences a few times, and one big car show. He'd been squired around town by other executives. That had never cost him a cent. Things had certainly changed since those halcyon days.

He parked the car across the street from the hotel, hoping to save some money from not parking in the basement of the hotel. Twelve dollars a night? No. He used the center entrance, the fancy tiled foyer, then the curved stairs to the right, and walked along the balcony to their room on the second floor. He knocked on the door a coupla times, then used his key card in the slider thing and opened the door. Lucy was sitting on the nearest sofa, looking at the flat-screen TV across the room. Oprah Winfrey was on, babbling about some drivel with some other Hollywood trash.

"Hey, hon. How was your day?" Lucy looked up at him as he leaned down to kiss her cheek.

"It was all traffic, all the time, Luce. How you doin'? Did you get lunch?"

"No, I fell asleep watchin' a movie last night. I heard you leave this mornin'. Thanks for not wakin' me up. That flight wiped me out, and all that airport noise kep' wakin' me up." She yawned again. "That Cantina opens up at five, it's a free dinner and drinks. You wanna go there instead of goin' out for dinner?"

"We can if you want to. There are some places down the road in El Segundo, a Sizzler and a coupla little indie places I went to when I was out here before. One o' the folks I talked to today said we should ask for a better room on the back side of the hotel."

———

Before they could leave the hotel, Lucy insisted that they go down onto the show floor behind the elevators at the elaborate three-story floral display and have their pictures taken together. Wade requested the assistance of one of the desk clerks as a photographer, a common request from out-of-towners. As the couple stood stone-faced a half-foot apart in front of the flowers, the clerk hoped he never got to the point in his new marriage. He wondered why people who'd been together for decades couldn't act like they actually *liked* one another. He looked at the tip the man offered him—a whole dollar—and almost refused it.

After passing the giant South Coast Plaza shopping mall and a number of stand-alone stores, Wade was tiring of Lucy's qualifications for actually stopping and shopping as she'd said she wanted to do. Finally, a little after five, he pulled into the parking lot of a South Bay Buca Di Beppo Italian restaurant.

He looked across the car at her and said, "Let's eat here. I've heard their ads. I understand it's quite good."

And it was. He'd ordered a carafe of wine to go with the elaborate course that they'd settled on, three courses that made him feel full, more so than any time recently. The wine helped his mood. He'd already decided on his cover story for the return to Georgia. They'd believe it, just as they'd bought the story he'd given after Jack and Beth had died. He was still a bit queasy about that situation, but the audience had been receptive, so it was worth another try. After dinner, he'd ginned up an argument with Lucy. Something about her nagging and not being able to hold a decision after one had finally been made.

18

Beverly Hills, California — 2004

Sylvia Tate stepped into her trailer inside Stage 11 at Warner's at 4:35 that afternoon and sat at her dinette table as the phone rang. The number readout displayed her home number. "Hello?"

"Miss Sylvia? It's Alma. How soon can you get home, hon?"

"I'm shooting 'til seven or so. Maybe later. What's wrong?"

"Oh, the swimming pool from that house up the hill broke open. There's been a small mudslide from there, and most of it's now in your side yard. It's raining, too. There's some damage beside the garage. Who should I call?"

Sylvia Tate suddenly realized the problem she had. "Okay, Alma? Just leave it alone for now. I'll try to leave earlier. Is any mud or debris getting into the house?"

"No, ma'am. Your garden at the side yard behind the garage is the main area that is damaged, and the patio behind the garage is covered with mud."

"Oh, okay. Just bear with me. I'll get there when I can."

Sylvia consulted with the production manager to determine the shooting schedule for her scenes. "Ted, can we push those to tomorrow? I have a situation at home that I just have to take care of ASAP."

"Sorry to hear that, Syl. Go ahead on. We'll handle it for you. You good for tomorrow?"

"I should be. The script girl gave me the latest revisions, so I'll catch up on those before tomorrow morning. I'll keep you posted. Thank you! My wardrobe will be in my trailer."

The veteran studio *handler* made a note on his pink shooting script and looked back up at her. "I'll pass the word. Good luck with the home thing!"

————

Forty minutes later, Sylvia Tate arrived home. She parked on the driveway and immediately walked to the side of the garage to find an extra layer of mud tapering taller toward the rear of the structure. She walked up the new muddy slope at the side of the house to the garden area where the real worry lay. She took an appraisal of the situation and then went to the garage to get the shovel that hadn't been used since that first time almost a year ago. It took an hour, and she had to re-wrap the rapidly deteriorating, and still odorous, contents. It was gross. She was thankful for the eight-foot boundary fence that blocked any outside view of the side of the property.

19

I spent the following Sunday afternoon with Lynn and her big-time jeweler husband. I had met Lynn during my second week in LA and had served my state-mandated two-year professional license apprentice period under the management of her law firm. That period had ended a few months ago when my *full-strength* PI license took effect. She and her husband were among my closest friends and confidants.

Lynn was also needlessly distressed by my continuing bachelor-hood, so she often attempted to set me up with her single female friends and associates. Each one that I had encountered so far had been nearly flawless in appearance and carriage, some of them borderline stunning, most of them recent law school graduates, some employed by Lynn's law firm, and all so far were native Ange-lenos from upmarket or prominent families. Therein, it seemed, lay the rub.

My decidedly middle-class upbringing and my cop career, brief though it had been, seemed to outweigh my master's degree in criminology. Further, the potentially tawdry aspects of my current snoop career did not meet up to these women's lofty expectations for a potential first or second husband. I know that sounds presumptuous and sexist, but it's also quite realistic and, on occasion, a bit tiring.

This afternoon, Lynn's candidate for a potential life-partner for me had parked her new silver Lexus SUV at the side of the driveway toward the rear of their idyllic Pacific Palisades property, in the usual guest slots next to the huge white frame garage. I'd been there before, so I took one of the other spaces and walked around the side of the white brick manse to the polished pale gray stone surface of the patio. The patio was immense, far larger than my first apartment, but then almost any intact standing structure out distances that dump. To the left, opposite the pergola-covered table, stood Jack and Lynn, each a vision of perfection and grace.

Lynn spied me and hurriedly crossed the space to hug me, in true Hollywood style. I don't mind that at all, really, because she's a very attractive woman and a close friend, but the *show* element of the gesture can get a bit grating after a few laps. Parties with this set can be exhausting. I don't need a hug every time I see a friend. In any event, I walked with her to the grill, where her husband, Jack, was artfully flipping a variety of succulent-looking steaks, sausages, and chicken breasts. The man's an artist working in his main trade, fine jewelry, but he's purely a badass when dealing with former animal componentry as well.

After we shook hands and he returned to his duties, he said quietly, "So Street, yet another chosen candidate from the ranks of SoCal's more desperate single professional women! I wish you luck."

I smiled. "Jack, buddy, I live to serve."

I left the outside kitchen complex and joined to hear Lynn and her friend Stacey under the slatted cover of the patio. Stacey was a very attractive woman in her late twenties, a willowy five-foot-nine ash-blonde. A former model, she was now a paralegal with a law firm in the same building as Lynn's offices. I had seen her in the building a year before as I was wrapping up my apprentice duties. She was recently divorced, so she had to share those issues. I guess

I was as cordial as I needed to be, but there really wasn't any *there* there, probably for either of us.

After the meal had concluded, about dusk—as the butane torches around the yard were lit—Lynn pulled me aside and suggested that we take a few minutes to discuss the Sylvia Tate matter. We sat with our wine glasses on the carved wooden steps of the circular stairway that would lead to the upper deck of the primary bedroom suite and talked quietly.

"Street, I've been thinking about Sylvia's brother, Wade. I wonder if perhaps he is pulling a major scam on her."

I concurred. "She and I discussed him at length as we were returning from Vegas. She spilled quite a few gems on him. He is not a nice guy, and she intimates that he screwed up his dad's businesses before the dad died. I think she also has vague suspicions about his possible role in their siblings' demise as well, even though she says it was just a freak accident, it's the way she says it. Most likely, he's just pulling a scam on her with regard to the values of the family's business properties. They made a big deal about the businesses being closed and the sites razed. I'd like to find some info on the transfer of those properties to the subsequent owners. I also think that Sylvia would cover the costs of the investigative effort if we asked her and told her of our suspicions."

I continued. "And there may be some issues with Wade himself, right here in town." I explained the late return of the borrowed Escalade, locating the damaged vehicle, and the bloodstains found inside the vehicle.

"Wow. This thing is really snowballing, isn't it?"

"So it seems," I said. "I'd like to set up a meeting, perhaps just a lunch, Sylvia, you, and me. She has a pretty good business mind. I don't think she will have any issues with expanding our efforts. There could be a considerable gain for her if our suspicions hold true."

Lynn frowned a bit and said, "You know how hard it is for me to get away from the office during the week. Why not just have her come to my office? We can take a half hour, order lunch in, tell her of our suspicions, see what she thinks, and explain the possible outcomes. If she agrees, you can do your thing from that point. Your efforts on her behalf will be officially sanctioned by my firm and managed from my office."

"That sounds good. Thanks for introducing me to Stacey too. Nice lady, very talented, great legs. Much like your own." I grinned.

"Why thank you, Mr. Street. I failed to detect any blue flame shooting between the two of you. That's okay." She grins her mischievous grin. "One of these days, Street, I'm going to fix you up with Miss Right. Just you wait."

"Hey, a work assignment, free food, and a promise of eventual matrimony. What more could I ask?"

———

The meeting with Sylvia Tate was set for the following Tuesday afternoon. She mentioned that she had auditions on Monday and Wednesday, so apparently, her professional prospects were looking up. On Tuesday morning, I drove to her home and waited by my Trailblazer until she came out of the house.

She greeted me warmly and said, "Street, why don't we take my car. You can drive, you're far better with traffic than I am."

I agreed, and we took her handsome metallic black late-model Lexus sedan from the garage. As I pulled it out of the space, I looked across at the covered Shelby Mustang, still there. The trip to West LA took thirty-five minutes in moderate traffic on Sunset Boulevard westbound, and we arrived at Lynn's office ten minutes prior to our appointment.

The meeting went as expected. Sylvia agreed to our plans and encouraged my trip to Georgia. An agreement was signed for Lynn's representation in the matter to include my efforts, and funding was agreed to. Sylvia seemed pleased to have support for the situation. She was a great assist in providing me with friends, family members, and social contacts in the area, and my plans were solidified quickly. We arrived back at her hillside home just before dinner time that afternoon.

————

My itinerary was set. To Georgia, I would go. That said, I now had a half-day to follow my instincts on the Arnie Lankershim matter—or lack thereof, really. I used the number that Suzanne had provided me and called Lizzie Totts's home number. I was surprised that there was an answer.

"I'm Elliot, Miss Totts's executive assistant. How may I be of assistance to you?"

I identified myself and tried to explain my situation. "Mr. Lankershim was Ms. Totts' agent for well over a year before he disappeared. I know they had a close relationship and had become friends and allies in the pursuit of her early career. I'm hoping that I can meet with her and discuss their working relationship. I'd also like to see if she has any ideas about his disappearance. I promise I'll be brief. I know she's busy."

Elliot sounded a bit bored as he responded, "Hold for a moment. Ms. Totts is at the pool, I'll ask her and be right back."

I heard as he walked the cell phone to the patio, pool, or whatever. There was some conversation in the background, apparently Elliot wasn't adept at finding *Hold* on the phone. After two minutes of indecipherable conversation, he returned.

"Mr., um, Street, does this meeting absolutely have to be in person?"

"I find that's the best and most efficient method of communication. I won't waste time for either of us, I promise."

He sighed, then said, "Very well. If you insist on one-on-one, be here at three o'clock. She will allow fifteen minutes. No recording devices, cameras, or firearms. Our security will examine you when you arrive. Do you have the correct address?"

I told him what I had, and he agreed. "I'll be there a few minutes early. Thanks for your help with this, Elliot. See you soon."

"Fine."

———

Faced with a huge property tax bill, mammoth operating expenses, and an uneven earning picture, Lizzie Totts had offloaded the expansive home in Nichols Canyon that her childhood earnings had provided her. She was now renting a smaller but still grievously expensive home in the depths of Laurel Canyon. The home had in earlier decades seen occupancy and ownership by some of the royalty of the Los Angeles rock music industry, but now it was just an old house with crappy insulation and questionable plumbing. Its kitschy charm was largely lost on the twenty-five-year-old celebrity.

I drove along Laurel Canyon Boulevard from the south side of the hills, finding the proper narrow turnoff that led to a narrow driveway, leading to the restored bungalow at the top of a crest tucked behind the commercial enclave, which anchored the eclectic foothill community. Legendary rock musicians had lived among these hills through the decades, and a few had even died there. Now the area just seemed old and cramped, and redevelopment was beginning to encroach, replacing kitschy shacks with McMansions stuck onto hillsides denuded of authentic vegetation in favor of the fake stuff chosen for color coordination.

I parked on the dirt that formed the surface outside the chain link fence at the construction site across the street, locked the Trailblazer, and found the quaint wrought-iron fence gate that led to the vine-covered home. It was an older place, lots of multicolor brick and a hint of rustic flavor that didn't, in my mind, match the image of its ever-trendy tenant. Undaunted, I pressed the doorbell. After a few seconds, the stained-glass paneled door opened, and a slight young man appeared.

He looked up at me and asked. "You're Mr. Street?" He stepped aside as I nodded and stepped inside. "Please come in, sir. I'm Elliot, Ms. Totts's executive assistant. She's on the phone, she'll be out in a moment. Can I get you anything? Water, a beer, something stronger?"

"I'm fine. Thanks." As I followed him to the living room, I asked, "How long have you worked for Miss Totts?"

He grinned and said quietly, "Oh, I'm the latest in a long procession. We'll see how long it lasts. Please have a seat, she'll be with you in a moment."

I sat on a tall rattan-topped stool next to the counter of the wet bar that formed the divider between the living room and the kitchen. The combined rooms were smaller than I'd expected, but the ceilings were taller. The walls were rough, an approximation of traditional stucco though too pale to be authentic. There was a random variety of photos around the room, but the east wall held a collection of photos of Lizzie Totts with a variety of other celebrities. Many figures in the entertainment industry kept their photo collections on *I Love Me Walls* to celebrate their fame or to use as a conversation starter for guests.

As I scanned the collection, trying to find someone, I recognized Lizzie Totts entering the room. Smiling, she said, "Well! Look at you!" She approached and extended her hand. "I'm Lizzie. And you are..."

"I'm Street. I'm a private investigator." I offered a card, she took it and looked at it without much of a response.

"What can I do for you, Mr. Street?" She was smiling at me. It was a great smile. I appreciated that.

"I'm looking into the disappearance of your former agent, Arnie Lankershim. I don't really have a client, it's more a personal curiosity. I know that he was your representation early in your career after you got out of the kids' programs. There is another of my clients who was also close to him, so the disappearance is still a mystery. Would you know anything that might help me flesh this out?"

She grinned as she tilted her head and answered. "That's an interesting choice of words, Mr. Street. Arn was really big on *fleshing out* his clients. He fleshed me out a few times. And actually, he was pretty good at that."

"I've heard that he was a busy guy. That apparently cost him the chance to start a family with this friend of mine. So how's the career going?"

"Oh, it's okay. I had an audition last week that may work out well. Have you seen any of my work?"

"I'm a bit outside your target demographic, I'm afraid. Get in a good solid dramatic role, I promise I'll watch. You are quite easy to look at, on or off screen."

"Thank you, Mr. Street. I feel weird calling you that. What's your first name?"

"Friends call me 'C.' It's the first letter of my first name. I've used that since I was a kid."

"And what is that name?"

I smiled. "I forget."

"That doesn't start with a 'C.'"

"Good catch." I changed the subject. "So Lizzie...please...do you know anything about Arnie Lankershim's disappearance? I know it's been a while, but you were one of the last people to spend any significant time with him. Any ideas?"

"No, not really. He was worried about what that woman he lived with was going to think when he came back that weekend. I guess I kept him distracted."

Oh, I'll just bet. Lizzie Totts was wearing a rather modest white one-piece swimsuit that somehow wasn't all that demure with her inside it. I was rather enjoying the visit, but concentrating on anything other than her was becoming an issue. "So you have no other opinions? There's nothing that comes to mind?"

"No. Sorry. He was a nice guy and a good agent. He got me several good contacts that have paid quite well. I liked him. I wish he was still around. But as far as his disappearance, he dropped me off here on his way home, and that was our last contact, ever." She looked from the floor back to me. "So, Mr. C, are you married?"

"I'm not. I've been working on building my business, serving my apprenticeship until a coupla months ago. That all keeps me busy. I'm always looking..." I smiled.

"Looking is harmless, C, and it's free." She stepped toward me. "Give me a call sometime. Let's go see a movie or something. It'd be good to have a friend from outside the grind."

"Thanks. I may take you up on that." I rose from my stool and started toward the door. I turned toward her and smiled. "Thank you for your time, Lizzie. Take care."

20

After I cleared my calendar for the next ten days, I researched the itinerary. I made contact with the local lodging in a neighboring county at Sylvia's suggestion, and after studying the area a bit, I made arrangements to rent a new Mustang from Budget at the Atlanta airport to drive while I was becoming accustomed to the surroundings. Those *exploration* miles can add up fast.

Sylvia had described her hometown as a town in which most everyone drove a white pickup, and I gave that some consideration. I didn't want to make myself or my *stranger* status all that obvious. I did a quick online study of Georgia governmental operations to obtain contact information for the attorney general's office and state police agencies in the event that any of our studies bore fruit.

When I asked Sylvia about a local contact with potential insight on the family's business operations, she handed me a list of five people, two of them relatives, and told me that I might have my work cut out for me. She wished me luck. Turned out, I'd need it.

My trip to rural Georgia had a couple of goals. For Lynn, I wanted to uncover any possible financial malfeasance on the part of Sylvia's brother, Wade, proof of an effort to hide the value of the commercial property holdings left to them by their father. Additionally, for Sylvia, I wanted to determine the circumstances behind her siblings' deaths. I was hoping that with the latter effort, I would come up empty.

I hadn't spent any appreciable time in the Deep South, other than the occasional trip down I-95 from Jersey to a Florida vacation at Cocoa Beach during my adolescent years. I knew I had a lot to learn about the area and the locals. There I would be a fish out of water, and the water was going to be deep at first. I had a list of potential contacts courtesy of Sylvia, but I knew that the names on that list could be somewhat dated. I had brought Sylvia's copy of the local phone book from a decade prior, which would provide business locations as well as a few home phone numbers of pertinent local citizens. Slow and steady seemed the best plan, and I hoped I would fit right in with the natives.

I flew out of the Long Beach Airport to Atlanta, hoping to avoid the endless, miserable clot that is LAX. Atlanta's airport was at least as dreadful as the one in LA but far more modern than LAX and more spread out. It took a solid hour before I could get to my rent-a-car. With an upgrade due to the flight, Budget set me up with a dark red V6 Mustang coupe that looked decent and ran well. Later in my efforts, after I got the lay of the land there, I would probably supplement the driver with the *less suspect* white F-150 since every other vehicle on the road seemed to be one of those.

I drove north on I-75 until I found the off-ramp to the state highway that would lead to Hyde County. I would stay in a well-reviewed bed & breakfast one county to the west while I did my poking and prodding nearer the stomping grounds of the Hawkins clan, Gadsden County. I checked in to the B&B, a charming, eerily quiet immense century-old southern mansion, a half-mile off the wide four-lane turnpike that led to my future temporary stomping grounds. The owners/managers were a quiet couple in their sixties, locals since birth, who seemed curious about their most recent temporary tenant, me. After we got acquainted and I unpacked my bags, I went for a drive to start exploring my subject area.

My first impression of North Georgia was that it was almost

solid trees. Southern California was not so adorned, my native New Jersey much less so. The scenery was quite pleasant and varied, but it took a little getting used to. The air was clean, the breezes were less balmy than at home but far more fragrant. The quiet, almost everywhere, was something I'd never really experienced anywhere I'd ever lived. I liked it here so far.

Another element I noticed was an abundance of *yard cars*, vehicles that were abandoned but somehow never made it off the owner's property. There were plenty of those in Jersey, but they were usually wrecked or much older than the ones I was seeing here. Zoning restrictions and the neighborhood busybodies would prevent any such assemblage on my own stomping grounds, as would my own sense of decorum. I'd never thought of myself as a *neat freak*, but the presence of decade's worth of derelict vehicles would break the limits for me.

My first stop for the evening was the sheriff's station in Gadsden County. The station itself was a block-long two-story block and stucco affair that looked a bit too ambitious for the size of the population that it served. I approached the front desk after being buzzed in and soon found myself in the office of the shift commander, Senior Deputy David Cale. The stout Black man looked at my California PI license and started his queries. His heavy accent accompanied him.

"Welcome to Jawja, Mistah Street. This yo fust tam out here?"

"Yes, sir. I'm liking what I see so far."

"Excellent! Where ya stayin'?"

"I'll be at one of the local B&Bs for the next few days." I skipped the specifics in the interest of *personal security*, realizing that I had no idea who I could and couldn't trust.

"They's some nice places aroun' here, I'm sure they'll take good care o' ya. Now what can we help you with?"

"Well, for the moment, I'd like to see the accident report for a car crash from a year and a half ago. I understand it was one fatal after a projectile was dropped from an overhead pedestrian crossing. A truck was hit, driver was pronounced on-site. His sister was transferred by air ambulance to Atlanta, mortally injured, she passed a week or so later." I paused and handed him the list I had made of the details.

"I remember that quite clearly, Mistah Street. That was a bad one. You say you have some questions about it?"

"I do. It's nothing specific at this point. I'm just curious about the conditions and the elements of the accident. The victim's sister is a friend in California, and she has questions about the location and the circumstances surrounding the crash."

Deputy Cale cleared his throat, scratched his chin, then said, "Oh, I remember that one. It went down out on the turnpike during my shift. The crash site was actually just outside the city jurisdiction, so we were called in ta hep. Ma boys did a good job, but ever'-body there that night did everything they could ta save that poah girl."

"I understand that. I'd like to see the accident report as well as take a look at the crash site, see if anything calls out to me."

"Tell ya what, Mistah Street. Hows 'bout you come by tomorrah, 'bout ten, I'll give you the Dep'ty that was primary on that same crash. Ah'm sure he can tell ya anythin' you need ta know 'bout it. I'll pull the file and pitchas and leave 'em out for ya too, the emma-lope will have yo' name awn it."

"That sounds great, Deputy. I really appreciate the effort."

"Glad to oblige, Mistah Street. We don't get a lotta big city PIs roun' here, we'ah happy ta help." He paused, then said, "Just's long's ever'body minds their manners."

I smiled at that last bit as I rose from my chair. "I'll try my best." The deputy reached across the desk to shake my hand. So far so good. I left the sheriff's station and drove west toward the town, crossing the Fairwater city limits line five minutes later. Aside from what appeared to be a little local street racing on a side road approaching town, there was less than nothing going on in the small town that evening.

The Fairwater Town Square was tastefully retro, with a humongous courthouse front and center on the square, nicely maintained red-brick-surfaced intersections, and dozens of storefronts, mostly antique shops and boutiques for the local females. Side streets off the main square displayed a few dozen attorneys' offices. County offices were in another part of the town.

There seemed to be no franchises or national brand names in the downtown proper, but following the sparse traffic, I did run across a brightly-lit Sonic drive-in a half-mile farther out. Having seen no other familiar offerings of dinner, I took a space under the canopy and ordered a truly mediocre hamburger with extra cheese and extra pickles. Seems the days of hard-boiled private eyes dining at posh eateries in big cities had passed me by temporarily. After washing down the alleged sandwich with a large iced tea, I drove back to the B&B, intending to call it a night.

———

At the B&B, the proprietors, Alicia and Todd Graves, had other ideas. They were sharing a glass of wine with their guests, so I took a few minutes to partake. The wine was excellent, from the North Carolina vineyard of a famous NASCAR champion, and the conversation was quite pleasant and instructive. One of the couples was returning to visit family in the area after moving to central Florida in their retirement. Gary Ludlow was a former furniture store owner from Fairwater. The best part was, he had known, been friends with, and/or had done business with literally everyone in town. I would have to play it by ear for a few days, but he could turn out to be a great asset to my work in Georgia...if I could trust him.

My B&B lodging was quite pleasant; an immense bedroom suite, close to seven hundred square feet, with areas set aside for rest, relaxation, and media, and a bath suite that I would emulate when I tackled my guest bathroom at home later that year. There was even a fireplace, a gas unit controlled by a switch on the wall. A double glass-paned door opposite the entry opened onto a very pleasant deck overlooking the impressive garden maze that made up part of the property's expansive backyard.

The evening ended after a great shower with me deeply situated in a mammoth king-size bed that enveloped me for nine hours without an inch of movement. I hadn't slept like that, ever.

21

There was a calming effect to that early southern morning that I had never experienced anywhere else. I could hear birds chirping outside the window, along with the gentle rustling of the large oak and ancient magnolia trees outside my bedroom. Twenty feet from my balcony, atop a ten-foot pillar, a Hummingbird feeder was a popular hangout for those amazing creatures.

Even better, it was as if the varied aromas from the expansive kitchen one floor below were piped into my suite. I quickly showered, dressed, and went downstairs to find a serving table full of visually and aromatically fascinating foods. I didn't realize how hungry I'd been after having barely eaten the day before, but I fixed that situation in grand style that morning.

As I was wrapping the morning's project, Gary Ludlow tapped me on the shoulder and asked, "Mr. Street, can I borrow you for a couple of hours this morning? I'd like to show you around my old hometown."

———

We were in my rented Mustang. I had let Gary Ludlow take the driver's seat. This was his turf, as he explained early in our travels. "Forty-one years in the same location. I'll show you my place when we pass it. From what I hear, the people who bought me out ain't doin' all that well. They're younger, o' course, so hopefully, they'll get their rhythm after a while. Takes some time, and usually a little pain, to learn the ropes o' business nowadays."

"You're right about that. You knew the Hawkins family fairly well?"

He looked across at me. "You might say that. I started buyin' cars from the daddy just as soon as I could afford the payments. My first second-hand delivery truck came from 'im, along with maybe a dozen after that one. After that, maybe fifteen other personal vehicles over a thirty-year period. Got my kids started buyin' from 'em too. I loved those big ol' Pontiacs, lemme tell ya."

I smiled. "We have that in common. What kind of guy was the dad?"

"Aubry was a good, solid businessman, just not overloaded with personality. He grew his holdings as time went on, pretty much ran the vehicle business in the entirety of Gadsden County for years. The city bought all their cars and trucks from 'em. Cop cars, municipal vehicles, pickup trucks, even mowers and construction machinery...all that stuff. Soon as he could afford to expand, he expanded inta farm equipment. Got a lot o' out o'town bis'ness too, some from all the way to Atlanta."

"Sounds as if he knew his stuff. Did you know his daughter, Ann?"

"She's the one went to California, isn't she? Beautiful girl as I remember. Her younger sister took after her in appearance. My middle son and that younger girl dated for a while when theys in high school." He grinned at the thought. "Really pretty girl."

"You were around here when the son and daughter had the car crash?" I asked. I was starting to appreciate the *everybody knows everyone else* element of the local scene.

"That was jus' sad. I was a deacon at the church they attended.

Aubry, the daddy, was hurt by the deaths because he wanted to pass his business on to his kids. I could relate ta that. Hell, we all want that, Mr. Street. I wanted the same thing, but my kids jus' wasn't interested when the time came."

"That happens. Do you know much about Wade, the oldest son?"

"Hmmph...more'n I want to. That sonofabitch put well over a hunnert people out of work just after his daddy died. Closed those businesses up within a week of the funeral. You know what that did to any *other* business that depended on their customers bein' *employed*? We carried some of our own accounts, doin' our part tryin' to help people out. All of a sudden, a lot o' wage-earners, mostly younger couples with families, were cash-strapped an' late on their notes. We were as lenient as we could be, but it hurt, lemme tell ya."

"Could you show me the business locations? And you know where the crash occurred?"

"Sure thing, Mr. Street."

For the next hour, we traveled around Fairwater, with Gary Ludlow providing chapter and verse on the ins and outs of small-town Georgia life in the new century. He drove by the former locations of the Hawkins' businesses. Most of the locations were now bare land, with a few in the early stages of redevelopment.

"Gary, where would the building permits be taken out? Is that city? County? What?"

"That would require city building permits first, even for demolition, since the site is within city limits."

"So, I should check at the Fairwater City Hall, right there at the courthouse."

I had been taking notes on the addresses of the business sites. After we had toured all of those, I asked about the site of the crash that had taken the lives of the Hawkins siblings. Gary drove to a divided four-lane highway, the *turnpike*, a few miles from the city square.

As he pulled to the side of the road, he explained, "That was a gawker's paradise for a couple of weeks. The pickup landed way over there. It left the road right about there," he pointed to the end of a curb that started maybe an eighth of a mile back. "And it landed up there, on its roof."

"I see." I snapped a few photos of the site.

After the tour, Gary drove back to the B&B. On the way back, he gave his opinion on the recent and not-so-recent history of the city in which he had lived for decades. He was less than charitable about the father and son Hawkins. By the time we parted company, I fully concurred.

I had to ask, "One last question. If one wanted to know more about the Hawkins family and their dealings around town, the eldest son in particular, who would I talk to, and who *should* I talk to? Who could I trust?"

"Well, now. Let me think about that for a bit. Small towns are secretive places, Mr. Street, but the inhabitants on occasion gossip like a minivan full of eighth-grade cheerleaders." He chuckled at his own joke. "I'll get back to you in a day or so with my verdict." He smiled. "I promise you the wait will be worthwhile."

"Thank you for that. I look forward to hearing from you."

My problem with the explanation being given for the crash was that there was no way the vehicle was impacted by the concrete chunks under the pedestrian overpass and continued almost a thousand feet before leaving the road and crashing. That just wouldn't happen in the real world unless they were traveling at very high speeds. That had supposedly not been the case. The impact had to have happened *after* the car passed the overpass. That translated to straight vehicular homicide, not just some crank kids dropping stuff off the bridge. *That* translated to someone needing to be captured and tried for those crimes. But who would have had reason to take that drastic an action against that seemingly popular and certainly docile pair? And how should I proceed in finding that perpetrator?

———

Mark Hawkins was a first cousin of Wade and Sylvia, and the first name on the local contact list that Sylvia had provided me. There was apparently no love lost between the cousins or the sisters who had birthed them. They had not spoken to one another in years, despite living less than fifty miles apart. Hey, that had happened in my own family. Not all that big a deal. Mark had worked as service manager for the Pontiac/GMC dealer that Wade had closed down. As an accredited journeyman mechanic with factory certification and a service manager for over a decade at his uncle's dealership, he seemed to be someone with a knowledge of the subject at hand and the authority to observe and manage a situation.

I called ahead and made an appointment to meet him at his home. On the phone, Mark came across as a friendly guy with definite opinions. In person, he was much better. I pulled onto the driveway of the mature brick-and-frame two-story, parked at the rear of the house, and walked to the garage at the back of the property. A nice pepper green '70 Pontiac GTO convertible sat nose-out on a pair of jack stands in the first garage, getting my attention right away.

As I approached the garage, a tall man with a ponytail and graying temples looked toward me. He wore a pair of faded black khakis and a Jeff Gordon graphic T-shirt. He extended his hand and smiled as he approached me. "You're Mr. Street." It was a pronouncement, not a question.

"I'm him." I approached, and we shook hands. I looked at the GTO. "I'm impressed. The front view of the '70 GTO was one of Pontiac's best ever. This is beautiful. Which powertrain do you have?"

"It's a Ram Air III. Not originally that way. I ordered the parts and built the motor to that spec a few years ago. I'm thinking of converting to EFI in a year or so if the systems prove to be dependable."

"I have a '69 at home in California." I related the story of building my GTO. "It's in the paint shop right now."

"Sounds cool, Street. You didn't come all the way across country to jaw about cars, though, did you?"

"I did not. I'm looking into the business situation that your cousin Wade has created here, and I may have a question or two about the accident that killed Wade's two younger siblings."

"You are not the only one, Mr. Street." He wiped his forehead with his sleeve. "Let's go sit in the shade on the patio and talk. Would you like a beer?" He opened the ice chest that sat in the shadow of the garage.

"Sounds great. Let's."

A few minutes later, sipping Michelob from frosted bottles, sitting on weathered redwood picnic table benches, Mark opened the topic of Wade's business practices. "Soon as the old man kicked the bucket, ol' Wade went on a tear. He shut down all the businesses and put all of us out of work. I imagine you have heard about that."

"Yes, I have, from several sources. You worked for the car dealer, right?"

"Yes sir, I started when I was seventeen, a week after my high school graduation, sweepin' up the shop an' parkin' cars for the managers. I got all the right training, put in a lot of hours, and worked my way up to service manager for five brands by year fifteen. I had twenty-seven years on the job when the axe fell. I was lucky, my wife and I had resources set aside. She works for the city, and she makes real good money. I feel real bad for a lot of the other workers though. This shit came at us like a bolt outta the blue."

"How long after the layoffs did he start razing the properties?"

"That started about a week, maybe ten days, later. One day they were boardin' up the showroom, the next week they're knockin' it all down." He chuckled. "Hell, it was a waste of good plywood, too."

"What was his reasoning behind all of that sudden action? Any ideas there?" I took a sip of beer.

He frowned and pursed his lips, then said, "Near as I can figure, Mr. Street, this is a small town an hour's drive north of Atlanta. The grand municipal *daydream* that Wade shared with a few of the city fathers is that Fairwater needs to become a go-to destination for well-funded big city types tired of the traffic and the rat race. Rumor says they want to build a bunch o' tilt-up crap to lease out for tech centers, light- and medium-duty industrial facilities, and stacked-box-style condo projects, all built on the sites of his previously successful, thriving small-town businesses. Fantasy versus reality and fantasy took the day, but the real-world folks here in town lost out big time."

I asked, "How long would it take to cancel the franchises? That would require legal assistance, and it'd take time. Was there any inventory that had to be sold off? Where did the unsold vehicles go? There had to be some time that elapsed in order to get the wheels rolling on the closures, right?"

Mark said, "The new cars and trucks were all sent to the auction down in Atlanta and sold off as soon as Aubry passed. They were all sold at a loss, from what I heard. I'd like to have snagged one or two of them myself, but they were taken off the property in a heartbeat."

I continued, "But all of that didn't happen overnight, right? What I'm getting at, Wade had to have started the process to cancel the franchises before Aubry passed away. Did he have that power?"

Mark answered, "I'm not privy to how the business was structured, and I wasn't paying much attention to Wade by the time the ax fell, but I'd imagine you're correct about that."

"Was Wade the first, or one of the first, or perhaps the only, business owner to take such drastic action?"

"Oh, make no mistake, he wanted to start a trend, but he jumped the shark. Other business owners saw the shafting that Wade gave the people who had supported this town's local businesses for decades. They may have decided to hold off for a while. Lotsa local folks here in town agree that ol' Wade made a straight-up asshole move."

I asked, "Who owns the Hawkins' business properties now? The sites have changed hands, right?"

"The signs tell of a corporate owner or manager or an LLC, whatever that is."

I wondered aloud, "That stands for Limited Liability Corporation. Where could I find out about the property transfer? Is that city or county, state or what?"

"The Hawkins business sites are all within the city limits, so the property transfers would be handled at city hall, right there on the town square, downtown Fairwater."

I asked, "Do you know anyone there who could help me?"

He drained his beer, put the bottle back on the picnic table, and smiled at me. "I know the one that *matters*, Street. I'm married to her. Want an introduction?"

"Absolutely."

"Tell ya what...I need to take the Goat out to check out the new shocks I put on it this morning. Let's roll into town, we'll stop by and see her."

"Deal!"

———

Mark and I moved to his garage. He took the car off the jack stands, dropped the top and idled the car out of the garage, then pressed the button on the sun visor to close the garage door. He piloted the car off his property, took a left at the street, and drove a quarter-mile to the intersection with the turnpike. There he turned right and accelerated. The mellow exhaust note reminded me of the sounds of my own GTO. It was a happy sound, one that I had missed hearing in recent weeks. We traveled west toward the outskirts of the town. Mark took a late right turn and drove toward the business district. Passing one intersection, I spotted the Sonic drive-in that I'd seen the previous evening, off to the west from our current route.

"Town's got eight traffic lights now. Soon it'll be Manhattan South!"

I looked across at him. "That's how it starts."

Mark found a parking slot on the east side of the massive beige Fairwater Courthouse, raised the convertible top, and locked the car. "We'll go up to the third floor. They just gave Annie a private office and a promotion, so we'll have a little privacy."

———

Annie greeted us in the hallway on the third floor. She was an attractive forty-ish blonde woman who had met Mark when she bought a used Firebird from the Hawkins dealership nineteen years prior. She knew her stuff, quickly establishing the transfers of the former Hawkins business properties offered themselves as sources for out-of-state business entities. Nevada masks the identity of principals in such formations, but in Nevada, the masking is effective. The Corleone family loved that part.

Annie smiled when I mentioned that. "You're right about that, Mr. Street. But, this is Georgia. The names may be secreted within Nevada, but they are *not* when the corporate entities are properly registered here in Georgia with the Secretary of State."

I looked at Mark and smiled. "Mark, my friend, I hope you realize that you married far above your station. This lady knows her stuff."

"Every day in every way, buddy!"

22

I'd made real progress today, but it also set me up for more and deeper work before I could leave Georgia. I arranged to meet the couple for dinner that evening, then Mark and I went back to their house. I left to visit the local coroner to do a little accident investigation.

The coroner's office was located next to the local hospital, an arrangement that had always made good sense to me. The assistant coroner, a young trainee named Jon Baker, met me at the door of the coroner's office complex. He had me cool my heels until his boss had finished the latest examination of someone who could no longer offer criticism about the care being offered. A half-hour later, the white-haired chief coroner passed me as he approached his office after he washed his hands in the industrial-size basin on the other side of the open double-width morgue entry door.

He approached me as he straightened his lab coat. Every coroner I'd ever met displayed random brown and maroon stains on the front of their smock. It's just part of the gig. This coroner, a veteran physician named Jason Crabbe, asked me to follow him into his office as he slipped his smock off his shoulders. He wore a subtly patterned light-gray dress shirt over a pair of dark-blue slacks and a pair of Nikes. He looked at my business card and then back at me.

"Los Angeles, huh? I spent a month there a few years back. Did a conference with the LAPD. Interesting trip. We got there just in time for a gang war. I'll spare you the details." He drank some coffee. "What can we help you with?"

"I'm friends with the older sister of the Hawkins brother and sister who died in a really violent car crash about a year and a half ago. I'm told this office did the posts on both of them. Do you have any memory of that session?"

"Sure. I was close with their father and mother. It was a very sad time, and I think those deaths put their mother in a downward spiral. She wasn't in all that great a shape *before* they died, but..." He exhaled, frowned, shook his head, and sipped some more coffee.

"I understand the brother took the brunt of the accident."

"Mr. Street, that was no accident. We were fishing concrete chunks out of that kid for an hour. It damn near decapitated him. Would you like to see pictures?"

"Honestly, no, but it's part of the job."

Jason Crabbe wheeled his squeaky office chair toward the file cabinets behind his desk, opened a drawer, withdrew a file folder, then selected a stack of color photos which he passed to me. They were cringe-worthy, to say the least. The young man's head and his torso above the rib cage were crushed almost to the point of being unrecognizable as human. The odd element was the addition of large chunks of the concrete block fragments that had done the damage. Though blood-soaked, the fragments of the block, with their sharp rectangular corners, were easily recognizable.

"Dr. Crabbe, how much concrete was found? Was it all weighed for volume?"

"You mean, did we fish it all out and see how much there was? Sure. Last sheet in the stack."

I looked at the sheet, which estimated that almost a pound of material had been taken from the corpse. "Wow. That's a lot."

"Add what was scattered around the cab of the pickup, including the material that injured his sister, I figure it's about a half-block." He looked at me and frowned. "It hit the windshield and broke *through* as it broke *apart*. Poor kids didn't have a chance. I hate doing those exams. Shit, I knew those kids from infancy. I went to the same church they did, raised my own family at the same time they were comin' up. Seein' a great kid like that in that condition really hurt, and it pissed me off."

"Okay, then you have an opinion about the matter."

"Sure. It was a full-on double murder. Some asshole targeted them, period. Timed that block to drop as he saw 'em comin'. Got off a lucky shot, sure as shit. Please pardon my language."

"No problem. What did the police say?"

"Typical lazy-ass backwoods amateur-hour horse shit, Mr. Street. 'It was just kids, tossin' shit off the pedestrian overpass, didn't know they'd hurt nobody, blah blah blah.' Makes me sick." He withdrew a stapled two-page typed form from the folder and passed it to me. "Of course, getting our local Roscoe P. Coltrane counterpart to wake up and pay fuckin' attention, maybe look past the easiest possible conclusion, is *far* too much to ask."

I deadpanned my response. "So wait…you're saying the *Dukes of Hazzard* was not a *documentary*?"

He smiled. "There are a depressing number of people in this town who are still convinced that it was, Mr. Street."

"Interesting perspective." I stacked the sheets together and asked, "May I get a copy of those sheets?"

"No problem, Mr. Street. Are you going to apply some big city criminal investigation technique to this matter, find the bastard who caused these kids to die?"

"Dr. Crabbe, I'm going to give it a hell of a try." I watched as he stacked the pages into his office copier. "Would you know where the vehicle was taken after the crash?"

He frowned, then said, "I doubt it's still around, it's probably been crushed or sold for weight by now, but you might try whatever insurance carrier they had. That information should be with an attachment to the original accident report, I suppose." He removed the pages from the copier, shuffled them, and put them into a fresh file folder, to which he stapled his business card. He passed that across to me and said, "Listen, man, if you luck out and make any progress on these murders—and that's what they were, make no mistake—you let me know how I can help. That was a good solid family. The daddy was a good friend for many years. We feel for 'em." He offered his right hand.

"Thank you, Doctor. I'm sure we will talk again."

————

I didn't really want to talk to the local police that day, so I took the car and drove around the town, trying to get my bearings. Knowing your way around in a strange locale has its advantages, and I expected that the hostility that might eventually be shown by allies of the current Hawkins patriarch should be taken seriously. Along my route, I revisited a few of the former business locations, noting the varying levels of construction preparation at each. Redevelopment was moving forward at a few locations, though seemingly not at a steady, ambitious, or accelerated pace.

It was a hot afternoon, so eventually, I stopped again at the Sonic drive-through. I picked a covered slot and snagged a large lemonade. I re-read the accident report that accompanied the photos and waited for answers to the questions that were rattling around in my head. None came right away, so I finished the lemonade and continued my drive.

23

The State Capitol of Georgia is Atlanta, which is lucky for me because all I had to do was tackle I-75 traffic for an hour the next morning. Atlanta resembles LA in many ways, including the immense amount of freeway traffic *every* hour of *every* day in *every* direction. I think there were more trucks on the Atlanta freeways, but perhaps that's just a mid-week thing. I made a few passes through the Capitol area before I found a suitable parking space, then I spent another half-hour finding the proper office in which to kill another hour waiting for the proper bureaucrat to order the proper underling to obtain the information I was seeking.

The material that I obtained for my efforts and all that waiting was a mixed bag. GeorgiaPrimeOne LLC, a foreign corporation located at a commercial mailbox address on West Sahara Boulevard in Las Vegas, Nevada, had acquired eight separate properties in the city of Fairwater, purchasing the holdings of the business entity that had been formed decades ago, just one day after the patriarch/owner's passing. Principals in the LLC structure were listed as Wade Hawkins, his father, his mother, and the two younger siblings. All of them, aside from Wade, were now conveniently past tense.

Judging from similar transfers I researched that afternoon, the amount of the purchase was about thirty percent of the appraised value of similar business sites anywhere in the North Georgia commercial real estate market. I gathered that declared value information from established liability and comprehensive insurance coverage, a state requirement for businesses in Georgia. I was catching on.

From Atlanta, I drove—slowly—back to the B&B in the late-afternoon rush hour traffic. Does Atlanta ever end? The I-75 north of the city was a great stand-in for LA County's 405 southbound on any Friday afternoon. The stop-and-go pace gave me time to think and consider my next steps. At the B&B, I changed into a pair of jeans and a Georgia Tech sweatshirt—I'd briefly gone shopping for *local appearing apparel*—and spent a half hour answering emails and returning phone calls regarding business back home. Just before seven pm, I called Lynn to update her on the new material. She concurred that by his subterfuge, Wade had put himself in a potentially serious legal lurch.

Problem was, how could I, an unlicensed player, a total stranger a continent away from my home turf, with no backup and even less familiarity with local laws, customs, and legalities, possibly gain sufficient traction to take down a local power broker and favorite son?

The next step, from my current vantage point, seemed to point toward proof of Wade's wrongdoing against his own sister. I was unsure of what penalties for offenses would be within the State, so I needed to bone up on Georgia law or make contact that would provide solid information regarding same. That, in turn, would require a level of trust that I had, as of yet, not acquired. I did, however, have a couple of potential leads for finding that.

In the interest of security, in advance of my plunge into the depths of Georgia criminality, I made a call to an ally of mine in LA. Zig had been a friend since my second week in town when I had sought out a location for small arms target practice. I've never been all that great a marksman, but I have great respect for the concept of practice makes perfect. Zig had helped me often with that. I had found his prosperous gun store in the flats of Burbank soon after my arrival, and he and I had been tight from the first day.

Zig was a sixty-ish Vietnam-era Air Force veteran who, like me, had wanted to live in California since he was a little kid. Once he hit town, he had taken any job he could find, from movie extra to apprentice stuntman to technical adviser for a firearms wholesaler. That particular gig led to the acquisition of a near-bankrupt Burbank gun store which he pulled back from the brink. His store now had dealerships for five major gun makers, but the real draw for locals were the specialties.

Following the infamous North Hollywood bank robbery shootout in the late-90s, his shop on Magnolia Boulevard had become a go-to for *enhanced armaments* for law enforcement officers in need of potent firepower. His shops' capabilities included ammo loading and weapons training, basic-to-bad-ass.

I called Zig that evening, and we talked for a while. He promised that I would receive a *care package* by FedEx Air, since I hadn't been able to bring my own weapons with me on the plane. Better safe than sorry. I gave him the address of the B&B, and he wished me luck.

24

The next morning, after yet another sumptuous breakfast, I started driving with the intent of solidifying my thoughts and opinions regarding the car crash that had wiped out the Hawkins siblings. Eventually, I found my way back to the turnpike and found the accident site. A hundred feet past the pedestrian overpass, I pulled the car off the road and took a better look at the structure and the surrounding area. I leaned against the back of the Mustang and stared at the bridge for maybe five minutes. It was an impressive structure. The clearance markers indicated a sixteen-foot clearance height at the low point of the outer lane. The crest of the structure over the median strip of the highway arched maybe six feet higher.

A combination of steel and concrete made up the arched walking surface. Upright posts resembling chain link fence poles stood every ten to twelve feet across the span, and a tightly-woven chain link fence material spread the length of the walkway across the width of the divided highway. The mesh fencing was topped with spirals of razor wire a couple of feet below the roof.

I snapped a few pictures with my little digital Canon, then resumed the car and drove to the next exit from the highway. Two blocks off the next main route to the east, a residential cul-de-sac lined with modest older tract homes led to this end of the elevated walkway. I parked at the base of the hard-packed dirt pathway, walked to the crest of the walkway, and watched the traffic for a few minutes through the chain link fence. A small amount of sand, gravel, and assorted debris littered the walkway surface. Out of curiosity, I pushed on the chain link fence surface, finding it tightly bound every few feet at the bottom all the way across on both sides of the structure. I put the camera into *video* mode and shot the maximum movement of the fence mesh, then recorded my walk back to the car.

A couple of things were obvious: the fence material was sufficiently tight across the span of the walkway that there was no way a *trim-block* of structural support concrete block could be dropped from this structure. There might be space between the mesh to drop a rock of one-to-two-inch diameter, but nothing larger. Had the bridge been altered, updated, or improved since the Hawkins crash? I'd need to determine that before I started making waves or considering alternatives. My earlier study of Georgia state government structure told me that the State Highway Department would be the source of that information.

Soon a potential information source approached. As I sat in the idling rental car parked at the end of the cul-de-sac near the base of the elevated walkway downloading the fresh photos into my laptop, a dingy white Chevy Malibu slowly drove in my direction and parked behind me. The car displayed an A-pillar spotlight, and a narrow push bar hung from the front bumper, indicating a former marked police car turned unmarked and unconvincing. The driver let the car run at idle as he ran my plates.

After about ninety seconds, the driver's door opened, and a slim young man stepped out of the Malibu. As he shut the door, he straightened his uniform and walked toward my side of the Mustang. As he approached, I powered the window down and held my business card and driver's license for his perusal. He stopped at the rear line of my driver's door and leaned forward at the waist to look inside the car.

"Good afternoon, sir. I'm Officer Waverly, Fairwater PD. Could I please see some identification?"

I wiggled the fingers that held my credentials, and he took them, examining them for a moment.

"Reason I stopped, Mr. Street, we had some reports of an unfamiliar car parked here, and I was asked to check it out. There are two schools on the other side o' the bridge, so people here keep an eye out for strangers." He returned my ID and kept my card.

"Understood, Officer. I'm doing a little research for a client. It's simple observation at this point." I craned my neck to look at him through the window opening. "Would you mind if I stood outside the car and asked you some questions? You're local, perhaps you could help me a bit."

The officer backed up a step and said, "Sure thing, Mr. Street."

I opened the door and stepped out of the car. Standing next to him, he looked to be in his late twenties, about six feet, with close-cropped hair and a crisp uniform.

"So whattaya need, Mr. Street?"

"A little over a year and a half ago, there was a car crash. Supposedly, a concrete chunk was dropped from this elevated walkway. It struck a passing vehicle, caused a crash that was fatal to two. Did you work that one?"

"No, I was on vacation that week. I remember reading the report though. Pretty grizzly deal, but it was deemed an accident in the end."

"Okay, I've heard that." I gestured toward the bridge. "I'm curious, have there been any alterations to the fencing on this bridge since then? Was anything ever done to prevent a recurrence?"

"Hmm...no, as far as I know, this one is as it's always been. No one's changed a thing."

"Where could I obtain a copy of your department's accident report for that event? I'd like to see what your investigators had to say."

He withdrew a business card from his blouse pocket and handed it to me. "Well, you can get that from the PD. Here's my card. I work days this month. If I'm in the office, I'll handle that for you myself. Give me a call before you arrive, I'll meet you."

"Thanks. I appreciate the nod." I returned to the car as the officer resumed his unit and backed onto the street.

———

So far, so good. I was pleased with the way things were going here. Everyone was agreeable and cooperative at this point. It wasn't the first time I had seen an investigation progress with so little resistance, and I was not going to question my good fortune. I drove back to the B&B, changed into some more casual clothes, and called Lynn's law office in LA. She picked up on the second ring. She always does that. It's eerie.

She spoke cheerfully. "Hey, Street! How goes life in the small city?"

"Good. Our suspicions are showing fruit. As we suspected, the properties formerly occupied by the Hawkins business entities are under various stages of redevelopment. I've yet to determine their transfer to new owners, but if that's the case, ol' Wade is depriving his sister of substantial value of the parents' estate. I need to determine the current ownership of the properties, but the signs I see indicate the ownership is an LLC, outside the confines of the great state of Jawja."

Lynn paused for a few seconds, then asked, "What state are the LLCs registered in? Delaware and Nevada carry the bulk of those, then you start looking at offshore. Any bets?"

"I'll let you know when I find out. I may have to do some research at the State Capitol to figure it out. I'm researching commercial real estate prices in the area, the properties look a bit large for the values that were assigned, and there's something else that I'm looking at as well."

"And that is?"

"Sylvia's younger brother and sister were killed in a car crash almost a year and a half ago. Freaky deal, a chunk of concrete supposedly dropped from a pedestrian overpass into their car, causing a rollover crash. The brother was killed instantly, the sister was critically injured. She lingered for a while before passing."

"Wow. That sounds...um..."

"Unpleasant, at the very least. Thing is, the fencing along the walkway of the pedestrian bridge from which the projectile was supposedly dropped is far too tight and restrictive to allow anything that size to pass through. That's a design feature intended to prevent that same style of accident or vandalism. This bridge, built in 2001 according to the dedication plate, is newer than the other bridges in the area. Those design changes were made in the '90s to prevent that type of vandalism. I am told that the structure is as it was before the incident. As a result, I'm seeing a straight, intentional vehicular attack completely different from the eventual official conclusion. I want to seek out the truth in the matter. I may have an ally or two in that examination."

"So your suspicions are taking shape. Shall I advise Sylvia of your progress?"

"Let's hold off on that until I have something more solid to tell her. She and Wade are going to be at odds over the financial affairs anyway, there's no need to raise false hopes on pure conjecture."

"Sounds as if you're going to be busy. Call me if anything else comes around."

25

I met Mark and Annie Hawkins for dinner that evening, and we chatted for a few minutes about his cousin. I had figured there was no love lost between them despite Mark's long employment under Wade, and I thought Mark might have an idea about a proper angle of attack. I also asked him if he knew of the potential whereabouts of the car involved in the Hawkins crash.

"It should've gone to the county impound lot after the crash. I know it was never brought back to the dealership. It would have been property of the insurance company until they settled the matter and/or their investigation is completed."

"That makes sense."

"I'll call around tomorrow and see if I can find anything."

"I appreciate that, Mark, but please be careful. You have to live in this town. I don't. I know Wade has some serious connections, and I don't want you to put yourself in an awkward situation locally. If there are toes to be stepped on, tell me where they are, and let me do the stepping. I can turn around and leave."

He responded, "Gee, Street, you're no fun at all."

"Depends who you ask."

"I'm surprised Wade's not back already."

"Can you show me where he lives? Where does he do business?"

He smiled and mocked shock with that question. "Wait, you expect *me* to be an accessory to your clandestine, extralegal, potentially criminal activities here on my home turf? You just warned me about stepping on the wrong toes."

I caught on instantly and carried the ball. "I'll let you hold the flashlight or something while I pick the locks." I paused for a few seconds. "Seriously, Mark, I just want to see where he lives and where he does business. I don't intend to burgle either place."

"Oh, darn," he said, deadpan. "Regardless, I'm in."

"I knew that."

Mark changed the subject. "You said you've looked at the accident scene."

I answered, "I have no idea who is involved with whatever happened here. The crash that killed your cousins may have been as it has always been described, but I have my suspicions. If you can give me some pointers, tell me who to talk to, where to look for information, who might turn out to be an ally, it would be a great help to me. I have a budget, and I'll pay you for your time."

"That sounds good."

"How is your relationship with Wade? Might running into him create difficulties for you or your family?"

"Nah. Hell, Street, Annie has as much pull in Fairwater as Wade has, and I'm sure that, at least lately, people here like us a *lot* better than they do him. *We* didn't kill a couple hundred jobs for no reason. We can certainly point you in the right direction. Are you packin' heat?"

"Not at the moment, travel restrictions being what they are, but I have a care package coming from a friend back home. Cop Glock and accouterments."

"That's a start. I have a basement gun room at home. I can loan you some of mine while you're waiting."

"Thanks for that. Does Wade have any protection here on his turf, anyone actively protecting him or his interests?"

"There are a couple of city councilmen who sided with him in his business closures. They have a few allies in the PD, but if that becomes an issue, there are others in that business who are certain to be on *our* side. Local politics can be rocky in small southern towns. The loyalties can be fierce. That's another reason you need me in your corner."

"You're hired."

Annie spoke up. "And if you have him, Mr. Street, you have me as well. I liked Jack and Beth. Their deaths have always smelled bad to me. They didn't deserve that. I want to help find out what happened to them."

Mark asked me, "What do you want to do first?"

I looked at Annie. "If you'd get me a list of locals I should talk to, it'd be a big help. I'm still trying to get an accurate read on this place." I turned to Mark. "And I need to find that car they died in."

Mark looked at Annie. "Hon, do you remember what we discussed on the way down here, that lady you mentioned briefly?"

Annie smiled. "Mr. Street, you understand that these cute little southern towns are hotbeds of small-town gossip."

"I'll take your word for it."

She smiled slyly as she continued. "And you've had face-to-face contact with Wade Hawkins, haven't you?'

"Just a couple of times, out in LA. He wasn't exactly a fount of personality."

She smiled. "You're a master of understatement. Would you like to meet his former side chick?"

My face must've belied my surprise. "You're kidding." I frowned. "Wade Hawkins? Side chick? The mind reels."

"Oh, you ain't seen nothing yet. She was one of his business interests for a while. She has a small bar out on the turnpike near the city limits. Wade financed her business license and paid for improvements in her business site. He may have even paid to build the whole thing. Every one of the business permits in this town comes through my office."

I laughed. "Annie, I knew there was a reason I liked you. You say they're past tense?"

"Yes. They seem to have ended about a year ago. He came to the office to change the paperwork from a partnership to an LLC that she had set up. He definitely wanted his name *off* the paperwork."

"Okay, you say you know this woman? And they are definitely a thing of the past as a couple, or whatever word is appropriate in this case."

"Oh yeah, they're about as *done* as you can get. It seems to have been an amicable but definite and permanent split."

"I'm impressed. Can you introduce me to this woman? Is she still in town?"

"She is. Let me do this. I'll text her and see if she'd like to talk to you. Last time I spoke with her, she was ready to scratch Wade's eyes out. You probably won't be able to shut her up. When I hear back from her, I'll tell Mark."

"Ask her to set an appointment. I'll meet her any time, any place."

"Call it done." She picked up a menu from the far end of the table. "What's for dessert?"

26

Chattanooga, Tennessee—2004

Lincoln Pride was released from the Hamilton County Jail in Chattanooga, Tennessee, along with eleven other inmates, at a few minutes after one am on February 11, 2004. The wee-hours release into the cool night air was a common practice with detainment facilities around the country. It enabled the facilities to collect an extra full calendar-day occupancy payment from the federal government. As the other new releases wandered out onto the street, Lincoln Pride walked to the closest City Bus Stop. He had a plan.

As the bus approached the dimly lit metal enclosure, the wiry young Black man stepped from his solitary place on the bench. He felt through the front pocket of his saggy black khakis for the coins to pay the fare. It would be the last time that he paid for local mass transportation. The bus rambled north through the historic areas of downtown Chattanooga before it turned toward the hilly areas to the east, the home to smaller but more affluent businesses and numerous educational facilities. Ten minutes in, as the bus trundled down a side street heading for the main drag of McCaullie

Boulevard, Lincoln Pride finally saw what he'd had in mind. He reached up to pull the cord to request a stop.

He stepped off the bus and walked a half-block back west through the misting rain to the wide property of Hamilton County Municipal Employees Credit Union. Powerful Mercury vapor lights scattered around the perimeter of the parking lot, perched atop thirty-foot poles, cast a dim pale blue sheen over the damp parking lot. The squat, beige brick building with the bright-blue hip-style roof stood at the center of the plot. Lincoln Pride silently walked to the rear corner of the building to a spot that gave him shelter from the rain as well as a view of the Drive-Up ATMs. It was eleven minutes after two that morning, and he was certain that he would have only a short wait before his prey arrived.

East Ridge Attorney Evelyn Stewart-Thorpe wheeled her two-week-old dark-blue Infiniti G35 coupe into the credit union parking lot fifteen minutes later and drove directly to the second lane of the drive-up ATMs. She was more excited to be starting a new relationship than she was to be ending her eight-year marriage. The divorce would be finalized in three days, and she was ready for the coming changes. She smiled when she thought that she and Harry, her partner since Law School until recently, both now had new girlfriends.

Evelyn centered the car in the second lane of the ATM aisles, stopped, and opened the car door. She knew that she could never reach the buttons on the face of the ATM through her driver's window of the new car, so she left the car idling and kneeled in front of the vertical face of the big metal box. She punched in her ATM security code and chose a $500 withdrawal to ease the course of travel for the next couple of days.

After Lincoln Pride casually strode from his concealment in the shadows of the building to the open door of the shiny new dark pearl blue car, he shoved it farther open as hard as he could. The door caught Evelyn sharply on the left side of her body and knocked her off balance. As she toppled, she hit her head on the edge of the ATM console and fell to the concrete pavement, where she was knocked unconscious. Lincoln Pride watched and waited as the cash machine whirred into action, and he grabbed the money as it appeared in the narrow slot. He then plopped onto the light beige leather driver's seat of the blue coupe and powered out of the ATM aisle, brushing Evelyn's right foot in its new high heel with the front tire as he drove away. The ATM area surveillance cameras showed the entire exchange, but on the video feed, Lincoln Pride was only a fleeting dark shape.

———

Less than ten minutes later, driving calmly and using all of the appropriate turn signals, Lincoln Pride took the freeway on-ramp to the I-75 southbound into Georgia. An hour later, cruising at seventy-five with the Atlanta R&B station on the stereo, Pride took an off-ramp toward a random small town, some place called *Fairwater*. Sounded innocent enough. He hadn't encountered a single Tennessee or Georgia State Trooper on the freeway south from *tha'Nooga*, but he knew the sharp new car, with someone who looked like him driving, was far too nice to not attract the wrong type of attention. At that point, it would become a huge problem for him.

He left the car at the parking lot of a Denny'—after wiping down the steering wheel, seat, and radio buttons—and casually walked inside to order a Grand Slam Breakfast. No more bologna and government cheese on stale white bread for him. After he finished the early morning meal, he went into the restroom for a *birdbath* before he paid the tab. Finally, he walked out of the restaurant, turned to walk toward the town, and never looked back.

He combined most of the stolen cash with his own money returned at his jail release, a shade over a hundred bucks, to get a week's room at a low-slung older motel in the town's *Black area*—an area too clean and quiet to be a hood, really—of this dinky-ass little town. Fairwater, Georgia, would be his new home for now.

Grand Theft Auto, Assault with a Deadly Weapon—her car—

Interstate Flight to Avoid Capture and Robbery aside, Lincoln Pride had decided that he would try like hell to go straight this time. He had just done a *deuce,* a two-year stretch in County Jail after the Sovereign Citizen *no driver's license needed, traffic laws don't apply to me* script that he'd tried on the Sheriff's deputy at a traffic stop before he tried to drive away from said deputy during that traffic stop.

Car chases are a lot of work, and they rarely end well. And when properly utilized, Tasers really hurt. The judge had been an old white dude who didn't play that shit. The charges bought Lincoln three years in County, with the possibility of a reduced term if he behaved himself. He had done so. The term of his county sentence passed fairly quickly once he got his head around being captive. There were lotsa *homies* there, and as in most jails, they didn't have too much mix with the *beaners*—Latinos—or the *woods* —Whites.

He had lucked out, landed a job assignment working in the County Motor Pool, cleaning police cars, removing emergency equipment from outgoing decommissioned vehicles, and doing oil changes on county cars, trucks, and SUVs. The steady work had helped the jail term pass quickly. He'd been good at that type of work, he'd learned a lot, and he'd enjoyed the work, so he decided to try to get a gig with that work in the role, if he could find anyone who'd hire him.

———

Pride vedged the first three days at the Blue Door Motel in Fairwater. It was an old bungalow-style motor court dating back to the forties, with fifteen separate units laid out in a *U* shape around a weedy, overgrown center island. Half of the shabby units had been taken as monthly apartments. The owners there, an older Black couple who reminded him of his Grands, seemed to like him and cut him a deal for another week after he played the role, explaining that he was freshly released from jail and was just lookin' for some honest work.

After he mentioned his fondness for *car work*, the couple suggested that he go see, "Mista Hawkins over at the Pontiac store. He's a good man. We known him for twenty-five years or more. Tell 'im we sent ya." After he'd checked in and taken a long shower and a longer nap, he spent some of his money on a twelve-pack of beer from the package store down the street. He tried to catch up on his sleep over the weekend and watched a SHAFT movie marathon on WGN on the ancient color console TV in the corner of the main room of the suite. He kept falling asleep while the movies ran, but he was impressed with that Richard Roundtree. Brother-man had it goin' on.

Lincoln Pride washed his meager wardrobe in the motor court laundry that weekend and bought a fresh three-pack of colored T-shirts from the nearby discount store. That next Monday morning, lookin' fresh, he walked three blocks to the Hawkins Pontiac/GMC/Saturn dealership, arriving at eight forty-five am. He asked the receptionist for Mr. Hawkins Senior, who had not yet arrived. His son Wade, standing nearby talking to a salesman, asked what the problem was.

"Oh, there's no problem, sir. I'm Lincoln Pride. I'm new in town, and I'm lookin' for some work. I have a coupla years recent experience doing light service on a lot of domestic vehicles; oil changes, lubes, and the like. Lotsa GM iron in the mix. Mister and Miz Brown over at the Blue Door Motel said I should come here ta see about some work, said they know your daddy."

Wade looked the other man up and down and saw nothing objectionable. "Our family has known the Browns for decades. They're good people. Tell ya what, Mr. Pride. You just lucked out. Give me a few days, I have an employee who's leaving later this week. Let me move some folks around, and we'll get you started in the service department. Go introduce yourself to my cousin Mark, there in the service department office. He's my manager there, you'll be working for him. We'll see you, let's say, Thursday at eight o'clock sharp?"

Lincoln Pride breathed a sigh of relief. "That'll work just fine, Mr. Hawkins. I'll see you Thursday." He extended his hand, the other man smiled, and they shook.

"Welcome aboard, Lincoln."

After two years in the can, Lincoln Pride had two real *breaks* going for him. That was the longest *streak* of good luck that he could remember having, ever.

27

The MoonGlow Bar was a flat-roofed concrete block structure between a used car lot and an automotive detail shop. It was painted a light beige with a wide bright-red door, front and center. There was a freshly blacktopped parking lot with newly applied, brightly painted yellow lines. A well-detailed bright yellow '02 Pontiac Firebird Trans Am convertible, a rare special-edition model from the final year of Firebird production, was parked off to the right as we faced the building. It carried a chrome license plate frame reading 'Hawkins Pontiac GMC' and a personalized license plate reading HOTGRL6. I parked the renter two spaces away from the Firebird, and Mark and I walked into the bar as another patron exited.

The interior was dark but sporadically lit in the style of small taverns anywhere. We took our seats at the bar as a sturdy woman with long dark-blonde hair approached. She smiled widely at us and greeted Mark. She looked to be forty-ish, with a tightly bound black leather top that squeezed her breasts high and narrow. I wondered if that was comfortable. A faded pair of stretched denim Daisy Duke cutoffs over broadly patterned net stockings and a pair of Adidas Walking shoes finished her look.

She had a few tattoos around her upper arms, a Marine Corps shield on her left arm beneath the shoulder, and another, a Harley Davidson trademark crest, on her right. Her hair looked to be well-maintained, her complexion clear, and her eyes shone bright green.

"Well, look at you, Mark Hawkins! How long has it been?" She smiled a wide smile as she reached across the bar and patted his hand.

"Been a while, Suze! You're lookin' good."

"On my best day, maybe, if you stand back a ways. Coupla beers for you guys?" She looked at me. "Any brand preference, hon?"

"Sam Adams?"

"Autumn blend. You got it." She went to the cooler at the side of the work area, withdrew a pair of bottles, and walked back toward us while popping the caps. "So, Mark, what brings you around?"

Mark leaned in and spoke softly. "Suzy, this is my friend Street. He's a PI down here from LA. He's looking into the business situation regarding *he whose name shall not be mentioned*. We know you and that guy were tight for a while, and he wanted to get your take on a few things."

She frowned. "Oh, really. Happy ta meet you, Mr. Street." She looked past us. "Well, now. Why don't you guys take your beers over to one of the booths, and let's have us a chat." To her staffer, she called, "Sarah? Take over here for a few minutes, okay? And get us a bowl o' pretzels."

Mark and I moved to the booth at the far side of the room and took our seats. Of the six booths on site, only two were occupied, the closest to ours by a middle-aged couple, the male in shirtsleeves, the woman in slacks and a red blouse. Her hair was tied in a tight bun, his head looked freshly shaved. We took our seats two booths away, and Susan Keeley took a seat opposite us. We spent a few minutes getting acquainted. It turned out that she had done her basic and some of her Marine duty in San Diego and knew some of the SoCal landmarks that I had frequented. She had migrated east to Dallas, Texas, with a husband after her enlistment ended, then to North Georgia after a divorce. She had family in the area and had been in town for the last six years.

She looked directly at me. "Ask away, Mr. Street."

"Okay. Did Wade ever discuss his plans for this town when the two of you were together?"

She was adamant. "He *always* had plans. He would never shut up about 'em. He was always gonna make the town a big deal so that all those folks down in Atlanta would notice. They'd move some major businesses up here, and they'd all have to come to him for...well, everything. All that stood in the way of all his plans was his dad, Aubry. 'Daddy,' as he called him, was old school all the way, 'Build slowly, be faithful to your locals, help others make their way to success.' Wade thought all that jive just got in the way of his own intentions. He was *all Wade, all the time*, and he could be one greedy bastard."

I had decided to take the *blunt* route in my questioning. "Except where you were concerned."

"Well, yes. He was fairly generous with me right from the start. I had been shopping for a cheap car to drive about a year after I arrived here. He had noticed me at the dealership, and we had talked briefly, but I was completely surprised later when he gave me the keys to that yellow one outside after we'd gone out for a month or so. He had justified it by saying it was traded for a new truck, and he didn't think it would ever sell at his dealership. It was basically a free car for me." She frowned briefly. "Not that I didn't earn the damn thing."

I smiled and asked, "He was *energetic*?"

"Well, yeah. More like *insatiable*. To look at him, you wouldn't think so, would you? He had been corked up for so long that he said I was his first real release in years. He said his wife was a cold fish, nagged him 24/7/365, and that they hadn't been together for years, blah, blah, blah. I'd heard it all before."

I interjected. "Susan? No offense, but I'm honestly not concerned with his sex life. That's not on my radar at this point. Did he ever mention his sister in California?"

Susan took the mild rebuff in stride. "Oh, you better believe it. I absolutely loved that hospital show that she was on. He was over at my place one night, I'd been watchin' it, and he pitched a fit when he recognized her. He made me switch it off. That sucked. I didn't know that actress was his damn *sister*."

"What did he say about her?"

"Just that she was a slut. Made me wonder what he thought o' me. That cooled us off for a few weeks, actually. He finally apologized an' we got back together for a year or so."

"What about his two younger siblings? They both worked at the dealership for Aubry. Did they ever come up in conversation?"

"Sure thing. Wade knew his daddy was fading, even before the mama died. He wanted to take over the businesses and make drastic changes. He had offered to buy both the brother and the sister out, and they had both refused. His little brother *loved* the car business, and he and Wade had words on quite a few occasions about that. The younger sister took that brother's side, so they were both standing against Wade."

"How did he react when the two siblings died in the car crash?"

"That was a little strange. He was...what...I guess *cold* is the right word. He was like, 'It was a freak deal. What can ya do?' You'd have expected a little emotion, but he never showed that to any extent."

"Did Wade ever display any tendency toward violence? Did he ever voice any desire to get even with anyone, in business or anywhere else?"

"Oh, he could be mean, and he got pissed off fairly regularly. I felt like I was his escape valve most o' the time. I think if he ever decided to go after someone, he'd just try to hire someone else to do his dirty work. He had the money to do so, and I'm pretty sure he could make the right connections if he wanted to."

"Were you surprised at the way he shut down the businesses after Aubry passed?"

"Well, I was just an observer by that time, we were not together anymore, but I paid attention anyway. He'd had that shit planned

for years. He would do the work on his laptop at my place sometimes. He was just counting the days till he could pull the plug on
his daddy's businesses. After his mama died, he was rooting for his
daddy to follow her as quickly as possible. Like when we went
somewhere, he would make certain that he left work—extra work,
really—for his dad anytime he could. We went on trips sometimes,
on very short notice, and he dumped all the normal workload on
his daddy."

"Where did you go on your trips?"

"Oh, Myrtle Beach a few times, down ta Miami once, sometimes
Atlanta just for a day or so at a nice hotel when he was feelin'
horny." She looked at me. "I was in it for the money and the good-
ies, Mr. Street, but trust me, Wade's performance in the sack
improved considerably under my guidance."

I wasn't surprised that the conversation had again taken this
path. I'd learned a few things about ol' Wade that came as a
surprise. In a way, I was glad that he wasn't as starchy as he had
presented himself in LA. That he had a *side chick* wasn't all that big
a shock—I'd seen that before with other seemingly upright,
unlikely guys—but that his had been someone of Susan's style was
a bit of a surprise. Their involvement seemed a matter of opportunity for him, a matter of convenience, access to influence, and
financial gain for her, and purely physical for both, but it seemed a
really odd mix nonetheless.

My real goal had been to get an idea of Wade's mindset on his
home turf, and that was coming through just fine. He wielded his
power freely here in both personal and business affairs and would
use his influence freely to push the locals around. I wondered how
that would transfer to the business dealings. I also wondered if
Wade would have had sufficient negative energy to incite violence
against his own siblings or anyone else. Time would tell.

Mark and I talked with her for a few more minutes and
polished off a bowl of decent pretzels. The die had been cast. My
opinion of Wade Hawkins hadn't changed all that much. I'd verified his business duplicity on his own turf. If I could show that he'd

cheated Sylvia out of a fair amount of the estate value, perhaps that account would soon be settled.

———

The younger man and his blonde girlfriend sat in their booth at the MoonGlow as the trio two booths away quietly continued their discussion, and the man listened intently to the casual conversation being held five feet away. At some point, they exchanged glances, and the woman whispered, "I'll call him and tell him."

28

One of the names on my list of *approved contacts* was the car dealer's longtime clerk and DMV lady, Dottie Yarborough. A feisty seventy-two years old now, she had worked for Aubry Hawkins from the very beginning. I made an appointment to meet her at her home in the older section of town. The home was a sprawling red brick ranch with a large heavily-treed lawn and a massive garden island in the front yard. She welcomed me into the living room and offered me a spot on the flowered sofa in front of a large framed waterfall painting.

"I just made a batch of sweet tea, Mr. Street. It's gonna be warm out today. Let me fix you a nice cold glass."

"Thank you, Dottie. Oh, and Mark Hawkins sends his regards." I took a sip of the sweet tea and instantly imagined it being brown-tinted pure sugar cubes somehow made liquid. It was all I could do to act naturally as the fillings in my teeth spun in my mouth as she spoke. I had asked her about her history working for Aubry Hawkins.

"All he had back then was a converted service station. He built everything he had from scratch, and when he was finished building one place, he'd start expanding what he'd just built. He was easily

•

the smartest businessman in this whole town." As she spoke, I sat the almost-full glass of tea on a convenient pad on her coffee table.

"You worked for him from start to finish."

"I did. Thirty years and change. He started me at forty dollars a week, and I know there were times that he had a hard time writin' *that* check. When he was able, after he became prosperous, he was very generous with me. We took care of each other, make no mistake. And I absolutely loved those two younger kids of theirs. That young Jack was set to run those businesses himself in a few more years, and that Beth? She was sharp as a tack. She had wanted to take over my job whenever I retired, and she would've been good at it."

"I'm working for the older daughter, the one who moved to California."

"Are you? She's just a beautiful girl. What's that she calls herself now on that TV show she was on for so long?"

"Sylvia Tate. She legally changed her name over a decade ago."

"That's right. She's Sylvia Tate now. What a great actress she has become. We used to watch her on that hospital show every week."

"She's become a friend. I'll tell her what you said." Now I smiled and said, "I notice, Dottie, that you didn't mention Wade Hawkins in your fond talk of the Hawkins family."

Dottie turned emphatic now. "Well, there's a reason for that, now, isn't there, Mr. Street? If you've been in Fairwater for over an hour, you know what people here think of *that* man."

"Did you ever hear any friction between Wade and Jack? Were there ever any arguments between them at the business?"

Dottie answered, "Oh, certainly. That happened about once a week with them."

"Did Aubry know of the problems between the brothers? Did he ever enter the fray or comment?"

"I think so. He had his own issues with Wade. As Aubry faded after his wife passed, ol' Wade started his power trip. He started hoggin' the trade-in cars and trucks for his own dealer over on

MLK, paying lowball prices for them. I saw all the numbers and called him out a time or two. He didn't pay me any attention at all."

I asked, "Do you recall the accident that killed Beth and Jack?"

"Oh yes. Their mother was just devastated by their deaths. That's what killed that poor woman. And get this, while the parents were in Atlanta with her before she died, Wade was already back at work rippin' his daddy off. That just made me mad. When I called him out on it, Wade told me to mind my own business, called me an old bag. I'll show him an *old bag.*"

"Wow. Remind me never to piss you off, Dottie." I smiled. "I think I have what I came here for. I may contact you again soon." As I rose, I said, "You've been a great help with my work."

As we walked toward the door, Dottie patted me on the back and said, "You go out there and kick Wade's ass, Mr. Street. He deserves it!"

29

My primary goal that morning after meeting with Dottie was trying to locate the vehicle in which the Hawkins siblings had met their demise. Mark Hawkins had suggested that we do a title search for the car if we couldn't get help from the police department. Since I didn't know who I could trust at FPD, I sought another source. The accident report that the coroner had given me had the car's serial number, and I found an online site for VIN and registration searches. Punching into the Georgia DOT Motor Vehicles site, I determined that the car had not been legally sold or re-registered, nor had it been recorded as being destroyed.

I called Adam Waverly, the Fairwater police officer from earlier, and asked that we meet away from the department if possible. He was out on patrol that day, so he suggested a parking garage a few blocks from the town square. I backed into a perimeter slot. He was still wheeling his tired Malibu, which he nosed in so that our drivers' windows were close together.

He looked across at me and extended his hand, filled with a file folder. I took the file folder. "Here ya go, Mr. Street. I made you copies of the official report and of the on-site photos. I hope they help you."

"I'm sure they will. Thanks."

I opened the manila folder and was greeted by a set of actuality photos of a red, two-wheel drive Chevy or GMC pickup, a sporty short bed, wide-box model modified in the style I'd often seen on the West Coast. From the appearance of the custom rims and the lack of body emblems, I speculated that it had probably been the young man's *toy*. It was laid on its roof on the grass shoulder of the highway over fifty yards from the overhead walkway. The young man's body had been trapped under the cab, his nearly-obliterated cranium lying at an impossible angle from the trunk of his body. Subsequent photos showed the car from various angles and determined the path of its travel. The photos supported the conclusions made in the official printed report and vice versa.

A couple of questions popped into my mind. How fast had this truck been traveling at the time of the intrusion of the concrete into the cab? The path seemed to have been straight until a little after the truck passed the median K-rail barrier that extended fifty feet or so beyond the overhead walkway, then it made a sharp right turn onto the grass surface beyond the shoulder. A shallow drainage ditch caused the path to sharpen, prompting the truck to bottom out and causing its front tire to dig into the surface. That started the problem. The truck started a medium-speed rollover, probably two rounds. The driver, probably mortally injured by the concrete, was by now beyond input. He and his sister were just along for the ride as the truck spiraled out of control.

Looking closely at the photos of the truck, I caught something that didn't make sense. There was a fairly deep crease in the sheet metal on the driver's side ahead of the rear wheel. There was a vertical smudge of white paint in front of the passenger side door. That damage would not have been part of the harm inflicted in the rollover crash. Odd. I filed that image and information in my mind for future reference.

That afternoon I went back to the B&B and sat on the deck outside my suite, watching the hummingbirds hover around their feeding source. I replayed the available scenarios regarding the accident, finding none that even remotely made any sense. My conclusion was that the accepted explanations were pure fantasy. There had to have been a second vehicle involved in the event, and that vehicle was probably also the source of the concrete projectile that had murdered Jack Hawkins. That, in turn, translated to two occupants, a driver for the suspect vehicle and a *handler* for the concrete. Those perps now deserved the proper attention.

———

I called Adam at the PD and made an appointment for late that afternoon, parked in the *civilian* portion of the department's lot, and made it through the gauntlet of metal detectors inside, eventually landing at his cubicle in the large segmented office. He greeted me with a handshake and asked, "You need anything to drink? Coffee? Bottle of water?"

"A bottle of water would be great. Thanks."

The young officer returned a moment later, tossing me a bottle of locally-branded water before taking his seat. "So, let's see, Mr. Street, you wanted to look at the final conclusion report for the Hawkins' crash." He tapped a few keys on his laptop and waited as the nearby printer whirred to life. "I gotta ask you, man, how do you like LA? I've always wanted to check that place out."

"I felt the same way growing up. Come on out, I'll show you the high spots. It's a great place, but I fear it's changing, and not in the right direction. It may have already peaked." I took a sip of water. "The weather may be the biggest draw at this point. Clear and seventy-four degrees every day is hardly ever a bad thing."

"I get that." He looked over his shoulder, then turned his swivel chair to grab the still-warm, curled copies from the tall copy machine. He stacked them and then put them into an open manila folder.

"Here ya go, pard. I took a look at the report earlier this morning. It looks as if the concrete coming through the windshield initiated the crash."

I responded, "Of course. But where did the concrete come from? Look at the claimed source. There's no way that anything that big could have come from that overcrossing." I took the photos I'd made of the bridge and showed them to him.

"Wow. You may be on to something there, Mr. Street."

"Additionally, there is damage to the sheet metal of the Hawkins' pickup that does not align with the accident damage on the other side of the truck's body. That truck was *dead sharp* earlier that same day. It was Jack Hawkins' pride and joy. He kept it pristine. That added damage happened along with the concrete coming through the glass and killing that man. Count on it." I had become adamant in my presentation of my theory, maybe a bit too much so. I looked past him to see other officers in the room watching our conversation.

"You make some good points, Street. We'll try to take another look at it. Thanks for coming in to see me."

I left the PD confident that I was making progress but knowing that I had probably created an additional problem or six.

30

In an effort to locate the wrecked truck from the younger Hawkins' fatal accident, I referenced the obsolete phone books that I had borrowed from Sylvia. The list was short, there were three towing, salvage, scrap, and/or *junk* yards listed. I called the first number, to be told by the robot voice that the area code for the number had changed. Using the updated area code number that I sourced from the local business cards I was collecting, I made a second call and a connection.

"Ace Towing and Trading, this is Luke. How may I help you?"

"Hi, Luke. I wonder if you can answer a question for me. Where around Fairwater is the storage facility for insurance companies for vehicles that are still under investigation after an accident?"

There was a slight pause and some background noise, then, "That's about three hundred feet from where I'm standing right now. Is there any specific vehicle or accident that you're searching for?"

"Yes, sir, there is. My name's Street. I'll be there in half an hour. Are you still located on Union Street?"

"It's called MLK Boulevard now. They changed it a few years ago. Yeah, same street number, though. Ask for me when you arrive, there are five of us working here. I'm the manager. My name's Luke."

"Thanks, Luke. I'll see you in a few."

———

Junkyards, for numerous reasons, all seem to have their own distinct aroma. In this instance, the atmosphere was permeated with a fragrant mix of antifreeze and all of the old oil that had permeated the ground. The truly-devoted eco-Nazis in California would've had a collective stroke. There was a hint of mold and usually a stiff mildew aroma as well, not that unusual in an area where it often rained. The office was a dingy, aged light-turquoise single-wide mobile home with white trim. Think Jim Rockford's place but less glamorous. A covered front porch, double the width of the trailer itself, stood along the side of the hulk. I recognized *Luke* right away, a squatty balding middle-aged fellow in weathered gray coveralls who resembled the actor Ned Beatty except for his horn-rimmed specs. I introduced myself and showed my credentials. Luke took my investigator's license in his hand and held it close to his thick glasses. "Yes sir, that looks like a real California license all right. I lived out in Santa Ana for a few years back in the seventies. Helped that big ol' Pick-a-Part outfit get started. We worked our asses off, then the boss sold it off, and we got shafted, big time. No sir, I don't miss nothin' about that place but the weather."

"It has its moments. Thanks for seeing me, Luke. I'm looking for a red late-model GMC pickup that was in a fatal rollover crash a while back. May be booked under *Hawkins*. It's an insurance deal."

"Sure. We got that one. Insurance company's been payin' storage for a long time. I don't mind if they don't." He stepped off the porch and said, "Follow me." As he started walking toward the rear of the property, he said, "Yeah, we've had that one for a while. There's nothin' usable on it, so if it clears, it'll sell at auction and get crushed, sold for weight."

At the rear of the site, there was a row of corrugated metal sheds of progressively declining condition. Inside the third one was a long jagged shape covered with a threadbare blue plastic tarp secured with a half dozen bungee cords. Luke stepped beside the shape and started detaching the Bungees. After the cords were unfastened, he stood behind the vehicle and snapped the tarp away. He'd clearly done this before.

The truck had started life as an '06 GMC short bed single cab, bright-red, with custom wheels and a modified lowered suspension. Trash bags and plastic sheeting were taped over the former space of the windshield and absent side windows, and a printed rectangular label carrying the BIO warning was applied to the plastic sheeting on each side. I pulled the bags away and saw more white plastic, the interior airbags that had gone off on impact. The roof had been crushed downward to the extent that the first responders had used the Jaws of Life to remove it. After the rescue and recovery, the separated roof had later been laid atop the cab, favoring the right side of the body, which itself had an upward twist favoring the passenger side front corner.

The accepted narrative was that the projectile had entered the truck cab after being dropped from the overhead pedestrian walkway—an impossibility given the construction of the bridge itself. The shattered windshield, laying back over the roof of the truck, still displayed the jagged rectangular gash at the entry point of the projectile. The chunk of concrete had killed Jack Hawkins instantly, and the truck had left the highway and flipped onto its roof, with a substantial portion of the damage concentrated on the passenger side. Fine.

What then explained the gouge into the sheet metal of the driver's side of the truck? The damage had not come from the rollover accident. The height of the damage, well above the truck's lower body character line, indicating a raised vehicle, perhaps a four-wheel drive. A faint black half-round tire burn that had not been visible in the too-dark crime scene photos from the evening of the crash also caught my attention. I shot images of each side of the uncovered corpse of a truck with my Canon, attempting to copy the angles of the original pics.

Luke had stood quietly as I made my examination. I asked him, "Luke, has this vehicle been here since the time of the crash?"

"Right here, Mr. Street. Came in that same morning. Prominent victims, sure-fire insurance hassle, we put it here as soon as it came in. It'll stay here as long as they pay the storage fees."

I stood back from the truck to get a wider view. "Thanks for that, Luke. That's all I need. I'll help you wrap it back up." I gave him a business card. "If anyone else shows interest in it over the next few days, please give me a call."

I helped Luke lift the weathered, threadbare blue tarp over the body and watched as he re-attached the Bungees. We walked back toward the front of the yard, chatting about business and the weather. I regained the Mustang and drove back toward the town square.

31

Mark Hawkins and I sat at his weathered redwood picnic table, tackling the woes of the world around us. The considerable difficulties with current national politics had already been settled with considerable agreement. The stories of things and people concerning the tragedies of 9/11/01 had been exchanged, and the loss of Dale Earnhardt had been mourned for a few moments, all over a quiet Saturday afternoon with a cooler of beer handy on the patio next to the table. Mark's wife had taken their two youngest daughters to the mall for a heavy-duty shopping session. Free at last, free at last.

Mark and I had invested a couple of hours in preventive maintenance on his ever-present Pepper Green GTO. The oil change had been his job, the installation of the modern radio had been mine. I had completed a similar task in my own '69 Goat prior to my cross-country trek a couple of years earlier, so the job wasn't all that difficult. With the engine lubed and the tunes flowing, it had been time for some serious leisure as well as a bit of random discussion.

After opening another cold one and passing it to me, Mark asked, "So, how are you adapting to small-town living?"

"It's bearable. I could see living somewhere like this if I had a family, and maybe a different line of work. Speaking of work, tell me more about your cousin Wade. You know far more about him than anyone else I've encountered."

Mark took a long drink from his Michelob. "Well, lessee...he was the oldest of our cousins, first of the generation, so he saw himself as the leader of the pack. He's four years older than I am, and he had a coupla years on his sister. You say she changed her name to Sylvia? We hadn't seen her in years until all of the family funerals. Anyway, Wade's dad had him walking alongside at every step of the family business right from the start. Boy was working in the shop doing oil changes when he was ten years old, and he always tried to work his ass off to please Dad, but his dad never really showed any confidence in Wade's work, even after Wade finished college."

"Where did he go to school?"

"University of Georgia, but he was on a shoestring budget. Aubry hadn't gone to college. He'd built the businesses he had from absolute scratch, and he wasn't that big a fan of higher education. A couple of his earliest sales managers at the car franchise had been MBAs, and they'd screwed him over, so he was sour on the whole concept of a college degree."

"And yet Wade never struck out on his own? He never just moved on to a different situation?"

"He probably didn't have the initiative or the energy to step up and get it done. He didn't want to start from the starting line when he could start from midway down the track. Dad's word ruled, A-to-Z, in Fairwater. Wade also married very early. He was twenty-two, his wife was twenty. She came from a family that was even more remote and less emotionally solid than Wade's. They were just waaaay too young to get married, and they married the wrong people."

"There's a lot of that going around."

"Yeah, and it was made worse by the fact that Lucy hated her in-laws with a passion that burned brightly for over twenty years. She could suck the energy out of a room in seconds."

"Lotsa that going around as well."

"Not to the degree that Lucy took it. It got to be embarrassing after a few years. She would give her own version of chapter and verse about her in-laws to anyone who would listen. Eventually, if she was going to be at a family event, other people would find a last-minute excuse to avoid her at the event or perhaps just avoid the event altogether. I did that myself a few times."

"Not fun."

"Not even close. Now Wade's folks were not perfect by any means, and Aubry could be a little cranky, especially in his later years, but they didn't deserve the trashing they got from Lucy. No one on the planet would."

"Why didn't Wade just divorce her?"

"I think he wanted to. He had someone on the side once or twice, but that never lasted very long. Small towns talk a lot, and maybe he just didn't want any of that extra baggage. Eventually, he just went back to work. Stayed busy 24/7 and improved the business a bit. He's the one that added the later franchises and grew the dealership beyond the farm store-style truck-and-tractor dealer to a nice multi-line small-town car dealer that had connections in the farm implement field."

"Sylvia showed me pictures of the businesses. They looked pretty decent, if a bit *quaint*. How well did they keep up with trends and fashions as business changed over time? I know that GM would have wanted them to relocate to a business park, and I know that Wade and Jack had words about a buyout."

"Well, Fairwater was changing, as were the times. As the town grew, the customer base wasn't as trustworthy as it had been. Some random hometown guy's word was no longer necessarily his bond. Uncle Aubry got shafted a few times, and Wade called him on it. He had to go out a few times and lay down the law, do some repos and collections, and on occasion, he had to get tough. A few folks got tough back at him, and that just pissed him off worse. Wade wanted the old man out of the picture, but that wasn't going to happen voluntarily."

32

Fairwater, Georgia—2005

Wade Hawkins answered the phone at 1:14 am that Tuesday, and he wasn't happy about it at all. He'd retired early that evening, he'd described himself to his wife as *beat* and turned in before nine pm, and she knew better than to bother him.

He snapped into the phone receiver, "WHAT?" and listened for some answer. "Mr. Hawkins? I'm Officer Larry Taylor with the Fairwater PD. Sir, we need you to come to the hospital right away. There's been a serious accident out on the turnpike. We need to talk to you. Do you need someone to come pick you up at home?"

Wade Hawkins frowned and said, "No, I'll come to the hospital on my own. Give me twenty minutes. Do you have any details? What happened?"

"Please, sir, just meet us at the hospital."

———

Wade Hawkins' new pearl-white Escalade rolled into the driveway and parked under the portico at Fairwater General Hospital twenty-five minutes later. He stepped out and walked toward the waiting police car, a new silver Yukon that he'd sold the city just three months before. The young officer intercepted him at the entrance of the ER.

"Mr. Hawkins? I'm Officer Taylor. Thank you for coming down. Um, sir, I'm sorry to have to tell you that there's been a serious car accident out on th' turnpike, and your brother Jack was fatally injured."

The news took Wade by surprise. He stepped back and asked, "How?"

"Well, sir, it looks like some kids was droppin' stuff off the pedestrian bridge over the turnpike. We've seen it before, just not this bad. I'm very sorry for your loss, sir. Jack was a friend of mine. I used to race with him a few years ago. He was a good man."

"Thank you, Officer. Where is he? Can I see—"

"Um, sir, I wouldn't recommend that at all. I was on-site out there. I wouldn't wish that scene on anyone. Sir, there was a young woman in the truck with him. Do you have any idea who that would've been?"

"Oh god. That was probably our sister, Elizabeth. Beth. Oh god. Um, I'll have to call my folks. Is she here in the hospital?"

"No, Mr. Hawkins. She was taken by air ambulance to the trauma center in Atlanta. I can get you the specific address if you wish."

Wade Hawkins took a deep breath, trying to regain some semblance of composure. What to do first...he thanked the officer and turned back toward his car, his head still swimming. He and Jack had differed greatly in style and, he thought, substance, but hearing this, that his brother was gone, struck him dumb. First step? Call Dad.

———

The next two weeks were practically a period of mourning for the Hawkins family and many in the town of Fairwater. Beth, their baby sister, a surprise child conceived just after her mother's fortieth birthday, was hanging on by a thread at the ICU ward at Atlanta's biggest hospital, purely a victim of circumstance. The sparse traffic on the dark turnpike late on a weeknight had left the crash site unattended until one of the neighbors near the western-most base of the elevated walkway, taking a late night stroll with his German shepherd, had seen the carnage, probably a half-hour after the crash. Due to the delay in the discovery of the accident scene, Beth was belted into her seat in the crashed pickup, upside down, unconscious, seriously wounded, and bleeding out. That situation had done her profound harm.

Aubry Hawkins and his wife had stayed at a hotel near the Hospital in Atlanta, practically camped there, for their daughter's final ten days of life. When they returned to Fairwater and brought her back home, the elderly couple displayed an air of total defeat and despair, one that the gathered employees had never before seen. Genuine tears were shed by the entire staff as the business came to a halt for a third week.

The older sister to the two felled siblings, now using the name Sylvia Tate, arrived in Atlanta from Southern California on the second day of her sister's hospitalization. Her TV series was on hiatus, so her presence in Southern California was unnecessary. She was in town for well over two weeks. She abandoned any *celebrity* status by spending all her time with her parents. She had been closer to Beth than to any of her other family members, and she had played the *home* card very carefully.

Her middling medical training in preparation for her role in the network medical series gave her doubts as to the outcome of Beth's situation. In the end, she was correct in the bleak expectations that she never once voiced on this turf.

The combined funeral for the siblings was a quiet and dignified affair, practically a social gathering for the town in which the deceased family members had grown up. By the end of the services, Aubry's wife appeared far beyond her sixty-five years. The long-term estrangement between Sylvia and her parents was effectively ended. They were actually speaking to one another in lengthy conversations for the first time in her memory.

Wade, predictably, remained standoffish. After the funerals were over, he just wanted to get back to running the businesses. He wasn't much for sentiment, and there was work to do to catch up from the three-week respite. He was starting to see Aubry slowing in his words, responses, and reflexes, and he put that factor to work quickly to his own benefit.

33

Lincoln Pride was nervous, more so than he could remember being at any time in his entire life. He had been asked to *frighten* Jack, Wade's younger brother. The planning had taken a long time. Lincoln didn't know about *frightening* people. He had met and talked to Jack a few times at the car dealer, and those had been pleasant encounters. This whole deal had gone sideways when his helper, that lame-ass white boy who'd come along this time, tossed a half-block of concrete from the passengers' side window of the raised 4x4 pickup onto Jack's truck.

The red truck had slammed against the passenger side of the four-by, and Lincoln could feel the wobble as the smaller truck rubbed against the heavy tubular bumpers and the wider tires of the taller rig. Then the red pickup veered away in the opposite direction and left the road off to the right, digging in and flipping as it left the road. Lincoln Pride had floored his gas pedal and left the area as quickly as possible, not wanting to see the result but knowing it would be bad. At the garage, he dragged the big dumb white kid, Ryan Tabor, out of the truck and beat him to a pulp. Pride knew that now he'd have to run, and that the injury that they had caused to Wade's younger brother would be an inexcusable crime.

Then again, Lincoln knew that Wade had never seen or met the *helper*. He had also never given Lincoln a direct assignment to coerce or intimidate Jack after the buyout offer had been refused. Lincoln decided he'd disappear for a while or at least make himself scarce. He felt bad for what had happened, but given time, he thought—hoped, really—that the situation might work out for him. He was relieved that for the next two weeks, Wade was preoccupied with his younger sister's hospitalization, her eventual death, and the siblings' funerals. He didn't give much thought to the fact that he'd had a hand in her death as well as Jack's.

Lincoln Pride was thankful also for the new conjecture, the *official* opinion that the projectile had been dropped from the overhead walkway. There had been a spate of that type of vandalism in the counties surrounding Fairwater, a fact that, along with the lazy police work done by the Gadsden County Sheriff's Department, may well have saved Lincoln's life.

34

I was talking to the owners of the B&B that Monday morning when my cell rang. I recognized the number. "Officer Waverly! How you doin'?"

"I've been better, Mr. Street. Seems I have been seen talking with this PI from California a little too often, and the brass took offense to that. You are considered a troublemaker and a pot-stirrer here in Fairwater. You've been looking into the Hawkins car accident, poking into people's business, and prodding for information. As a result of your *aggressive activities* and my alleged collaboration, I have the next ten days off."

"Aw, man. I'm sorry to hear that. Is there anything I can do to help? Can I talk to someone?"

"No need, Mr. Street. Actually, I was wondering if you need any help with your poking and prodding."

"Wow. Um, first? I'm sorry they did that to you. I didn't mean to get anyone into any trouble."

"I'm still trying to decide how much I care. Look, Street, I think you're on to some seriously crooked shit here in this town; the accident, the sudden destruction of the Hawkins businesses, the shifty operation of his new businesses, and some other stuff I know about. I'm open to helping if you have space for a wingman."

"That's an interesting offer, Adam. Let's meet somewhere for lunch and discuss it, see if we have any common ground. Any recommendations for lunch?"

"My go-to is Quinn's on Seventh Street. There's plenty of privacy, and the food is great. I'm there once a week at least."

"That'll work. One pm?"

"One it is. See you there."

———

I'd had enough experience with governmental politics to understand *how some things work*. Despite the illusion of friendship with Adam and a few others, I was still uncertain of who to trust in Fairwater, so I shifted into *caution* mode. I left the B&B and made a careful search of the Mustang, looking for bugs. Finding none, I drove into Fairwater, arriving at the real estate office across from Quinn's Restaurant on Seventh Street at ten-twenty that morning. I chose a parking space with a good view of the restaurant parking lot and kept a sharp eye out for police cars, clandestine surveillance teams, SWAT trucks, and other potential threats. None appeared, so maybe I'm really not that big a deal to these folks. Hope springs eternal.

At five minutes before one, Adam's handsome late-90s silver Camaro convertible pulled into the parking lot of Quinn's Restaurant. As he stepped onto the front porch, I started the renter and drove across the street into the parking lot. I joined him in the foyer of the restaurant as he was being led to a booth toward the rear of the room. We took our seats, ordered our beverages, with mine carefully specified as *unsweetened* iced tea after the earlier trauma at Dottie's house.

As our beverages were delivered, I started the conversation with an obvious question. "Can you tell me what your department knows about me? You inferred that they've been keeping an eye on me."

Adam smiled. "Good eye, Street. You seem to have poked the bear when you started asking about the Hawkins accident. Outsiders get noticed in small towns. My sergeant saw your name on my event report after the first time we met out there that day just off the turnpike. He called me into his office and gave me the third degree—who were you, what were you asking about, *who* you asked about, and he gave me a directive about telling him any time you and I talked. Second meeting, he warned me. He had decided I'd been a bit too friendly with you. Third mention, they've been keeping an eye on *me*, and I'm the bad guy for talking to *you* without mentioning the contact to *him*, hence the suspension."

Well now... "Wow, I had no idea that I had caused you that much of an issue. Sorry about that. But, actually, it clarifies one thing...your sergeant is the guy I have to be careful around. Maybe he's one of the *Hawkins' faithful* that I should watch out for."

We gave the waiter our orders. The hot roast beef sandwich and sides that Adam ordered sounded good, so I asked for the same thing. When in Rome...

Adam smiled. "I wouldn't worry about that all that much. I'm six years on the job here, and I may be close to a change. Tell me what you need to accomplish here. Let's see what common grounds and interests we have."

I was glad to get on with the job. "Okay. I have two concerns, up from one when I arrived seven days ago. My initial interest was determining what Wade Hawkins had done regarding the estate settlement that he brought to his sister in California. Granted, he brought her well over eight million dollars, net. But after well over three decades running some of this town's biggest businesses, after the deaths of the other two siblings, and after the supposed sale of the family's property holdings, that eight million seemed a bit low. Granted, this is a small town, but property values for a decent commercial property anywhere in Georgia are not at bargain-basement level."

"Okay, I agree with you on the property values here. I know I can't afford a decent house here in town on a cop's salary."

"So after I arrived, I also started looking at the conditions surrounding the fatal crash of the Hawkins siblings. Sorry, your department and the sheriff's crew both dropped the ball big time on that deal. There is no effing way that event occurred in the manner that the reports claim. Maybe at some other pedestrian crossing bridge in the area, just not from *that* one. The truck in the wrecking yard and the pedestrian overpass above the turnpike both render that explanation an utter impossibility. That truck showed collision damage that *did not* happen in that crash."

I called up the photos I'd taken at the wrecking yard.

"Do you see the tire burn and the body damage on the driver's side in this image? The 'official' photos from the time of the event didn't show that damage because they were too dark. What happened there? I'm thinking a direct, intentional vehicular attack, and *that* translates to double vehicular homicide."

Adam was still looking at the images on the camera. "I could see that."

"Have you done any accident investigation on the job here?"

"Hardly any. I've been stuck, mostly doing traffic control at major crashes. Rank has its privilege, and I have had no rank to speak of. At a small-town PD like this one, lotsa the time, there's not a lot goin' on." He sipped his Coke. "You were a cop before you went to California?"

"Oh yeah. Five years in Atlantic City. We did a little of everything there, from traffic control to homicide investigation, with a few drive-by shootings thrown in from time to time just to keep everyone awake. That's a tough place at times. Count your blessings for being spared some of that stuff. Do you have aspirations to a higher climb up the law enforcement ladder?"

As our food arrived, Adam explained, "I'll finish my criminology degree next year. We'll see where that leads. I wouldn't argue with a change of scenery and a pay boost."

The food at this place was excellent, and I decided that this would not be my last visit to Quinn's. The conversation veered off into other areas until the food was gone. As the dessert plates were being cleared, Adam said, "So, let's get to work. Where do you want to start?"

"This town is your turf. I need to revisit the sites of the Hawkins properties that were razed after the father passed away. I have a map that I want to mark off to see what's connected, to see if that says anything to me. Then I'd like to see any other properties that Wade Hawkins owns, anywhere he hangs out. Show me the high spots in Fairwater from an insider's perspective. Give me the tour."

"Call it done, Street. Let's take my car. PD has its eye on that Mustang."

———

The next two and a half hours with Adam as tour guide taught me a lot about Fairwater, Georgia, and probably a bit about small towns in general. All was not as it seemed. First, the Hawkins business properties were all within a few blocks of one another, and it appeared that most of the properties dividing those sites were smaller, older, less productive, and might be acquired at modest cost. They were largely the sites of simple structures and businesses that could be cleared easily. Obtaining zoning waivers from sympathetic city fathers wouldn't be any hassle for Wade Hawkins. I wondered what the end game would be, but *building the foundation of a local empire* seemed a good possibility.

Among the Hawkins businesses that were *not* closed, the biggest was the MLK Avenue *pot lot*, Wade Hawkins Motors, and the title loan business located a block away. Adam parked in the lot for the Subway sandwich shop across the street from the car dealer, giving us a good vantage point for observation of the location. The car lot occupied a former service station and displayed thirty vehicles of varying appearance and condition in three rows. The best-appearing of the cars, a shiny black five-year-old Toyota 4-Runner, was parked on a metal ramp placed diagonally at the corner of the property. The former corner gas station had been repainted in tasteful beige tones with dark red trim. The long rectangular forward canopy was festooned with triangular flags and banners. As low-end small-town buy-here-pay-here used car lots go, it was fairly impressive in its appearance and appeared to be fairly busy.

I had been curious to see the possible staff parking for Wade's businesses, curious as to how and by whom the businesses were run. The car dealer property showed nothing special there when we first arrived, so we decided to give it another look later in the day. Adam moved the car a block down the street to the parking lot of a former McDonald's location, now serving as a sparsely-attended Indian café, Curry Central, across from the storefront location of Hawkins' title loan business. The parking lot there had a better discovery for my purposes, Wade Hawkins' very own white Cadillac Escalade, parked squarely in front. We sat there for twenty minutes after Adam went into the café to order some drinks. Three customers came and went from the loan office in forty-five minutes before Wade left the office and departed in his Escalade. Adam fired up his Camaro, and we followed at a discrete distance.

Wade Hawkins was nothing if not *busy* that afternoon. By five o'clock, he had made five more stops. Three were the sites of his family's former businesses, where he consulted briefly with attendants and employees, and the other two were local banks. There was not a smoking gun to be seen at any of the stops.

Adam was a careful and attentive surveillance tech. The repeated appearance in the rearview mirror of the same silver Camaro convertible for an extended time period would be troublesome for almost anyone had the image been repetitive, but he made impressive efforts to change the car's frontal appearance. At various points in our travel, he lowered the convertible top. We donned baseball caps while traveling roofless. At other points, he varied the frontal lighting profile of the car, running lights becoming low beams, high beams, and the Z28's driving lights, while also expertly varying his lane and distance positioning. Similar methods had been taught by law enforcement agencies for decades, but I had seen very few operatives ever apply them as energetically, attentively, or effectively as Adam did that day. The guy had chops. At quarter-after-five, Wade Hawkins pulled into the driveway of his home on Tenth Street, Northwest. As we drove past, convertible top and tinted windows raised at this point, Wade stepped from his car and walked to the front door of his home.

"What do we do now, Street? Looks like he's done for the day."

I said, "How 'bout *It's Miller Time*. The MoonGlow is a bit down the road, I'll buy."

"You're on."

———

The MoonGlow parking lot was empty late that afternoon, which was odd at very best, but Susan's yellow Trans Am drop-top was parked in the same slot where I'd seen it days before. Adam pulled in behind it and stated the thoughts that we shared. "Something's up here."

We walked toward the car and immediately spotted the blood-stains on the concrete sidewalk beside the car. Adam pointed at the dark smear on the side of the door under the side view mirror, the painted casing of which was also smeared with a bloody handprint. The sidewalk showed a smear of blood that looked a little like the shape of a forearm. Someone, I could only assume at the time to be Susan Keeley, had perhaps been severely injured here, probably one-to-two days before.

I looked at Adam. "This is your turf. What do you suggest?"

"I'm going to call it in. At least get it on the record as a crime scene."

He raised his cell phone to his ear after punching in the non-emergency number for the PD. He held up a finger and mouthed, "*Wait.*"

"Kevin? Adam Waverly. Hey, man, I'm at the MoonGlow Bar out on the turnpike. We have a crime scene here, someone's had the crap beat out of them, and the bar itself is closed tight. You need to send crime scene out with one patrol unit, at least get it documented for when we find a victim." He paused to listen. "That's right, no victim present but plenty of blood evidence and a chunk of concrete through the windshield of the car." Another pause, then, "Okay, buddy, I'll be here to verify discovery. Thanks."

I had been concentrating on the blood stains and hadn't even noticed the gaping rectangular hole in the windshield. Maybe I was slipping. I went to the Camaro, grabbed my camera, and took some images of the scene before I started to hear the distant sirens.

"Adam, I'm going to skip being a discovery witness for this one. I'll meet you at the Denny's three doors down when you're done here."

"Good idea."

35

I asked, "What's up? How'd it go over there?"

"It's the typical bureaucratic falderal, hurry up and wait. That's how they work. While I was waiting for their brain waves to kick in, I made a few calls and found Susan Keeley."

I was surprised. "Where is she?"

"She's in the hospital, fifteen miles south, down in Tyler. Check out here. Let's go see her."

———

The Tyler General Hospital was a sprawling three-story affair that sat among hundreds of trees on a three-acre parcel near another idyllic small southern town. We parked in front, walked to the main entrance, then to the front desk.

The receptionist/nurse looked at me and smiled. In her smooth southern accent, she asked, "How may I help you?"

I smiled back. "Looking for a friend of mine, Susan Keeley. I think she checked in yesterday, maybe the day before, and I need to check on her."

The woman looked at her computer screen and said, "Keeley,

yes. She's in two-eighteen." She pointed to her left. "Take the elevator, turn to the left at the nurse's station."

"Thank you, ma'am."

———

Room 218 was a semi-private affair that was dimly lit and eerily quiet but for an occasional *beep* from an electronic monitor next to and slightly to the rear of the bed. The bed was reclined maybe thirty degrees so that Susan could watch TV. The speaker on the TV was on the headboard of her bed. Her head, above the whiplash collar, was propped on a pillow, her mouth was open slightly. From her grimace and the labored sound of her breathing, I could tell she was in pain. As we entered, she looked up at me.

"We meet again, Mr. Street." Her voice was weak, and her jaw didn't move when she spoke. She smiled and spoke through the right side of her mouth. "Sorry I'm not a little more presentable. The past two days have been a little rough. The only bright spot, now I can talk without moving my jaw. Me and Jeff Dunham. Yay me."

"I can see that. We went by the MoonGlow and saw the aftermath. You had us worried. When did this happen? Do you know who attacked you?"

"It was what, two nights ago after I closed up. I walked to the car and saw the windshield, then *pow*! The lights went out. Who's your friend?"

"This is Adam Waverly, he's a PD officer in—"

"Fairwater. I've seen him in the bar a time or two." She blinked a couple of times and whispered, "Hi, Adam." She lifted her good arm and wiggled two fingers.

He nodded and said, "Ma'am."

Susan looked at the rolling table next to her bed. "Mr. Street, can you hand me that glass of water? And put the straw in it? I dry out real quick."

I did as requested and handed her the plastic glass. She sipped and looked back at me.

I needed some information. "Susan, help me out here. Do you have any idea who attacked you? Is it someone you've seen before?"

She sighed heavily and said, "No, but I know it's a message sent from far above *my place*. This was Wade telling me to keep my damn mouth shut and stop talking to outsiders, folks like you."

"If that's the case, I apologize, and we'll try to get you compensated for your suffering. How did you end up in this hospital? We would have expected you'd be in Fairwater."

Through her wired jaw, she responded, "Oh, no way. I have a friend who works here. When this happened, I called him, and he came and got me. It's a better hospital anyway, and it doesn't have Wade Hawkins' eyes and ears everywhere."

Adam asked, "What is the damage? You look like you took quite a pounding."

Susan smiled again, then she winced and mumbled, "Thanks. You should see it from my side. Broken jaw, shattered left knee, five broken ribs, various cuts and bruises, and a concussion. This goddamn whiplash collar may come off tomorrow. Other than that, I'm just peachy." Her breathing was labored as she added, "The semi that ran over me survived without a scratch."

Adam asked, "Do you know who did this to you? Do you recall a voice? A face? Anything?"

She blinked again, and even that looked like it hurt. "I didn't see a face, everything came from behind me, real sudden like. Whoever did it, he has some serious moves. Once I was down, he started in heavy. It hurts a lot in many places. He was very thorough."

I commented, "I understand. Is there anything you need? Anything I can do for you?"

"Well, how's my car?"

"Needs a windshield. Everything else will clean up fine."

Her *good side* frowned. "Maybe it's time to let that one go down the road. I'm not all that big a fan right now."

I smiled and said, "Hey, it's not the car's fault. Hang on to it. As cars go, it's even a decent investment. They're not making any more of them. Or, here's a thought, maybe just sell it to me." I paused and added, "Kidding! Speaking of money, are you insured for hospital care?"

"Oh, I'm covered. Only costs me ten bucks a day or so to be here. I figured there'd be a holdup or a robbery at some point, maybe someone would shoot my ass. Shit, that would probably hurt less than this and mean less time off work." Now she sighed and closed her eyes for a minute. I took the hint.

I laid my business card on her rolling table and said, "Susan, we're going to let you rest. Here's my card. You need anything at all, any time, give me a call. I'll check in on you in a day or so. You stay in touch." I turned, and Adam and I left the room.

As we waited for the elevator a moment later, Adam asked, "So tell me if I'm getting the vibe here. She had been Wade's main squeeze for a while, and after they split, she was supposed to stay silent about him. She talked to you, someone saw that. Wade found out and had someone rough her up."

"That's pretty much it. Whoever did this, though, left another hint, the concrete through the windshield. That's the same thing that killed Jack Hawkins. Maybe it's a trademark." The elevator door opened, and we stepped inside. "So that's two deaths, and one attempted murder using the same MO."

Adam responded, "And you're convinced that Wade Hawkins is the initiator, the financier, whatever."

As the elevator door opened, I looked at him and said, "The technical term for all that is, *The bad guy*."

"Thanks, Street. I'll try to remember that."

36

Atlanta, Georgia — 2005

It had been a long day in Atlanta at the dealer auction for Jack Hawkins, but he was happy with the outcome. The dealer's lesser trade-ins, at least the ones he'd sent south before Wade could get hold of them for his *pot lot*, had sold and brought decent money. The market was improving. He also had a line on a few cars that customers had requested. He was gaining *cred* with the crew at the auction house, and he was proud of that.

He'd picked Beth up from a job fair that she had helped manage for the previous two days, and she was anxious to get home to her apartment in Fairwater. Her new boyfriend, a paralegal at one of the local law firms, had been texting her, telling her how much he missed her. She had commented about this to Jack, who showed her no mercy. As she approached the truck, Jack marveled once again at how both of his sisters had been born so beautiful while he and Wade were barely average in appearance. Beth was petite with dark-blonde hair, an excellent physique, and an infectious smile, another element of her makeup that he had long razzed her about.

As she settled into her seat in the pickup's cab, Jack began his teasing with a barrage of questions. "So, how's that grimy boyfriend of yours doing? Is he still calling you ten times a day?"

Beth smiled and rolled her eyes. "He's down to three times a day when he has a break at work. Apparently, they don't give much of a lunch break if you're below a certain level of employment or tenure."

"Ah, so he's a *sweatshop lawyer*. Fascinating! How will he ever support you and the eleven flawless children you'll have with him?"

"Oh, it's eleven now, is it? HA! Well, if this family is to perpetuate, *someone* has to create a progeny, don't they?"

"A 'Progeny'? What the hell's that? I was talkin' about you and whatsisname havin' kids."

"It's the same thing, o' master of typos. Your vocabulary really is microscopic, isn't it?"

"Why yes, it is. And why not? C'mon, girl! We live in *Fairwater, Georgia*, and I fit there quite nicely. Not *Goodwater*, mind you, not even *Decentwater*! No, just *fair*. It's like the city founders didn't know the meaning of the word *meh* yet. It's like, 'Hey guys, Let's not commit to adequacy or anything drastic when we name the town, okay? Fairwater will suffice." Beth laughed at the accuracy of the descriptions.

Jack had driven to the northbound turnpike after leaving the I-75 with its Atlanta traffic, and he was glad for the respite from the noise and clutter of the big city and the freeway. His longtime project pickup truck was almost where he wanted it, he just needed a few new bits to reach completion. It looked great, it ran beautifully, and it handled like a sports car, so he'd reached his goal for now.

Jack looked in the mirrors as he drove and noticed the glare from the lights of a big obnoxious, lifted pickup approaching at fairly high speed in his inner lane. Jack fingered the turn signal stalk and changed to the outer lane as the white truck rapidly gained on his position. He thought, *What's this guy's major malfunction?*

Jack held his speed steady as he waited for the taller vehicle to pass, but as the truck drew alongside, it slowed to match his speed. Jack could see that this was a Dodge pickup from the mid-eighties, the newer sculpted body style like he'd seen the hero on one of those old TV detective shows drive. The truck was now alongside the red pickup, so he looked up to see if it was someone he...

Just then, the windshield in front of Jack Hawkins exploded, glass shards and broken concrete chunks everywhere, and the truck veered left, rubbing its side against the white truck's tall tires and catching the large-diameter step bars that hung below the cab. After jumping a foot off the pavement after hitting the sidewalls of the tires one last time, the lowered pickup took a hard right turn. Beth was screaming at the horrific vision to her left as the projectile continued through her brother and smashed the rear window out of the cab. By now, the truck had started its sickening turns and flips, ending on its roof in the damp grass almost a hundred feet from the side of the highway. The truck continued running at its cruise control speed setting until the engine died from fuel starvation. A pillar of acrid white smoke rose from the wreckage as the engine expired from oil starvation.

In the cab of the white Dodge 4x4 out on the turnpike, the driver elbowed the passenger savagely, screaming, "What did you do?"

He took one final glance back toward the carnage before he sped off, hoping—no, praying—that no one had seen.

37

I returned to the B&B that evening, considering my local options, but I also wanted to know what the outside opinion was, so at quitting time out west, I called Lynn. I caught her as she was taking delivery of her new car, a dark silver Aston Martin coupe. I had seen the photos when her husband had asked her to select the car, and with the special-order accouterments specified, the delivery had taken a few additional months. Neither of them were shy about getting specifically what they wanted...that's just the way the wealthy are sometimes, though Lynn and Grant were far more pleasant about their affluence than many I had met since arriving in California.

With the celebration of the acquisition completed, the discussion turned to the situation in Georgia. I had sent the information about the property values and the probability of Wade's fraud against his sister to Lynn the day before, and she had questions for me.

"How do you want to proceed with this, Street?"

I answered, "Well, regarding the estate issues, I figured I'd leave that to you. I don't quite stack up to you as a great legal mind.

Should an examination of that matter happen as a legal issue brought by the State of Georgia or California, or what?"

"You should discuss that with a local attorney there in Fairwater. Do you think you can find one that won't side with him due to his local influence?"

"I'll have to ask my best local adviser. He's Wade's cousin, and he worked at the family's car dealerships for decades, so he got shafted the way many of the other locals did. He is not a Wade Hawkins fan. Many others here are on the same side."

"That sounds positive."

"It should be."

"Are you making any headway on the accident investigation?"

"Some. My suspicions regarding the accident itself are all but proven at this point. I have an ally from the police department who is in my corner regarding that. He actually got suspended because he was talking to me too often. He's a good guy. Thing is, in the scenario that I have in mind, there had to be a new player, someone who actually caused the accident, and that person is, at this point, a total unknown."

"So you don't think it was an accident at all."

"Absolutely not, unless flying concrete is a regional phenomenon of which I am unaware. Thing is, Wade wouldn't sully his hands doing anything like that himself, so we're looking for yet another unknown entity, a hired gun, or more accurately, a hired chunk of concrete."

"What should I tell Sylvia?"

"If you talk to her, just say I'm making progress on all fronts."

"Fair enough. Stay safe and keep in touch."

"You too. Happy Aston Martin."

"Always!"

———

I spent most of that evening at the B&B. The hosts had a discussion group going, but I retired to my suite when the topics turned to the proper maintenance of grandchildren. I hope to be so equipped at some point in the future, but at the present, my mind is on the work at hand.

———

I was at Mark Hawkins's house the next day for lunch, helping him install a new aluminum radiator into his '70 GTO. The radiator was securely bolted to its mounts, and he had just finished fastening the bottom radiator hose. I was pouring a fifty-fifty mix of water and coolant—what used to be called *anti-freeze*—while he tightened the metal collar around the ends of the upper hose when the topic of conversation turned to the various investigations that I had started.

"So, Street, what's the latest on Wade?"

"Well, he definitely shafted his sister with regard to the value of their parents' estate settlement, probably by at least a coupla million bucks. We have to talk to the State Attorney General's office in Atlanta, but there's a chance that action could be brought in California as well. Maybe not though, since the cheat was engineered and implemented here."

"You had asked about Jack and Beth's crash. Have you come to any conclusions there?"

"Many more questions than conclusions. I found the truck, and it shows extra damage that hints that there was some interference in its travels before the crash, but that would be next to impossible to prove in court. It wouldn't point back to Wade in any substantive way, even if circumstances said he was the shot caller."

"But you still think he had a hand in it."

"That depends on how angry and determined he was at the time. I'm still curious about a motive that Wade would have had for acting out against Jack. I know that they had argued about a potential buyout. Is Wade the type who would take action if a potential adversary didn't instantly buckle under? And would he dare take action against his own family? That car crash was *not* an accident that came out of the blue. I'm seeing a full-on vehicular attack with official excuses and explanations to fit. Add that to the attack on Wade's former side chick, Susan, just a couple of days ago. She's not in as bad a condition as Jack and Beth, fortunately, but perhaps not for a lack of effort. One common thread between the two events is a concrete block through a windshield."

"Ouch. That could hurt."

"If applied at speed, certainly. In Susan's case, the car was parked, and the broken glass was clearly a warning. Just some conjecture here, Mark. Let's say Wade had issues with someone, be it a repo, a past-due loan, whatever. Is there anyone you have seen or heard of that he would hire to do his dirty work? Is there anyone a little *hinky* in his orbit?"

He smiled. "You're using *hinky* as a technical term, right, Street?"

I nodded in agreement.

"There were probably a few through the years, but the most current, the most recent, would be young Mr. Pride." He put his empty bottle on the patio and opened another. He passed another to me as well. "You're probably on to something there. Wade hired this guy, Lincoln Pride, as a lube jockey for the shop. I didn't mind that at all. I needed the help, but Wade hired him with no application and no vetting whatsoever. In the office, Dottie ran a background check on him after a week or so. Turns out the clown had been sprung from the jail up in Chattanooga just a few days before Wade hired him. Granted, Wade hired him because he was a friend of a friend, and Pride was certainly decent at the work he did when he was workin' for me, but c'mon, man...maybe let's have a few basic standards, okay?"

"How long did he work for you?"

"He was there for a couple of years full-time, then Wade started using him off-site. He started by sending him out to help with repossessions, sometimes in the early mornings. There weren't a lot of problems with the usual clientele, but Wade had relaxed the standards for selling and delivering vehicles, especially lower-level used cars. He'd accept smaller down payments more often, and he'd qualify people with lower credit scores as well. That eventually caused problems—more repossessions, more cars that just disappeared, more cars impounded for being uninsured. Short strokes, Wade was sloppy at running a business."

I asked, "How did Aubry respond to all that?"

"Poorly. Understand, Aubry was always a diplomat if there were late payments from customers. He was an artist with getting people with financial issues back on track. We rarely had to go to court or go get someone's car. When Wade started his own place, that *pot lot* over on MLK, they were rolling anyone with a pulse and getting stuck with four repos a week. That is *not* the way to do the car business. That's just tacky."

"Just speculating here, you think Wade would have sent this Lincoln Pride out to do his dirty work, maybe getting a little too rough with people?"

"Without a doubt, Street. Eventually, I started seeing repoed customers come to the dealer, either to settle their bills or just collect the personal stuff out of their cars. We started seeing them with black eyes, bruises, a couple of 'em looked like they'd been through the war. That legendary Hawkins diplomacy with regard to financial dealings was a thing of the past. His dad would never have stood for that kind of crap."

I asked, "What kind of guy was Pride? You worked with him for a while. What was he like?"

"He was a pretty basic guy, I guess. He never really looked past the surface, and he would just say funny stuff at times. I once asked him how it felt to be named after a great president. He looked baffled, and he asked, 'Who's that?' I said, 'Abraham Lincoln, of course,' and he came back with, 'Nah, man. I was named after the Black dude on an old TV show *Mod Squad.*'"

I laughed. "Ouch! Well, how could anyone live *that* down?" I took a sip of beer and changed the subject. "Dottie, the DMV lady at the dealer, told me that Wade had opened a title loan business in that part of town too."

"Sure! He was totally devoted to keeping poor folks poor for as long as possible. That's my technical definition of *asshole*."

What are the chances that this Pride guy is Wade's thug in Susan's case, using brute force to tell her to keep her mouth shut?"

Mark grinned. "Oh, maybe eighty, ninety percent."

"That's what I'm thinkin' too. I'm gonna call young Officer Waverly, see if I can get some traction with him in that direction. Thank you for the input. I owe you one."

"Anytime, Street."

———

I spent the rest of the afternoon studying the legal system in Georgia. I had done a bit of research and found a small private university forty miles from Fairwater that offered a fairly healthy and well-respected law school. I called ahead and arranged for an hour with an experienced law professor. She kindly explained a few of the ins and outs of the state system. Her conclusion was that since Wade's estate cheat of his sister was planned, engineered, and perpetrated within the boundaries of the great State of Georgia, any legal actions against him would also be better handled here as well.

She passed a name of an accounting and estate inquiry supervisor at the State Department of Revenue and gave me an idea of the proper format of an inquiry into the Hawkins business operations and property transfers. I was a little nervous about approaching such a situation, but the information I gathered helped assuage my fears.

Driving back to the B&B, I decided that this was a conclusion that I could live with. Sylvia Tate had plenty of money, and a protracted legal fight over a few more million could get boring in short order. My bigger concern was that someone, let's say *parties unknown*, had murdered two people and attacked a third using similar methods. On the surface, there would appear to be no commonality, no *connective tissue*, between the two events other than the method of attack. Then again, *on the surface* wasn't my preferred area of examination.

No one in Fairwater would expect any beyond-the-obvious, against-the-grain exam of the accident site *or* of the wrecked truck by a total outsider, and certainly, no one would suspect that the evidence of the concrete, the common element at both sites would be discovered, or that connection made.

Yay me. Now all I had to do was prove it.

38

Wade Hawkins was tired. This trip and all its elements had worn him out, and waiting for the resolution was truly annoying. He was probably taking his impatience out on his wife. He had listened to Lucy's constant complaining for the last hour as they drove trying to find a shopping venue that suited her. He had long since stopped *hearing* her in such situations, and he often had to ask her to repeat her requests or even the general subjects she was discussing.

Finally, at a lengthy stoplight at another wide unfamiliar thoroughfare, Wade cut loose. Loudly, he said through clenched teeth, "Luce, I didn't bring you all the way out here to have a fight. Could you please just ease the hell up? Just for a goddamn MINUTE?"

She came back with a predictable response. "Wade Hawkins, your filthy mouth is neither welcome nor needed here in this car. I can understand proper English quite well."

Wade winced for maybe the fifth time since their drive had started. The wine was having its effect on him, and he returned to his previous thought pattern. He wanted it to be done once and for all.

Two minutes later, Lucy looked west from the car and said, "Will you look at that sunset! It's orange! Oh, let's stop and get a picture of it." Somehow, as usual, her request was actually couched as a demand, so Wade made the turn toward the Palos Verdes Peninsula scenic overlook that he'd scoped out earlier. Three miles further on, he pulled to the open parking lot—they would be the sole car on the property—chose a space, and parked. Lucy was already walking toward the top of the stairway. "Hurry up, Wade! Take the picture!" Somehow, again, her voice sounded like a screeching feral cat.

He closed the driver's door of the big car, took his Nikon digital camera from his pocket, and walked toward her. Lucy stood at the front of the upper platform of the segmented stairway that led to the beach fifty feet below. Wade smiled his stiff smile, stood ten feet from the platform, and snapped the photo after setting the automatic camera to flash. The only way that Lucy would show up while her back was to the sunset. She'd always been really soft on how stuff works, and he had always ignored that element of her makeup. Now he wondered why he'd done that.

"Luce, let's go down toward the beach, get some more shots down there." He motioned toward the stairway. At three levels toward the base of the stairway at the beach, there were square platforms, maybe fifteen feet square, built for the convenience of an aging citizenry, some of whom would want to take a short rest on the climb back up to the parking lot after visiting the beach to take pictures of the orange sunsets. Whatever.

As they ascended to the beach, Lucy commented again and again about the beauty of the fast-diminishing sunset. At the second of the landings, a large rectangular base with a 4x4 wooden railing anchored at three places across its length, he said, "This is a good one, Luce. You can see the ocean better from this lower angle."

As she turned to look at the view, Wade stepped forward in a single long stride. He put his hand in the center of her back and gave her a solid push. Over the railing she went, somehow twisting at the waist to manage a disgusted look back at him as she toppled from sight below the platform. The fall was silent. She landed hard on the rocks below, her head tilted at an impossible angle, her eyes open, her mouth agape in a sudden pain that she would never voice.

Fearful of witnesses, Wade Hawkins rushed to the base of the stairway to the body of his fallen partner of over twenty years. He didn't feel a lot, no loss, no grief at the sudden alteration of his life's path or his impulsive act. This time he really was numb. He stepped up on the small rocks at the base of the cliff and looked down at her broken body. At least this had been a quick death. Mindless of the blood that he gathered on his hands, he checked for a pulse—there was none by then—and he brushed her eyes closed. Then he stood, brushed the sand off his trouser legs, and made one more look for witnesses. Seeing none, he mounted the stairway for the long, steep climb back to the parking lot.

His climb made him tired as well as worried a bit. Back at the car, he sorted through the debris that she had accumulated in their one trip in the Cadillac—mostly retail receipts and the ticket from their dinner. He wadded it all up and walked it to the trash barrel fifty feet away.

Then by chance, his attention diverted to the mercury vapor lights that lit at their preset time at sunset. He looked up at one light pole and noticed a dark square shape near the top, just below the light standard. There was a small red light at one corner of the box. A camera? Oh, shit. He hunched down under his baseball cap and hurried back to the Escalade, concerned now that the excuse of a sudden impulse for his recent action might be useless. He started the big white wagon and powered out of the parking lot with his bright headlights on, something to maybe blind that camera, but the front bumper caught a low metal fence post on the way out. He heard the grinding sound and felt the nudge for a couple of seconds, then powered through, smoking the tires, rapidly escaping the parking lot that had now turned incredibly hostile.

He manhandled the Caddy at the quickest possible rate back north, finding the westbound Imperial Highway exit from the 405 in a little over a half hour. He made the transition to ride alongside the busy, crowded LAX hangars and runway for a mile until the turn for the hotel came up on the left. There was a group of fully-lit California Highway Patrol cruisers and their attendant officers at the turnoff and a wrecked late-model Mitsubishi Eclipse coupe off in the grass beside the road. Wade tried his best to look innocent as he passed the disturbance. Through the open window, he heard someone say, "Car Chase," and it put him at ease. They weren't there for him.

When he reached the hotel, he steered the big car down the basement entry ramp and stuffed it into a darkened space at the far corner of the underground parking garage. Then he walked to the bank of elevators and waited patiently for the lift that would take him to his room. He took a shower and changed his clothes, even taking his nice new wool slacks to a garage-level dumpster in a plastic trash bag after he found a single dark bloodstain on the left knee.

Wade set and rehearsed his story for the desk clerk. "I have been called back home on urgent business matters, and we will be checking out really early in the morning. Could I settle the bill now so we don't have to deal with it tomorrow morning?"

The desk clerk, a slight young fellow with dyed spikey blonde hair and an earring—Wade wondered if he was one of those *gays* he'd heard of—smiled and asked, "How did you enjoy your stay in California?"

"Oh, we did most of what we planned to do."

The clerk smiled a bit too readily and said, "Oh, I know how that is. There's never enough time, is there?" He slid the ticket toward Wade. "Sign here, sir, and have a safe trip back home. Come back and see us again."

Yeah, Wade thought to himself as he scribbled his name, *fat chance.*

———

Wade Hawkins didn't sleep at all that last night he spent in California. The reality of his act against his wife started to take its toll on him. He had visions of her final glance back at him as she toppled over the railing after *the push*. In his waking hours during his last night in Suite 432 at the Embassy Suites South, LAX, he imagined a brutal capture, a SWAT team surrounding his hotel room and dragging him out bodily, then him suffering a gunshot in the back as he started his final break for freedom, running across the wide street in front of the hotel. He realized that simple daydreams did him no good and could do great harm. He needed to concentrate on the things that he was facing, and he had to, above all, keep his stories straight and in order.

His official line was well-practiced. He had been called back to Georgia on an urgent business matter and would fly out as quickly as possible.

His wife had, quite by chance, run into some close friends from college in Georgia. They lived in Huntington Beach and had lived out here for ten years or more. They hadn't seen one another in a dozen or more years and decided to spend some time together. His wife wanted to stay and visit in California and would return home in a week or so.

He hadn't known her old friends, had never met them because they hadn't met until well after college graduation. We talked on the phone just last evening.

How did she die? Oh my god! She's actually DEAD? Noooo! *What am I gonna do?*

———

Wade left the Embassy Suites South the next morning at six twenty-five in a taxi. They used friggin' Toyota Priuses as taxis out here. That was ridiculous, though it had plenty of room and was really quiet. He flew out of Long Beach Airport—a much more expensive flight due to shorter notice—with a connecting flight to Atlanta from Dallas/Fort Worth, a facility even larger and less workable than the Hartsfield Atlanta nightmare. He had a ride arranged from Atlanta to Fairwater, a taxi again so that he wouldn't have to pay to rent a space to park his car for as long as he was away. In the end, he didn't think he saved anything at all. That's kinda how that whole trip had gone.

When he arrived back in Fairwater, he was really glad to be home, back in an area, a town, where he was in control of...well, pretty much everything. That he hadn't slept a solid three hours for the past forty-eight didn't change a lot until he triple-dosed his sleep meds. That put him down for a solid six dreamless hours until he awoke at five the next morning. He took a shower and spent an hour in the home office checking phone messages and making notes for contacts after business hours that next morning.

39

The cell phone rang as Lincoln Pride was getting out of the shower that morning. He heard it ring as he was walking to the night table and picked it up at the fourth ring.

"'Lo."

The voice on the other end was familiar. "Linc? Wade Hawkins."

"Welcome back, boss. How was California?"

"Dirty, crowded, busy. Everything that keeps it from being a vacation. It's always good to come back home." He sipped some of his orange juice. "We have some repos coming up this week. Can you meet me at the lot later today so we can set a schedule?"

"Sure thing, Mr. Hawkins. What time you want to meet?"

"Let's say eleven o'clock. That work for you?"

"Sure thing. I'll see you then."

———

Lincoln Pride had to wait outside of Wade Hawkins's office until ten minutes after the hour. The secretary had him cooling his heels in the outer office, telling him, "He's on his phone, it may be a while."

"I can wait. He called for me." Eight minutes later, Wade appeared at his office door, smiling his thin smile.

"Linc? Thanks for waiting. Sorry that took so long. Come on in, have a seat. I have to return another call, I'll be right with you." Wade stepped aside as the younger man entered the office and took his seat at the front of the desk. Lincoln had always liked that office. There were wall posters adapted from classic car advertisements framed on the walls, refugees from the showroom of the car dealer that had been razed. Lincoln had become accustomed to the dealership structure and enjoyed his work there when suddenly, just after Mr. Hawkins, Sr. had passed, the dealership had been closed, and the buildings boarded up less than two weeks later, the whole facility had been leveled.

Finally, Wade ended his call and looked across at the younger Black man. "Lincoln, how would you like a new job? You know that I've come to count on you to help me handle some difficult areas of this business. That means a lot to me, so I think you've earned this." He reached across the desk with a check in his hand.

Lincoln Pride looked at the check and withheld a gasp. The check read $5000.00. It was more than he'd ever held in his hand at any given time, ever. "Um, wow. Thank you, Mr. Hawkins. I really appreciate this."

"Oh, I know you do, Linc. Your modesty is one of the things I've come to admire about you. Oh, and please, call me Wade unless we're among customers or other folks in a business or public setting, okay? All my executive associates do that."

"Yes sir, Mr....I mean, Wade." He smiled uneasily.

Wade ignored the answer and plowed on with his spiel. "Fine. Now, as we're going forward, I'm going to need you to handle all of the repossessions for this lot and any collections or repos for the title loan business as well. We have a solid effort going now, it's finally showing a profit, and I have to work extra hard to keep it that way. I have some big plans for this town. You're in line to do very well for yourself in the near future if you want to. Can I count on you?"

Lincoln had never been talked to like this by anyone, aside from in the Army, before he got bounced for sloughing off during tech school. That old Drill Instructor probably hadn't been all that rough in retrospect, but Lincoln Pride didn't let anyone boss him around...until now...because now he had at least a little taste of fat money in his hand.

"Mr. er...Wade, I'll do anything you need done. Just ask." Before the meeting ended, the pair had also arranged for Lincoln Pride to have a car of his own for the first time in recent memory as part of his monthly compensation. He chose a clean silver 1990s Chevy Monte Carlo that looked pretty sharp but didn't stand out in traffic. A low-key car was valuable in case he had to follow some deadbeat or park and surveil some other deadbeat. He detected a theme.

40

"Mr. Hawkins? Mr. Wade Hawkins?"

"Yes, this is Wade Hawkins." It was a little after four that afternoon. He'd been expecting the call.

The voice was all but flat but also assertive. "Mr. Hawkins, this is Cameron Sheedy. I'm a deputy investigator with the Los Angeles Sheriff's Department's Lomita Office. Sir, is your wife one Lucille Hawkins?"

"Why, yes, she is."

"Mr. Hawkins, do you know where your wife is right now?"

"Certainly." He started the spiel he'd practiced. "She's in Los Angeles visiting with some of her college friends. We were out there last week, I was there on family business, and she came with me. She'd never been to LA. One evening we were at supper, and she ran into some college friends. They hadn't seen each other in years. She's staying out there for another few days visiting with them. I expect her back home in a day or two." He had used his rehearsed earnest tone up to this point, now he switched his tone to cautious. There was silence for a few seconds, then quieter, more slowly, with the requisite pauses, he asked, "Umm...may I ask why you're calling? Has something happened?"

Cameron Sheedy pursed his lips, lifted his eyebrows, and shook his head as he looked across the desks at his partner, who was listening on mute. "Well, Mr. Hawkins, I'm sorry to inform you that we found your wife's body the day before yesterday. She is deceased."

Another pause, then, "Excuse me? Did you say..."

"Yes, sir. Your wife's body was found at the base of the stairway near an overlook above the beach on the Palos Verdes Peninsula. She had fallen from a landing on the stairway that leads down to the beach."

"Oh god...no. Please tell me this is not true. We've been together for more than twenty years. I don't know how... Are...are you sure that it's her?"

"Oh yes, Mr. Hawkins, we are certain. I can put you in touch with the coroner's office so that you can make arrangements to bring her remains home to...where are you located, Mr. Hawkins? Where's home?"

More slowly now, and quieter, Wade Hawkins said, "I'm in Fairwater, Georgia. We're eighty miles north of Atlanta. Yes, sir. Please give the coroner my number."

"We will do that. I'm very sorry for your loss, Mr. Hawkins. Please call me if you have any further concerns." As he replaced the receiver on its cradle, Cameron Sheedy looked across at his partner slash protégé, Ed Steele. "So, young Mr. Steele, what did we just hear?"

The younger deputy investigator said, "Too many specifics, not enough curiosity? No plans for coming here for retrieval?"

"I have taught you well, young pup. He killed her, sure as hell." He turned to his computer monitor and typed a few words. "I can't believe how dumb that guy was. His wife just magically appears at the bottom of the stairs. No empty car in the parking lot, no explanation of how she got there? Maybe rural Georgia doesn't have cameras every fifty feet and constant, obsessive video surveillance of public sites." He shook his head as he closed the folder.

On his monitor, the video ran, showing grainy images of a white

SUV arriving at the parking lot at the Palos Verdes overlook shortly after the rain stopped. The vehicle stopped in a marked slot near the stairway, and momentarily a man and a woman exited from their respective doors. Chatting as couples will do, but never actually *touching,* they made their way to the stairway leading to the beach.

Cameron Sheedy tapped a few keys forwarding the video to the point where the male of the couple reappeared. He walked to the SUV and opened the passenger side door. He cleared the vehicle of random items which he took to the trashcan across the parking lot. At one point, he looked up at one of the several cameras that surveilled the parking lot. He flinched, then pulled his cap further down on his head. He returned to the car, started it, and drove off the parking lot, catching the front fender on a post at the edge of the exit ramp as he drove out. The dusk light would have rendered the license plate invisible, but for the fact that the vehicle's lights operated automatically at a certain ambient light level. Cameron paused the video, copied the license plate number onto his notepad, then keyed his cell to make another call.

When the connection was made, Cameron said, "Deputy Sheedy, Lomita Office calling for David Cale."

There was another pause, then, "This is David Cale."

"Deputy Cale, I'm Cameron Sheedy with the Lomita Office. How ya doing?"

"Every day's a peach, Deputy Sheedy. How're things down by the beach?"

"Doing well, I have a report from you from last weekend referencing a Cadillac Escalade found at the...Embassy Suites up by LAX. Has some blood stains? Damage at the front corner?"

"Yes, sir. Owner had it out as a loaner, it's back at the owner's property now. Turns out he's a licensed tow yard for the State."

"That's convenient. Well, it looks as if the same vehicle is prime on surveillance video relating to a Palos Verdes death, probably a 187. Lady from Georgia. Has the car been processed yet?"

"We're done with it. There's really nothing to see other than blood smears on the passenger's side of the front seat. Crime scene says it's female blood. There's not really all that much of it. The doer had blood on his hands, just swiped across the leather. No prints, just smears, but we have a couple of solid latents from elsewhere in the car. The owner has it back at his place in impound for the duration of whatever investigation is deemed necessary. We have the name of the person it was lent to, though he let a client of *his* take it. It's secure until we say otherwise. Primary's a PI, name's Street, he's up in the Wilshire district. Want his number?"

"Absolutely."

————

My phone rang a little after seven that evening. I didn't recognize the number, but the 310 area code said quite a bit. A Deputy Cameron Sheedy from the Lomita Office of the LASD was calling about a certain Cadillac Escalade and the guy who'd been driving it.

"Thanks for the call, Deputy. I can't say I haven't been expecting it."

"Oh, really. Tell me about that."

"Yes, sir. I just arrived in Georgia on business. You're calling about a Cadillac Escalade with some blood smears on the leather of the passenger's front seat. The owner gave you my name as the person he lent it to a few days ago."

"Yes, Mr. Street. That's right. You have a name to give me with regard to that vehicle, don't you?"

"Why yes, Deputy, I do. Name's Wade Hawkins. He's a party to my own work here in Fairwater, Georgia. He hot-footed it back home a day or two before I flew out here myself."

"Well, okay, Mr. Street, you have one up on me. Looks to us law enforcement professionals here in the Lomita Office that Mr. Hawkins is a person of interest in the death of his wife."

I smiled into the phone. "Ah. That Wade is one busy cat. How may I be of assistance to you, since I'm here on the ground on ol'

Wade's home turf? Do you have any plans to come have a chat with the boy?"

"That is not likely at this particular moment, Mr. Street. Our travel budgets don't allow us to hop on a plane at a moment's notice like you private tickets do. How 'bout you keep an eye on him for us and let me know what you see? It might take a week or so for us to get out there to talk to him."

"I expect I'll be here at least that long. As I said, ol' Wade's been busy on his home turf for quite a while, and there are several issues for which he needs to atone."

There was an audible sigh. "Well then, Mr. Street, sounds as if we're on the same page. How 'bout you call me or email me every forty-eight hours or so with progress reports on Mr. Hawkins?"

"I'll be happy to." We exchanged contact information then I had to ask, "How's the weather out there?"

"Cloudless, seventy-three degrees, slight breeze from the coast, as usual. There?"

"Fifty-eight and rain, all day."

"Ooh. Sounds...um..."

"Oh, it sucks. I know."

41

Wade stopped Lincoln Pride outside the used car dealer as he parked his car. "Hey, Linc, can I talk to you for a minute?"

"Sure thing, boss." Lincoln Pride was surprised when Wade motioned that they would walk toward the rear of the property. They stood between two repossessed late-model Yukons at the rear boundary when Wade stood close and put his hand on Lincoln's shoulder.

"Linc, I need an assist with something. I hope you can help."

"Tell me what you need, boss."

"There's a woman who's causing me some grief, Linc. I need someone to get her to shut the hell up about me and my personal business. We were close for a while, a while ago, and now she's talking to outsiders about me and my affairs. Do you know of anyone who could get tough with someone like that, impart the message, and then stay quiet about it themselves? It's really important to me, buddy."

Lincoln Pride had never heard Wade Hawkins refer to anyone, certainly not himself, as *buddy*. He decided to play to the audience. "Well, yeah, Wade. I do know of someone. It might cost you a bit..."

"Money's not an issue, Linc. I just want results. I don't need to meet the person, you're my sole agent in this thing."

"I can get it done, Wade, no problem. I know just the guy."

"That sounds good. How soon do you think we could get this handled?"

"Coupla days. I'll let you know when it's done and get you photos as proof."

Wade Hawkins reached into the inner pocket of his suit jacket and withdrew a long white envelope. "Information is inside with the downstroke on the fee. Let me know when it's done." He looked from side to side, then added, "Thank you for your help with this, Linc." He squeezed the taller man's shoulder, then turned and quickly walked back toward the front of the property.

Lincoln Pride waited for a few seconds, then walked back to his car. Sitting inside, he slit the envelope and saw a piece of paper with a name, Susan Keeley, and an address, the MoonGlow Bar on the turnpike. He folded the note and withdrew the bills, counting out two thousand dollars. He was impressed. This whole *thug* thing might work out after all.

————

Lincoln Pride drove to the MoonGlow Bar at half-past nine that evening with the intent of checking the location and securing his target. After a few minutes in the parking lot, he decided on his tactic and walked inside, taking a stool at the bar.

The middle-aged white woman with the long dark hair, the big fishnet stockings, the leather bustier, and the short shorts smiled and asked, "What are you drinkin', hon?"

Within ten minutes, Lincoln had determined that this woman was his intended target. He had seen her a time or two before the *real* car dealer closed, and he remembered changing the oil on her yellow Trans Am convertible a couple of times. That car was easy to remember. He downed a couple of tall drafts and some peanuts, had a few minutes of small talk with Susan, then paid the tab and left a tip before he bade her goodbye.

Her last words to him were, "You come back and see us."

As he walked out the door, he thought, *Oh yeah. Without a doubt.*

———

Lincoln Pride rolled past the construction machinery storage lot the next morning, one of the areas where Wade's dad's businesses had been knocked down a while ago. The driveway was open, but there hadn't been any discernible traffic in recent days since there were no tracks through the dried mud. He drove onto the property and parked the silver car toward the rear of the plot. This was one of the lesser plots of land in the Fairwater business district, and the warehouse that had taken the space for decades had been an eyesore, used as a parts depot for the company's farm implement business.

Various remnants of farm and construction machinery were scattered around the weedy two-acre parcel, but the location was also used to conceal repos and vehicles that had been damaged at some point in their service. A few derelict police cars were parked at one corner, and the tired Dodge 4x4 that Lincoln had used in the fatal crash of the Hawkins siblings sat at one corner, hidden from sight behind a rusty pile of farm machinery.

Lincoln wasn't certain what he was looking for or frankly why he was looking here. He figured he'd know it when he found it. Five minutes on site, he found *it*. That dumbass white boy he'd had along with him a while back had tossed a half-block of concrete from the side window of the 4x4 onto the lower pickup that Jack Hawkins was driving. Instead of hitting the hood and giving a good big scare, the chunk of block had gone through the friggin' windshield, killing both occupants. That had been an accident, and Lincoln was sweating it until the final declaration of *kids tossing stuff off the bridge* had become the official narrative.

He had seen the block thing used before though, and he

thought it would be a suitable tool this time. The car wasn't moving, and the owner would be otherwise distracted—getting the shit beat out of her. She might not even notice the car till later. He selected a fairly clean quarter-block from a pile at the rear of the lot and put it behind the seat of his car. His dark hoodie, a pair of leather gloves, and a good hiding place behind the MoonGlow would be all he'd need now.

———

The next night, Lincoln Pride parked the Monte at the back of the parking lot of the Denny's three doors to the south from the Moon-Glow. No one ever paid any attention to the back of those parking lots. Up in 'Nooga he'd even used one when he picked up a hitch-hiker girl a few years before. That'd been fun.

The sign on the front door of the bar said that it closed at two, so at ten till, he had walked calmly across the back of the adjoining properties and waited behind the back corner of the building. Susan Keeley came out fifteen minutes later, and *the job* took less than ten minutes, start to finish. Easy money.

42

When I returned to the B&B that evening, the owner stopped me at the front desk. He smiled and said, "Mr. Street, you have a package. I put it in your room as soon as it arrived."

"Thanks. I've been expecting that."

As I stepped away, he asked, "So are you getting your work done here like you hoped?"

"It's working out just fine. And I really like staying here. You run a tight ship, and the breakfasts are magnificent."

"We're glad you're enjoying your stay. Our wine and cheese evening fellowship starts at eight, I hope you'll join us."

"I appreciate the invitation. See you then."

———

As I entered my suite, I saw the FedEx box sitting on the end table next to the sofa. My friend Zig had promised me a care package. He called it a *Glock-in-the-box*, per our phone conversation earlier in the week. I broke the seal and opened the box to find a fresh Glock Model, a nice polished semi-automatic pistol with a pearl grip, and a nice black woven leather shoulder rig that I had ordered a week before I left home. A second layer of bubble wrap lifted out to reveal a backup piece, a black .22 Smith with an ankle holster in dashing black leather. A couple of boxes of Zig's special-loaded bullets, the same loads that I'd used for the last year for practice at his indoor gun range, lay at the bottom of the box. The man had my back.

I took a shower and changed clothes, then made my daily call to Lynn at six o'clock. She answered as usual on the second ring. "Hey, Street!"

"Hi, cutie. How's tricks?"

"Same stuff, different day, C-man. How're things in the land of peaches?"

"Making progress. Did you get any more information on the Hawkins' wills?"

"I talked to Sylvia this afternoon. She confirmed that each sibling had the same conditions in the parents' will. Upon the parents passing, the survivors would each get an equal share of the parents' proceeds. Just as I had expected."

"So Wade would profit substantially with the demise of his siblings."

"Yes, he would. Substantially. I would suggest though, that any actions against him be initiated within the State of Georgia. That's where the plan was formulated and executed. Do you think there's anyone back there who could be trusted to follow through with any real legal action? Is everyone in Fairwater under his thumb?"

"Not everyone. My contact at the State AG's office in Atlanta may be interested in taking a look, and I suspect there are a few attorneys in town who could show an interest. I'm tight with one of the cousins, so I'll pick his brain and see what he says."

"Is anything else happening back there?"

"Seems Wade Hawkins may be getting tired of hearing that I'm in town poking around on his turf. He may decide to offer resistance at some point."

"Are you prepared for that?"

"Pretty much. Got a care package from Zig today."

"That's good."

"Always. So how's the new Aston?"

"It's great. Very pretty, very techy, and quite fast." There was a pause and some background noise, then "Gotta go, Street. Duty calls."

"Make it all happen, Lynn. We'll talk tomorrow."

———

After answering a few emails and returning a phone call regarding a potential new client, I donned a jacket and went downstairs to the lobby, where the other guests were starting to sip their wine and nibble their cheese and crackers. The wine was again from the NASCAR legend's winery, and the cheese variety included a great smoky Colby to which I could easily become addicted. Good stuff, all.

A few introductions were made, very nice folks, but I had decided to play it close to the vest, not sharing my profession or the intent of my visit to the area. I was just another vacationer, a potential newcomer to the area just checkin' stuff out...and as of mail call this afternoon, packin' heat.

———

The information from Lynn and Sylvia regarding the content of the Hawkins' wills didn't really answer any questions to me. I was starting to realize that Wade Hawkins was still largely an unknown entity. I didn't really see him as being *greedy*, as much as power-hungry. Greed could cause decent men to do bad things, always had, always would, but *power* could bring someone to take far worse, more permanent, and more harmful actions. Power hunger usually displayed more energy and willingness to do more harm than mere greed.

One of Adam Waverly's comments earlier that day stuck with me as well, his comment that the dark red rental Mustang was now a known quantity to the local police, at least those among law enforcement who were Wade-loyal. Later that evening, I called Adam and asked him to pick me up the next morning, and I called Budget to send someone to the B&B to pick up the Mustang. Familiarity, it seemed, was starting to breed contempt.

———

Adam Waverly had picked me up from the B&B at seven-fifteen that next morning and had taken me fifty miles to a huge Ford dealer in the tiny burg of Winder, Georgia. This was another time-warp town, home to countless antique emporiums and even one ancient three-bulb traffic light on a side street off the town square. Regardless of the aged aura of the town itself, it was also home to the gargantuan Ford dealer, where I rented one of countless white North Georgia F-150s, a vehicle that would seemingly render me nearly invisible in this part of the country. There was still an issue that Adam pointed out as we waited for a traffic light to change.

"Okay, Street, now that you have the requisite white Ford F-150 pickup, rendering you a natural on any road in North Georgia, stop and look at the traffic and tell me what is wrong with this vehicle. What makes *this* white F-150 stand out like a sore thumb from all the *other* white F-150s that you see?"

I watched the passing traffic for a moment and made a guess. "Rollbar and lights above the cab? Custom wheels?"

"Nope. Nothing bolted on, just a natural addition from the vehicle being driven. I know you California guys are all clean freaks with regard to your cars, but here in *you all country*, we are not similarly impaired. We let our cars, and especially our trucks, get *dirty*. To a lot of people, the dirtier, the better. You wanna look truly natural in rural Georgia, or many other areas of the South, go out and get an inch-thick layer of good ol' Georgia mud on this thing."

"This is your turf. Point me in the right direction."

And he did. The forty-mile circuitous ride around Winder took over an hour because we took two-lane, rural routes, side roads, and the occasional random path to nowhere, mostly on roads that were unpaved. Sliding sideways in loose muddy dirt after a rainstorm was easy, fun, and happened at relatively low speeds so that we did not end up in the ditch at the side of the road, in far *deeper* mud. Adam explained that his dad had often taken him on Saturday morning sojourns down a variety of *flingin'* roads through the local wilderness, with the car sideways through curves, developing a close father-son bonding with every slide. I was jealous.

43

Eventually, I dropped Adam back at his car at the Ford Store, and we both headed back west toward Fairwater. I drove my deceptively filthy pickup back to the B&B. Along the way, I decided to consult again with Dottie, the most dependable of my background information sources regarding the ins and outs of the Wade Hawkins empire. I suggested that we meet for lunch. She suggested a small coffee shop two blocks off the town square, at a time slightly later than lunch, so as to avoid the prying eyes and ears that had caused so much trouble recently.

I arrived ten minutes early and took a seat near the rear of the dining room, waiting for Dottie to arrive. She was right on time, smiling as she recognized me sitting at the rearmost booth, facing the front door. We were the only guests in the place.

Quietly, she greeted me and took her seat. She smiled and said quietly, "Mr. Street, I'm really glad you called me. I have thought of nothing other than Wade Hawkins since you were at the house. What else have you found since then?"

"First, we have determined the language of the Hawkins parents' wills. With the other siblings out of the picture, he splits everything with his sister in California. He may have had a hand in

the accident that killed his sister and brother. There's more as well."
I took a sip of iced tea, again, carefully unsweetened.

"Seems the news hasn't become common knowledge here on his home turf, but I got a call yesterday afternoon. A loaner vehicle that I set up for Wade to use during his vacation in Southern California is the same car on video at a parking lot near the coast. His wife's body was found at the base of a cliff. She had fallen from one of the stairway landings."

Dottie frowned upon hearing the news, put her hand to her mouth, and mumbled, 'Oh, no...'

I continued, "Wade's on video surveillance leaving the car with Lucy, returning alone, taking trash from the car, and finally driving away. He's not accustomed to being under surveillance like so many Californians are. It sounds as if they have him cold, but I know he's a powerful guy here. He's bound to have legal help on his home turf if he needs it. Do you recall the local attorneys that he used back when you worked for him? Can I get a list from you?"

"Well now, Mr. Street, do you want the *pro-Wade* lawyers or the *anti-Wade* lawyers? I know 'em all."

"Who should I talk to if I want to take Wade Hawkins down locally?"

Dottie looked at me, wrote down one name on her Post-it note, pulled it off the pad, and handed it to me. "One name, Mr. Street. Just one name."

"Okay, thank you for that. Now, let's say Wade wanted to collect money, repo a car, or perhaps send a definite message, stopping just short of a threat?"

"Again, you're looking for one man only, Mr. Street." She wrote on another Post-it, handed the single sheet to me, and said, "Lincoln Pride."

I accepted the note. "Tell me about him."

She related the brief history of Lincoln Pride and Wade Hawkins. Starting with the impromptu hiring and continuing to the closure of the dealerships. "I heard that he kep' working for Wade after the dealers were gone, doin' collections and repossessions for the title loan and the used car lot over on MLK. I also heard that he could get rough doin' that work, Wade doesn't care about his customers like his daddy did, and that's a damn shame."

"Did their dad have any idea that Wade was doing that type of business?"

"Oh, I think he did. I think that may have been one of the things that finished him off. He and Wade had a few closed-door meetings there toward the end, and they got pretty loud on occasion, with Wade doing the yelling. He was just *cruel* toward his daddy, and I know that Aubry was really hurt there toward the end."

"I've come to expect that from Wade. Did you ever have any dealings with Susan Keeley?"

It took a moment for the name to click. "Yes. I did the DMV on that car Wade gave her. I knew he was cheating on his wife."

"Yep. Did Aubry know about the car that Wade gave her?"

"I don't think so. He woulda blown his top. I'm pretty sure Wade either paid that invoice himself or covered it up really well. That car had been traded on a new truck, and Wade didn't think he could ever sell it on the used car lot. People here want trucks and SUVs, sports cars like that, and convertibles especially, just take up space."

"Did the dealer ever get an audit from the State DMV? Was it known as a straight-up operation? I know that some dealers attract attention from the bureaucrats, and it can be a nightmare for them at times if they're not clean as a pin."

"Aubry kept all the dealers' operations really clean. That was part of my job. You see, the DMV in Georgia used to cover the farm implement dealers as well as cars and trucks. We never had any problems while Aubry ran things. I heard that Wade's used car place had some issues not too long ago."

"New topic. Do you know if Wade had a Life Insurance policy covering his wife?"

"Lucy? Of course. She was covered by the company employee policy. Wade kept her on payroll for a *no-show* job. That happens a lot in small towns and small businesses. Don't tell anyone."

"My lips are sealed," I smiled.

She looked at me, and her demeanor changed. "Mr. Street, are you going to make certain that man pays for all of this?"

"Dottie, I'm going to give it a hell of a try. Thank you for the word on Lincoln Pride. That helps me as well."

"You're certainly welcome, Mr. Street. You go get his ass too."

44

Lincoln Pride answered his cell when he saw that it was Wade's number. He heard, "Linc? Wade Hawkins. Thanks for taking care of that assignment I gave you. I need to talk to you about another person, and there's another repo for you from the car dealer. Get back to me when you can."

Lincoln Pride had slept late after his early hours visit to the bar owner. He looked across the bed at the nightstand, part of the furniture he'd bought for his apartment after he started making *real money* from his job at the Pontiac dealer. Then after he was tapped to start doing repos for the new lot over on MLK and the title loan store, his income had doubled, then tripled. It wasn't always the same amount, so he had to learn to budget, but he had done that well enough after the first week or two.

He had negotiated for the pickup. First, it was a cheap *get* for him, then it turned out to be a little *hot* after that dumb white boy caused that crash. He had parked that one for three weeks at the machinery yard until he thought it had cooled off a bit. As a replacement, he snagged the gray Monte Carlo, which was easier to drive and better on gas anyway. That was a factor when he had to stake out a house waiting for some deadbeat to come back home.

He had parked the truck back at the storage lot for the duration, and no one had ever objected. He went back after a week, during a queasy session when people were talking about the fatal crash, and removed the license plates—just to feel a bit less nervous about being found out.

Lincoln had long since gotten the hang of this repo thing. He'd find the person, using the existing paperwork, he'd talk to them and explain the task at hand, he'd get the keys to the subject vehicle and get the hell outta there. He'd been in the same position a time or two, and he knew that these people knew that they were up for repo. He always had a wingman with him, if only to stand silently behind him, look *stern*, and maybe drive the repoed car back to the yard. He had found that if he was a statesman, he could smooth over the anger of the repo subject with words of hope and a promise that if the account was brought up to date, a new agreement might possibly be struck and the car returned. That hardly ever really happened, but hey, if it worked in the moment, so be it

The helper was instructed to stay quiet and in the background unless things went sideways. Lincoln had learned early on that alcohol was not a good element in the discussions at the repo location. He'd had three fistfights and three different backup guys, all paid in cash at the end of the evening out of his own pocket. He didn't care much for that part of the deal, and he wanted to fix that in the next fee negotiation.

At ten-twenty that morning, Lincoln returned Wade Hawkins's call. Wade sounded calm but busy. "Hey, Lincoln. I'm up to my ass in alligators today. How 'bout you come by sometime this afternoon? I have a repo from the lot, and there's another fella needs a talkin' to. Lemme know how much you need for all this stuff, but don't stick a gun in my ribs, okay, buddy?" There was a two-second pause, then "See you then. Gotta go."

———

This fenced-and-gated annex next to the formal car dealer display and inventory service facility, right there on MLK, was apparently a storage lot for inventory awaiting delivery or service or, as I soon learned, vehicles that were freshly repossessed. The array of stored vehicles was wide, from a late-model Bonneville to a couple of older trucks. Many appeared to have been there for a while, displaying rain-streaked dust and dirt on their windows. No problem there, but where were the rest of the vehicles?

What about the wrecks, the burned-up cars, the real junk that any business of this type has to deal with? And since the Hawkins stores were also farm and construction implement dealers, where was the inoperative debris from that operation? Was there a separate property used for that purpose, or did Wade dispose of that debris as soon as it appeared? I decided to follow my hunch and consult my maps again to figure out Wade's other potential hiding places.

45

Adam and I were sitting at a table at Quinn's again, having another lunch, another hot open-faced roast beef sandwich with mashed potatoes and rich brown gravy with a three-inch ear of corn on the side, all steaming hot as the plates arrived. After the initial chow down, I asked Adam for his memories of Lincoln Pride.

Adam said, "Name's familiar. Remind me who we're talking about."

Between bites, I said, "Black guy, tall, thin, thirty-five-ish, works for Wade Hawkins. Does some repos and collections. My other informant says he gets a little rough at times."

Adam smiled as the name became familiar. "Oh, yeah. I remember him. I stopped him over on Twelfth for a burned-out taillight, maybe a year ago. He was totally baked. He started in with this Sovereign Citizen script, 'You don't need a driver's license,' then went into 'I'm not driving, I'm traveling,' that drivel."

"How did you handle that? I ran into a few of those in Jersey."

"Well, I made it into a joke. I looked in the car and saw that he had an automatic transmission. I asked him if it was an automatic. 'Sure,' he says. I come back with, 'Tell me, what does that 'D' there on your shift quadrant stand for?' He didn't have an answer for that.

I continued, "See, now, if you had a stick, you could say you were traveling. With that 'D'? You are definitely *driving*."

"Clever. I'm impressed. What was the resolution?"

"The shift supervisor wimped out. Gave him a fix-it ticket for the light, confiscated the pot, towed, and impounded the car because he was in no shape to drive. One of his buddies came and picked him up. I saw him driving the same car two days later with the tow yard markings still on the windshield."

"How much pot did he have on him?"

He laughed. "Oh, I asked him that. There was shake *everywhere*...on him, all over the car, out*side* the car...he was in pretty bad shape. Standing next to the car made my eyes water. He just answered, "All of it." The shift super had dealt with him before and told me to just let him walk, tow the ride. I found out then that Pride works for Wade Hawkins, and the Hawkins' name has big-time pull in Fairwater. That name was always Pride's *get out of jail free* card."

"There were other encounters with him?"

"I think he had a few others. I can make a call and check if you wish."

"That would help a lot as long as it doesn't get you in any more hot water with the PD."

"I'm not worried about them. I'm looking at other options for employment. I'll take you up on a reference letter if the offer is still open."

"Consider it done."

Adam keyed his phone, asked for his most dependable coworker, and within five minutes had the desired information written on his notepad, copied onto another sheet, and slid across the table to me. "That's his last known address as well."

I smiled. "Well done, sir."

———

We rode across town toward Fairwaters's version of *the hood* in the muddy truck, making the trip and finding the proper address within ten minutes. The secondary address, that of Lincoln Pride's girlfriend, held a modest tract home in what had been a development of pre-assembled tract homes built a half-century ago on concrete slabs on medium size lots. The trees in the front yard of 3004 Acklen Drive towered over an unkempt lawn. The house had undergone modifications in the ensuing owners and decades since its initial plan. A carport at one end had been closed in and another annexed. There were two front doors, each at a slightly different level. The vinyl siding and the roof looked fairly fresh, but the home's mismatched finish offered a distinct *amateur* appearance, and it was the least presentable home on the otherwise tidy street. A dark silver Chevy Monte Carlo filled the driveway. It displayed a Hawkins Pontiac GMC license plate frame.

Adam offered as we drove past the house, "That's the car I stopped that evening."

I answered, "Good to know. Thanks."

"How shall we take a closer look at the car and keep track of him?"

Adam offered, "Oh, I have ways of doing that. No sweat."

As we passed the house on the return trip, Lincoln Pride walked around the side of the house to his silver Chevy, got in and started it, then backed from his driveway and turned in the opposite direction from our route of travel. I made a U-turn at the top of the street and followed. The car was easy to spot because one of its tail light lenses had been broken, allowing the white of the inner reflector to show through. Adam agreed that if he'd been on duty, that would initiate another traffic stop and another fix-it ticket.

Lincoln Pride drove to a different neighborhood, made a delivery to the front door, then traveled to a small Walgreens store and bought some beer. While he was inside, Adam walked to the car and attached a small electronic tracker under the fuel filler door. He returned to the truck, and we watched. As he stepped into the pickup, he mentioned, "That's the kind of car I like at a traffic stop. Pot aroma from ten feet away will give you a contact high. Yeesh!"

Pride resumed his car, and we followed at a distance as he drove back to his girl's home. Adam sent the code for the tracker to my laptop. I verified it and put it to work for the next twenty-four hours until we made our next move.

———

I drove back down to the hospital to check on Susan. I was interested to see if her condition had improved—it had, slightly, but I also wanted some information on her potential attacker.

"Hey, lady...how's stuff?"

She smiled a little wider this time as she looked up at me. She still looked tired, but there was a slight color in her cheek—the one not bruised—that hadn't been there before. Her whiplash collar had been removed. "It's a little better, maybe a tenth of a percent or so."

"Your voice is a little stronger as well. You're a trouper! You'll be out of this joint and back to work in no time."

"I'm gonna give it a good six weeks or so. I have a good staff, a couple of 'em came by this morning. The MoonGlow is in pretty good hands for now."

"That's great news. Can I ask you about something with regard to *he whose name shall not be mentioned*?"

"Will it help you in your work? Will it help you round up Wade?"

I stepped to the door, swung it closed, then stepped back toward the bed and asked, "Did you ever know or have any dealings with a Black guy, Lincoln Pride? He's about thirty-five, thin, maybe a little *hinky* at times. He worked for Wade at the car dealer?"

She raised her good arm and scratched her bruised chin. "Yeah, I do remember that name. He was working for the service department and delivered my car to the front of the dealer after they serviced it once. He was polite, but he smelled like the inside of a bong. My car did as well for a few minutes. Made my eyes water till I put the top down. 'Course I'll use any excuse to do that."

"Well, who wouldn't? Sounds like the same guy," I said.

Susan continued. "He worked for Wade for quite a while. He was one of only two or three blacks working there. Wade could be kinda shy around Black folks, used to bitch about havin' to go after 'em for money."

"Okay...that explains something else. I have heard that Wade uses this Lincoln fellow for collections for the buy-here-pay-here and the title loan business."

"Well, there ya go. Blacks in a Black neighborhood are a lot more welcome and a lot less suspect than white faces, at least down here in the south."

"That happens everywhere, not just in the south. Tribalism breeds fierce loyalty."

"I see that a lot in the bar business." She took a sip from her water glass and looked up at me as she put the glass back on the table. "Wait. I think I see where you're going with this, Mr. Street. You maybe thinkin' this Lincoln Pride guy is my attacker? On Wade's orders?"

"You know Wade better than I do, Susan. You tell me."

She was starting to get my intent. "Nothing concrete, Mr. Detective, but I know he would hire other folks to do his dirty work for him. To come after me? I wouldn't put it past him for a minute."

I wanted to wrap up the visit and let her rest, so I opened one last avenue of discussion. "Before I go, did you hear about Wade's wife? She was found dead in California."

Susan paused for a few seconds, then looked up at me. "Well shit, Street, that doesn't surprise me one little bit. He'd wanted her out of the way for years." Susan shook her head at the thought. "She really didn't deserve that."

"Few people do. Thanks. I'll check back with you in a day or so." I squeezed her good hand and left the room.

Back in the truck, I called Adam and left a message. "Hey, Street here. Let's try to find a way to corral Lincoln Pride. I'm thinking that he attacked Susan at the MoonGlow. Call me back."

———

Three days after our initial conversation, I was talking to Cameron Sheedy from the sheriff's office in Lomita. He had brought me up to date on the investigation into Lucy Hawkins' murder—they were calling it that now—and I was trying to bring this little adventure to a close. I tried to keep the conversation regarding Lucy as specific and pertinent as possible, hoping to avoid unnecessary questions that would waste everyone's time.

Cameron asked, "Where can we find this Wade Hawkins, Mr. Street? We're working on travel authorizations to make the trip to secure the arrest there in his hometown. Think there'll be any issues there?"

"I wouldn't put a lot of faith in the local PD, Deputy. Hawkins has strong ties locally, including with the law enforcement here. You might want to have a chat with the State police. Staffs of both the Gadsden County Sheriffs and the local PD here seem to be in the bag with ol' Wade, with few exceptions. I have been warned."

"Do you think he'll flee?"

"He has the resources to do so, certainly. I have an operative who can help keep an eye on him if need be."

I could hear the murmur of conversation in the background, then, "Mr. Street? We will meet you tomorrow afternoon."

I gave them the address of the B&B and warned of the eyes that had watched and tried to corral me would be casting a wider gaze for them as well. "We'll make it happen, Mr. Street. We do this stuff for a living too."

46

Southern California — 2005

The shaking was sudden and sharp but, thankfully, very brief. Sylvia had been through earthquakes before, and she knew that this wasn't the worst ever, but it was bad enough to kick the breakers that turned the electric power in the area off for almost an hour. Still, the rains had been fierce lately. The ground was soft and easily movable when stressed. Looking out from the front windows in the primary bedroom onto the landscape of the city, she could see the lights on first-responder vehicles traveling in the darkness, and she thought that perhaps the effects had been more severe in other areas of the city. She hoped that the damage at Warners' and in the Trauma soundstage was at least manageable. They'd started filming again from the holiday hiatus and were working hard to regain the momentum that had made the show a success.

Arnie had been gone almost a year now. His absence had been a touchy subject at first. His disappearance considered a mystery by the LAPD until they tired of hearing the same story from Sylvia, his closest partner and confidant as well as an Emmy Award-winning actress. She had instant cred with the detectives, especially when they had interviewed her at home with the Emmys on the mantel behind her.

Her story had been consistent. She had planned their weekend well in advance. It was Arnie's birthday, his fortieth, and Sylvia had made elaborate plans as well to announce her pregnancy and propose marriage to him, with the exquisite Shelby Mustang given as an enticement for their union.

Arnie had suddenly changed those plans by spending the weekend with one of his clients, the increasingly notorious young starlet, Lizzie Totts. Lizzie was celebrating her twenty-second birthday the previous week. She was becoming famous for sharing her celebrations with random supportive men. Arnie could take much of the credit for making her famous, but his efforts had gone a little askew. She was in the process of joining other young celebrities who were *famous for being famous*, with little or no regard for any actual achievement or talent.

Arnie had *gotten his ashes hauled* numerous times that weekend, returning home Sunday afternoon at about four o'clock with an armload of roses for Sylvia, who wasn't having any of it. He had tried to apologize for his error in etiquette and had been rebuffed by Sylvia. They had argued. He had apologized repeatedly but had eventually just retired to the guest room for the night.

C'mon, the LAPD investigators had thought days later, What couple had never suffered and recovered from such an error in judgment? It was a natural part of married life. Granted, the average LAPD officer got divorced at least once, but c'mon, who hadn't?

The next morning, however, the guest room was empty. The bed in the room had been slept in at least part of the previous night, though the bed linens had been laundered by the time the site exam was performed by the LAPD. The garage space that normally held his car was empty. The expensive Shelby Mustang gift sat uncovered but otherwise untouched. When Arnie didn't return after three days, and after his absence from work had been noted, Sylvia Tate had taken time from her work at Warners' to report his disappearance.

After two more days, Arnie Lankershim's car had been found in a space in the newly constructed parking garage across Pacific Coast Highway from the entrance to the Municipal Pier in Huntington Beach. Surveillance footage of the parking structure and the adjoining shopping area showed him walking slowly toward the bright, white-sand beach in the early morning hours shortly before the area's numerous bars, restaurants, and tourist spots had closed. The cameras covering the beach showed that he had sat on the sand facing the ocean for an hour before his image had been lost in the darkness.

Arnie Lankershim's billfold, ID, and favorite sport coat were found on the passenger seat of his car beside the car and house keys. So much for domestic security concerns. A pair of black leather Rockport loafers, size ten wide, had been found near the waterline by an Orange County lifeguard. Ms. Tate had verified that those were Arnie's shoes, car, and belongings, evidenced by the walk-in closet off the primary bedroom that had an impressive door-mounted shoe rack filled with a dozen pairs of the same size Rockports in similar and varied styles. The man liked his shoes. Random clothing articles—shreds of a bloodstained dress shirt, a torn pair of wool dress slacks bearing his name on a dry-cleaner's label, and a single custom-patterned, initialed stretch sock suspected to be Lankershim's were found over the next two days at various points up and down the coast, in areas accurate to the tidal and surf patterns.

Three months after his disappearance, a request for a declaration of death was sent to the State of California and the City of Los Angeles. An official statement declaring Arnie Lankershim deceased would take another year to wander through the perpetually-clotted Superior Court System. Sylvia Tate and the newly renamed Silver Associates Talent Management Partnership, LLC shared the proceeds from his insurance policies.

The quake was considered a minor one and had done little

damage to most areas of the Los Angeles area. When she arrived home from the studio that evening, Sylvia had noticed that the stone retaining wall at the side of the property just inside the tall redwood boundary fence had broken—again—and that the slope below the wall had shifted—again—exposing the black plastic that had been used as covering beneath the plantings on the slope of the lot. Again, Sylvia donned coveralls and leather gardeners' gloves that evening to make the temporary repairs before the *real* gardeners arrived to tackle the erosion issue a week later.

47

As I drove onto the grounds of the B&B that evening, I saw an unexpected addition to the décor, a Gadsden County Sheriff's Department cruiser. I took my usual parking slot next to the building and locked the truck as I got out. The door of the dark-blue cop-spec Crown Vic opened, and a tall, younger officer stepped out. He stood beside the car, straightened his crisp uniform, and walked toward me as I approached the porch of the B&B. His nameplate read, "MASTERS."

"Mr. Street? A word, please?"

"That's two words, Deputy Masters. But hey, who's counting? What can I do for you?"

"First, show me some ID."

I pulled out my wallet and displayed the PI license and my California driver's license. I asked him, "Am I the guy?"

"Yeah, Mr. Street, you're the guy. A lot of people in Fairwater are becoming annoyed at your actions, and I have been asked to personally request that you stop bothering people. Nobody's done a damn thing to you, but that's not necessarily a permanent situation."

"What the hell does that even mean? Is that a threat? C'mon, dude, step it up a bit. Raise your game. Give me your best Rod Stieger impression, or at least be that fat guy who played the sheriff in the Dodge commercials in the late '60s. I'll wait here."

Now he stepped forward and pointed his index finger at me. "Street, you don't belong here, and you do not want to annoy any more of Fairwater's principals. Got that?"

I pointed back at him. "Nope. Ain't happenin' that way this time. And hey, if you think *I'm* annoying, wait 'til you see what's coming! That guy who told you to scare me off is gonna be shocked. Shocked, I say! But in the meantime, just realize that because you're *not* in Gadsden County anymore, you don't really get to tell me what to do. Now, you be a good boy and go tell Wade to clench up. His ride will arrive soon."

"Street, what the hell are you babbling about?"

"Wade killed his wife out in Cali. What, he didn't tell you? Uh oh! I let the cat outta the bag! Darn the luck!" I smiled. "Felony murder charges have been filed against Wade Hawkins in California, and they're coming to get him and drag his ass back out there."

Deputy Masters's facial expression changed, and his complexion reddened.

"Oh, whatever will you do? Now, see, if you *tell* him and he runs, *you'll* be liable for aiding the escape of a wanted felon. You don't want to do that, now do you? Of *course* not. So how 'bout you go back across the county line and make certain ol' Wade behaves himself until they arrive to talk to him. That's all on *you* now, Deputy."

Deputy Masters stared at me for a few seconds, then turned and walked back to his car. Over his shoulder, he said, "Later, Street."

I couldn't resist. As he entered his dark-blue Crown Vic, I called, "Y'all come back now, ya hear?" And I laughed. That part felt good.

———

The B&B held a cookout that evening, featuring some incredible steaks and a variety of fried catfish to which I could easily become addicted. I ate and drank my fill and had a great time talking with the other guests. I knew that I'd miss this place when it came time to leave.

I showered and turned in at about midnight and gladly slept off the effects of my gluttony with zero regrets. A bit after four that morning, I awoke. For whatever reason, I flashed on something that I'd seen in Fairwater a couple of days before. I called Adam Waverly's cell.

He answered groggily, "Yeah, Street, what is it?"

"Feel like a little adventure? Maybe a little skulking on enemy territory?"

"Mmm. Does it come with coffee?"

"Sure. You can bring all you want."

"Okay. Pick me up."

"Twenty minutes."

———

I drove to his condo and found Adam wearing jeans and a sweatshirt, standing on the porch with his thermos waiting for me. As he entered the pickup, he stretched.

"Where are we going?"

"I stumbled onto a remote storage facility for Wade's dad's businesses. It's something that Wade doesn't hold under his LLC. I saw, I dunno, maybe just the shadow of something there when I first found it, and I couldn't get it out of my head. If I have it right, it's the key to the Hawkins car crash. I'll show you when we get there."

On the dark, narrow, tree-lined side road off Seventh Street, two miles from the traffic of MLK and the town proper, I parked the mud truck parallel to the chain link fence next to the opening gate of the scrap yard for Hawkins Enterprises LLC and lowered the tailgate. As I climbed into the truck bed, preparing to hop over the fence, I asked Adam, "Do any of your professional cohorts ever roll by here in the middle of the night?"

After he landed inside the property, he said, "Not intentionally.

I don't think I've ever even seen this place. We may come out here if someone calls in for shots fired nearby or something. What the hell are we looking for?" He jumped off the pickup and followed me onto the property.

We approached the older Dodge 4x4 pickup, and I motioned. "That."

The truck stood out among the rusty scrapped farm and construction machinery and was probably the most recognizable object in the yard. It was at least twenty years old and had a pasty white paint finish that had seen better decades. The body panels didn't line up very well, and the passenger side front door wore chrome trim that indicated that it had come from a Dodge truck of a different vintage and trim level. I could tell that the truck had seen some rough duty in its life, but the elements that really interested me were the oversized tires, the wider steel rims, and the black powder-coated aftermarket step rail that hung below the body between the wheels.

I shone my penlight on the tires to see that they had suffered considerable sidewall scuffing. Most of the raised letters on the sidewalls had been torn and rubbed off. The paint was ground off the edges of the steel rims, and the round metal step rail that hung below the rocker panels displayed paint rubs that I strongly suspected would match the red paint that had scraped off the dented side of Jack Hawkins' lowered Chevy pickup. I pointed the signs out to Adam as I took images of the parts of the truck to compare to the images of Jack Hawkins' wrecked pickup. And as I opened the cab door of the truck? Concrete chips and one corner of a block.

"Fine, Street. Now what do you *do* with this? Where does it go from here?"

"I'd say, the criminal investigation division of the Georgia State Police. Know anyone there?"

"I'd like to."

"Me too. Let's go have a chat with them."

———

Showing up as a private ticket from out-of-state at the GBI offices in Atlanta, seemingly with our hats in our hands, was not a pleasant experience for anyone. It took two days, but we finally got their attention. The details of the Hawkins siblings' fatal traffic accident, coupled with my accumulated evidence of the causes of the accident, were deemed sufficiently *interesting* that it merited a closer examination by the Criminal Investigation Unit of the Georgia Bureau of Investigation. I strongly suggested that they initiate their Fairwater visit promptly, and they concurred. It took a while, but I was shocked that they were so agreeable. Score one for the visiting team. Yay me.

48

The next forty-eight hours were busy, as we kept an eye on Lincoln Pride and Wade Hawkins while talking regularly with the sheriff's deputies in LA regarding their progress in Lucy Hawkins' murder and the Georgia State Police with regard to Lincoln Pride. Expedited travel arrangements brought LASD Deputies Sheedy and Steele to Fairwater two days later. They teamed with the Georgia State Police to come to Fairwater, and Adam and I met them at, where else, Quinn's Restaurant in Fairwater. Cops gotta eat.

The coolest part for me was when the disparate law enforcement types, California and Georgia, showed up at Wade Hawkins' *pot lot* on MLK within an hour of one another. It was practically a badge traffic jam.

The Georgia boys showed up first, armed with a stack of warrants for Lincoln Pride, charged with two counts of first-degree vehicular homicide in the deaths of Jack and Elizabeth Hawkins and various charges, including attempted murder, regarding the attack on Susan Keeley.

Pride walked toward the disturbance grinning, curious about the disturbance, thinking that he would just be one of the rubber-neckers on site. This kind of stuff never happened in Fairwater, did it? He was not so lucky. Upon recognizing him, the Georgia officers quickly flanked him, wrapping a hand around each forearm and shoving him against one of Wade's trade units at the front of the car lot.

The lead GBI officer faced him and started reading his rights. "Lincoln Pride, we have warrants for your arrest for the murders of Elizabeth Hawkins and Jackson Hawkins and the attempted murder of Susan Keeley. You have the right to remain silent..." I'd heard it before, but it still sounded really good to me.

This was a big deal for Fairwater, with media coverage from Atlanta for the first time in anyone's memory. The local PD was called out to provide traffic control on MLK Boulevard. Adam stood with me, watching proudly from across the street.

Wade Hawkins played the shocked—shocked, I say!—onlooker and employer, denying any knowledge of the events but *truly grateful* for the fine work of Georgia law enforcement in solving the mystery of the cruel deaths of his beloved younger brother and sister. He even wiped a tear from his left eye as he spoke to one of the Atlanta TV reporters of his great loss. The guy was a real ham on camera.

Then the other shoe dropped.

Just after Lincoln Pride's arrest, after he took his place in the rear of the GSP Crown Vic, there was a stir of sirens on MLK as a pair of black Tahoes pushed through the barricades and onto the dealer's lot. I had stepped closer to the action after being advised of the arrival of the LA deputies and their GSP escorts. The rear doors of the first jet-black Tahoe opened, and a pair of crisply pressed tan-uniformed LASD deputies stepped out. That warmed my heart. The other doors opened to reveal a pair of civilian-suited officers on loan from a Georgia agency for this particular event. The second Tahoe parked close behind the first.

The older of the two LASD officers asked for the lead Georgia officer on-site and was referred to the FSD three-striper holding a position at the curb. Quietly, he showed his badge and said, "Officer? Cameron Sheedy, Los Angeles County Sheriff's Department.

This is my partner, Ed Steele. Could you please point me toward one Wade Hawkins and accompany me toward him? I have a warrant for his arrest."

The local officer frowned and looked a bit intimidated as he said, "Yes, sir. Follow me." As they approached the building, the local asked, "What's the warrant for?"

Cameron Sheedy looked at the taller deputy and said, quietly, without breaking stride, "First-degree murder. The man killed his wife." Then he turned to his partner. "Ed? Can you find our Mr. Street for me after we get this guy hooked up? I'd like a word with him."

The younger deputy grinned and said, "Sure thing, Cam."

The pair of officers walked past the assemblage of dealer staff and approached Wade. Cameron called out as he showed his badge, "Mr. Hawkins? A word, please."

There's a term that is used in law enforcement and the military, *command presence*. You hear the words stated with a certain level of authority, you tend to obey. Cameron Sheedy had it goin' on with regard to command presence.

Wade Hawkins looked past the employee he was speaking to, smiled, and said, "Certainly."

He dismissed the employee with a pat on his shoulder and approached the two deputies with his right hand extended. Cameron reached to the side of his belt with his left hand. As he accepted Wade Hawkins' offer of a warm handshake, he wrapped the other wrist with the first of his handcuffs. He then pulled Hawkins toward him and turned him ninety degrees, expertly grabbing the left wrist and cuffing both arms behind his prisoner.

I'd been a cop for five years, and I'd seen hundreds of people cuffed, but this was the most gracefully executed application of that hardware I'd ever seen. It made me smile.

Cameron finally spoke in a voice that no one present could ignore. "Wade Hawkins, you are under arrest for the murder of Lucille Hawkins. I am Investigator Cameron Sheedy of the Los Angeles County Sheriff's Department. We have an extradition order, and you will be coming with us. You have the right to remain silent. Anything you do or say may be taken as evidence and held against you in a court of law. You have the right to obtain counsel. If you cannot afford legal assistance, legal counsel may be provided to you at no cost. Do you understand these rights as I have explained them to you?" He waited for an answer, looking Wade straight in the eye.

Wade Hawkins answered, "I understand, Deputy. Please lead the way. Let's get this handled."

He walked to the Tahoe with Cameron's hand on his forearm and entered through the rear door. Deputy Steele reached in as Cameron backed out and secured the extended seat belt around Wade Hawkins. Ed slammed the door, and the pair spoke briefly to the State officers. I stood off to the side of the group and waited with Adam until Cameron looked in our direction and smiled.

He stepped toward us and extended his right hand. "And you must be Mr. Street. I recognize you from the photo on your California PI license. You're the one who got us into this deal, huh?"

"I'll take the blame if no one else wants it. Thanks for following through on it. He needed to get busted. You did good." We shook hands, and I introduced Adam to both Cameron and Ed.

"This was nice, efficient work from all involved. We have to get the hell back to Hartsfield International so we can get this clown back to LA. When you get back out west, let's get together." He handed me his card, I gave him one of mine, and we shared handshakes again. Then they boarded the idling Tahoe and left. I saw Wade Hawkins bend sideways in his seat and glare at me.

———

After all the activity subsided, I went back to the B&B to kick back for the evening and start to pack for my trip back home. I called Lynn and Sylvia to bring them up to date on the day's activities. Both seemed pleased with the outcome. I had to return the F-150 to Winder, Georgia, so Adam accompanied me on that trip after I gave the truck a thorough bath at the local squirt-it-yourself car wash. I still prefer really clean cars. Sorry, Georgia.

———

My flight back to LA was late afternoon the next day, so I met Adam for lunch at Quinn's and handed him a pretty decent check for his efforts on my behalf. He was considering an application to the Georgia State Police. I sent him a letter of recommendation a week later.

Mark Hawkins stopped by Quinn's and thanked us for *cleaning up his family*. We had one last toast of Michelob. Good stuff. At the Atlanta airport, I had to wait a couple hours for the flight. In the pub of our wing of the airport, the TV screen showed coverage of the arrests of the prominent city leader from the little town of Fairwater. The coverage made the town look almost perfect, with plenty of available area for expansion. It was presented as a great place to raise a family, especially now that these miscreants had been dealt with. Thinking about it later, I considered that Wade had wanted to make Fairwater a prominent town that would attract attention and promote growth. Maybe his arrest helped that happen.

49

After I returned to California, I kept up with the happenings in Georgia. I knew that I'd be subpoenaed to testify at the trials after Georgia won the tug-of-war over Wade Hawkins's murder conviction. The crime had occurred in California, but the victim and her husband were prominent Georgia natives, and the Peach State prosecutors made a good argument. I considered the fact that Georgia still occasionally carried out the death penalty as an advantage as well. Hope springs eternal.

When faced with the accusations involving the crash that killed Jack and Beth Hawkins, Lincoln Pride folded like a grandma's hankie. He hadn't really asked *the big dumb white kid*—who was unavailable for comment—to drop a chunk of broken concrete block into Jack Hawkins's pickup that night. It just kinda happened. He had used the same material though, all by himself, as a warning to Susan Keeley at the bar when he attacked her. That was just lazy. Susan's appearance at the preliminary hearing didn't help him a bit, especially when she arrived in the courtroom in her full medical regalia, still in her wheelchair. Lincoln's confession and apology may have helped him a bit, but the conviction was a slam dunk after the local familiarity of his targets was established. The testimonies, including my own, brought a quick verdict from the local Fairwater Jury. He drew a hefty sentence in the Georgia State Prison System, thirty-five years to life, and is said to be truly regretful for his actions. He seems to have adapted to prison life and already has a position in the prison motor pool.

Wade Hawkins pled innocent to the murder of his wife. That trial took longer to happen because his defense counsel asked for and were granted a change of venue. The trial took place in central Atlanta, so I was housed in a nice Marriott high-rise for three days when I went back to testify. Six hours on the witness stand at odds with a trio of hostile defense attorneys would have been fun, but for my being chastened by the judge for being disrespectful of said attorneys. Twice. In any event, Wade was convicted by the jury after two days of deliberation.

50

A year after the wrap of the Wade Hawkins ordeal concluded, I had
to go back to Georgia to testify in the sentencing hearing. Hawkins'
attorneys had won a change of venue for the trials, so this time, I
stayed at a high-rise Marriott in suburban Atlanta. The gang was all
there—Mark Hawkins, Dottie, Adam Waverly, and I had all testi-
fied in the criminal trial, and we had done a stellar job. As far as I
was concerned, Wade had gotten off pretty easy, two counts of
conspiracy to commit murder—his brother and sister—one count
of second-degree murder—his wife—plus numerous counts of
fraud, conspiracy, and collusion, regarding his property crimes and
cheating his sister.

A local trial in Fairwater was deemed a non-starter because so
much of the jury pool had been rendered jobless by Wade's own
actions. The pushover prosecutor in California had knuckled
under and sent the case of Lucy's death back to Georgia, the state of
her residence at the time of her death. I didn't really like that, but
the fact that Georgia will occasionally put a murderer to death
assuaged my annoyance.

Wade Hawkins, despite a phalanx of expensive and talented
criminal defense attorneys, was found guilty of the crimes of which

he was accused. During the criminal trial, I had said my piece for a total of six hours on the witness stand, four and a half sparring with an arrogant, *difficult,* and presumptuous young female defense attorney, describing the events that I had discovered and studied in Georgia.

My performance on the witness stand was excellent, if I say so myself, but the real harm was done to him by the testimony of Dottie Yarborough. Her emotional descriptions of Wade's murdered siblings and their eventual fate, coupled with his callous treatment of his late parents as well as the residents of the city of Fairwater, sounded such a ring of truth that even the snottiest of the defense attorneys had been wise to back off. The Atlanta jury took a week of well-publicized back and forth to decide Wade's guilt on all counts. Eventually, he was sentenced to thirty-two years to life in State prison. His fancy attorneys are promising a vigorous appeal.

Even before the criminal trial in Georgia, Sylvia Tate had settled the estate situation there. A forensic audit had been performed on Wade's dealings after his arrest, and Sylvia Tate had come away with another six million dollars in the settlement. She made out almost as well as the attorneys in that situation.

———

Back home in California in-between trips to Georgia, I had just made quick work of a divorce situation involving one of Lynn's bazillionaire clients by simply following her when she met her extremely limber twenty-four-year-old lover. The offending wife was fifty-two and—I'll be honest here—one of the least attractive women of means that I had ever seen in Southern California. Her *pet kid* was a brave specimen if ever there was one. After I snagged a plethora of photos of them together in numerous compromising... um...*positions,* I took the photos to Lynn and made an ultimatum —*no more divorce work*! Hey, there are some things you just cannot unsee.

Sylvia Tate was appreciative of the work we had done on her behalf and had become a friend. I would be invited to her location shoots for the TV movies that she was hired for, and there were some interesting situations that I was a part of. During my visits, I was occasionally called into duty to *run her lines* either in her dressing trailer on location or at home if she had a studio job. At one lunch session on a location shoot at West Covina, I had a long discussion with a writer about the legalities faced by someone in my business. I hoped that my input had some effect on his material.

There were some surprising invitations extended by her over the next couple of years, ranging from an invitation to be her escort to an art exhibition at the Getty Museum to one to go to a studio screening of a TV movie that she had filmed a couple of years before. Network management had changed during the film's production, so the airing of that material, as well as others, was delayed. Syl explained that studio and network management were ego-driven positions, and material green-lighted by the former crews weren't seen as priorities by the new crews. Who cares that product costing millions of dollars were stuck on a shelf for the interim? It all made me glad that I would never be a media executive.

Sylvia's influence on me deserved redress, so I introduced her to the wonders of NASCAR racing. Our first outing was at Irwindale Speedway, the latest of SoCal's diminishing array of motorsports venues, for a Saturday night of down-market adventure disguised, she said, as character study. I hosted her at a race in Las Vegas, using VIP slash skybox passes courtesy of a client of mine. She was the star of the show there, frequently recognized by the attendees, and we were invited to several later functions by those executives. I landed a few jobs from those contacts, so it turned out well. It's all about who you know.

We would occasionally join for lunch or dinner, usually during slack periods of work for either or both of us. Syl was always curious about my work and offered some salient observations about some of my dealings with people who seemed strange to me. I appreciated her perspective and valued her judgments as she did mine.

The topic of Arnie Lankershim's mysterious demise faded with time as our friendship developed. I was still curious, at times a bit doubtful, but also too busy to obsess on it.

I finished the seemingly endless GTO project after the back-and-forth trips regarding the Hawkins matters. I drove it sparingly, paranoid that it would face some damage, but I did take it to one of my lunches with Syl. It met with her approval, and that made me happy.

––––––

As time went on, my personal life had taken a turn for the better, at least on the surface. One day in the spring of '08, while walking out from my grocery shopping at Gelson's Market on Wilshire, I had seen a really cute young blonde woman back the rear corner of her black Mustang GT into the rear corner of my old Trailblazer in the parking lot. As I stood there, this stunning creature emerged from her convertible to survey the damage, and I confronted her. We exchanged insurance information and started talking. A week later, we had started seeing one another socially, and things just went from zero to sixty after that.

Cindy was an aspiring actress and had the advantage of being an absolute eyeful. She had arrived from her small hometown in Texas two years earlier and had almost instantly found jobs modeling in some local ad campaigns and working for companies displaying at trade industry conventions. I liked that she had a great work ethic and that she seemed to have an appreciation for me, my work, and my privacy. The sex was epic as well.

––––––

One idyllic Saturday afternoon a few months later, Cindy was at my place lounging on the patio, glistening in the sun, wearing a coating of sunscreen that I had quite enjoyed applying myself a half-hour earlier. Acting on her endless penchant for fashion, she had altered one of my old Shelby T-shirts to become an enticing and very skimpy top. I didn't mind at all. By then, I had modified my rear patio to include a barbecue grill and a wet bar. A nice 60-inch flat-screen TV was suspended at an angle from the ceiling of the canopy that extended from the back wall of the house. Two over-head fans stirred the air under the pergola roof.

I was tending to the needs of my GTO in the driveway behind the house. Its rebuild had been finished six months prior, and to my mind, it was nearly a work of art. We had been out in it the previous evening, driving to dinner at the pier in Huntington Beach. I was carefully wiping down the body with a soft microfiber cloth and a detail spray when I heard the talking head on whatever entertainment magazine show mention a familiar name.

"And in celebrity health news, representatives for *Trauma Center Hospital* star Sylvia Tate have confirmed the reports that the Emmy-winning actress has been diagnosed with stage four renal failure. She has now returned home after her hospitalization and is resting comfortably while under dialysis treatments."

I stared at the screen for a moment, then stowed the cleaning supplies under the car and went to the office to make the call.

Sylvia's assistant, Alma, answered the call. "Yes, Mr. Street, it's so good to hear from you. Sylvia's resting right now, but I will ask her to call you as soon as she's up. She has mentioned that she wants to talk to you. I'm sure she will call you later this afternoon."

I had mentioned to Cindy that I was acquainted with Sylvia Tate and that I had done some work for her a while back. Cindy had taken the initiative to study Sylvia's dramatic work and the history of her career. I filled in a few blanks but left out some of the details of my role in her brother's downfall in Georgia. Been there, done that, got the cast jacket at the wrap party.

The call came two hours later. Her voice was feeble, but she was definite in her intentions. "Street? Is that you?"

"Hi, Sylvia."

"Hey, buddy, I take it you've heard the news."

"Yes, Syl, I did, just a while ago. I'm sorry we haven't been in touch lately. I've been really busy with PI stuff. I saw your newest TV movie last week. You were stellar, as usual."

"Thanks, buddy. Hey, could I borrow you for a day or so? I have some statements that I want to make before the lights go dim for the final time, and I want a friendly recipient for them. When can you come to the house?"

"You're at the LA house?"

"Yes, we are."

"Is tomorrow okay? Noonish? If you want, I can bring some lunch from Jerry's Deli with me." The legendary Ventura Boulevard eatery had long been a favorite of hers.

"God, yes! That would be wondrous, Mr. Street. I have been on hospital food for three weeks. I need a rest from the *rest* that they impose on me."

"Great! Call it done. See you at noon. Oh, and there's someone I'd like you to meet. She's a fan of yours. She'll be coming with me if that's okay."

"Oh, absolutely! You told me about her the last time we talked. I would love to meet her!"

"See you at noon, Syl. Have a good evening."

————

We arrived at Sylvia's home the next day at noon after stopping at Jerry's Deli to grab the required eats. I knew from our earlier travels that Syl was a fan of Jerry's epic pastrami sandwich as well as the Reuben and the classic chicken soup. I agreed with all of those, so I loaded up, arriving with two giant white plastic sacks full of aromatic foods. When I rang, Alma answered the door, smiling as usual. Warmly she ushered us into the living room, taking the food to the kitchen counter and unpacking it.

Sylvia arrived from the stairway at the front of the room, and I was shocked at her gaunt appearance. She smiled, but I could sense that she was shaky as she walked toward me. "Street! Thanks for coming!" She walked toward me, and we hugged. I could tell her weight loss. She turned from me and spread her arms to embrace Cindy. "And you must be Cindy! Welcome!"

We walked toward the dining room table and Sylvia said, "I swear, Street, I could smell that wonderful aroma when you were halfway down the block!" She looked inside the bigger bag, then turned to me and smiled. "I know I'm going to pay dearly for this in a few hours, but it'll be worth every second. Let's eat!"

Syl seemed energized by the presence of what she called *real food*, polishing off half of a Reuben, a heap of potato salad, some dill pickle spears, and almost a whole bowl of chicken soup in the first of three sessions. She bragged to Cindy about my exploits on her behalf dealing with her rascally brother in Georgia. Cindy smiled and responded, saying something about me occasionally needing a cape. I smiled. I could feel my ego expanding, and it felt pretty good. Sylvia, at one point, took Cindy aside, and they spent over an hour discussing the ins and outs of their respective acting careers. Syl shared some cautions as well as some suggestions and recommended a couple of acting classes and theater groups that she knew of in the valley. I was impressed at her patience, and we both appreciated her guidance.

By five that afternoon, Sylvia's energy had waned, and much of the food had at last been done away with. Syl had a new worshipful acolyte in Cindy, and they were fast friends. I was glad for that. It was time to depart so that Sylvia could take her therapy.

As we walked toward the door to leave, Sylvia pulled me aside and whispered, "Street, please come see me tomorrow at two. I have some information that I have to give you. It will clear up many of the questions you've had for a long time. It's very important." Her breathing was becoming more labored as she spoke. I looked at

Alma, who shook her head in agreement and took Sylvia's arm to guide her back toward the stairway.

"Two tomorrow. I'll be here."

————

I had an idea about Sylvia's intent for the next day's meeting. I had long had my own ideas about the fate of Arnie Lankershim, and I thought I knew where he'd ended up. The truth of the matter and its conclusion were more detailed and strange than I'd imagined.

51

Los Angeles, California — 2002

When Arnie Lankershim dropped Lizzie Totts off at her house at the end of the narrow road in Nichols Canyon at three-thirty that Sunday afternoon, he expected something—a goodbye kiss, a handshake, an over-the-shoulder *thanks*, something that would indicate a response from her for the time they'd spent together. As the car drew to a stop in her driveway, she opened the door and hopped out without a word. He'd seen rush hour Metro subway departures with more emotion. All she'd really left was the faint scent of her perfume, courtesy of an early $1.5 million endorsement deal that Arnie had arranged for her.

They'd been intimate more than a few times that weekend, and he was amazed at her insatiable youthful energy and inventiveness. Arnie had especially valued the vision of her slowly emerging from the pool, au natural, the best of that move that he'd seen since the original, a stunning young Bo Derek 10 decades before. When he complimented her using that name, Lizzie had asked, "Who's that?" using her best ewwww tone. That was after he'd found out that she'd gone against his counsel and was talking with Playboy.

To salve his disenchantment over the Lizzie situation, he turned his thoughts to Sylvia. He knew that she was gonna be pissed about him missing their planned *birthday* weekend in favor of two days partying with one of his current favorite clients. Arnie knew what she'd wanted that weekend. He'd kept the thought of it at arm's length for weeks. They had talked at length in recent months about marrying and starting a family. Deep down, he knew that he had wanted that with Sylvia, but he had always used his career—and hers—as a stalling tactic.

Arnie waited in the turn lane for the traffic light at Mulholland and Laurel Canyon that afternoon after driving out of the canyon on the twisty Roosevelt Drive, and he decided to make amends. It was time. He drove down the wide curving north slope of Laurel Canyon Boulevard and was relieved to find that the high-end florist at the corner of Ventura was open on a Sunday afternoon. He smiled as he wondered if *reconciliations* were a major business segment late on Sundays for florists in affluent parts of LA. Could be. Arnie drove onto the parking deck and went inside, dropping a trio of C-notes on flowers. Lotsa roses. Roses would work. He also decided that he would pop the question just as soon as he could land a ring.

He'd make certain that he made a great prenup with a long *sunset*. The new associate on the next floor up was great at creating those. He and Syl had already made one another their next of kin for legal purposes, so the next step would feel almost natural. Convinced, he pulled onto the street that would lead him home for what would be the final time.

As Arnie drove up the slope onto the circular driveway, he saw that all three of the garage doors were open. Syl's light gold Acura Legend coupe, the one she'd had for six years now, the one he would replace for her soon, sat in the center slot. The outer slot displayed a new shape, a slightly taller car under a beige cloth cover. He was excited but wary as he left his Lexus in *his* slot and stepped to the covered vehicle. He pulled the cover from the front corner and gasped.

A little over a month prior, Arnie and Sylvia had taken a weekend and driven to LaJolla—La Hoyya—north of San Diego, for a long, reclusive weekend at an exclusive and very expensive hotel. Their suite overlooked the Pacific Ocean and came equipped with the calming sound of the surf meeting the beach far below. The Magnum bottle of Moet Hennessey champagne they had ordered from room service had helped initiate a passionate session of lovemaking that hadn't been equaled in years. Smiling, Sylvia had kept the empty bottle when they checked out.

On that Saturday afternoon, they had walked the streets of the affluent north San Diego County suburb, at one point passing a high-end collector car dealer's showroom. Among the eclectic mix of new and vintage Ferraris, Maseratis, and Lamborghinis, the dozens of examples of pricey foreign exotica—what Arnie had always called *froufrou cars*—was a stunning scarlet red 1968 Shelby GT500KR fastback that had captivated Arnie. He had seen these cars in magazines when he was a kid in Chicago and had always liked them. He had told Syl that they were now worth twenty-five times their original MSRP. He had probably laid it on a little thick that day. But shit, apparently, it had WORKED! He ran his hand along the length of the fender line, starting at the spoiler above the taillights, and walked to the front corner of the car. Magnificent.

As the shock wore off from what he'd discovered in the garage, Arnie stepped to his car, opened the rear door, retrieved the large bouquet of flowers, and entered the kitchen through the side door. He saw Sylvia sitting at the counter, staring at him. She was dressed up, one of his favorite outfits, that *snug* blue dress—maybe she wanted to get dinner out tonight—her hair was up in a very sophisticated do. She always looked *so good* when she dressed up like that. Then he saw how she was staring at him. She wasn't smiling, and he saw that there was a small semi-automatic pistol in front of her on the granite countertop.

Unsmiling and in a deep voice, Sylvia asked Arnie, "So, how was she?"

52

I arrived at Sylvia's home on the southern slope of the Hollywood Hills the next day at two, bearing gifts, again. I had acquired an extra DVD set of David Janssen's *The Fugitive* series, a series I knew that she had enjoyed and had used as a training tool early in her career. One of her methods was to copy and re-interpret the words and actions of the female characters in quality dramas. I had participated in her process of running lines during our acquaintance, and I appreciated the effort she had invested in her craft.

Alma greeted me at the door and ushered me inside through the living area to the patio at the rear of the house. Sylvia was seated in a recliner next to the large oval swimming pool under the pergola roof, wearing a long terry cloth robe, pink slippers, and a pair of huge sunglasses. She turned to me and gestured to the adjoining patio chair.

"Have a seat, buddy. The time has come."

"Syl, you don't have to do this. Fessing up isn't a requirement, at least as far as I'm concerned. There are better subjects for you to use as Father Confessor."

"Yeah, Street, but I like you, and I trust you. You're one of my best friends. We get along better than any of the show biz types I know. You also have a great sense of drama." She smiled weakly. "You're gonna like this. I promise. You might want to record what I'm going to say. There's a recorder on the kitchen counter."

I withdrew my digital recorder from my shirt pocket and showed it to her. "I came prepared. It's voice-activated, so start anytime you like." I pressed the on button and put the recorder on the table in front of her.

Sylvia cleared her throat and said, "Okay, I'm Sylvia Tate, and this is my account of events from my life. This will probably be my final statement, whatever that is called. Mr. Street will ask me questions to guide my comments."

I was now playing his by ear. Okay, so now I have to ask her questions. Fine. I jumped right in. "Sylvia, what happened to Arnie Lankershim?"

She looked at me as she spoke. "Oh, I shot him. He died instantly right there in the kitchen of the home I wanted to share with him for the rest of our lives. He passed on the offer, and he said the exact wrong thing. So I shot him."

Yeah, I'd kinda figured that. I had decided to just let her talk. Stream of consciousness often pays off well in confessions.

"He died instantly, just *Bang, plop, gone.* I'd seen scripts that dealt with *instant death*, and our medical adviser on the series had spoken of the surest methods to achieve that. It worked just as she had explained."

Sylvia took a long drink of ice water, then continued.

"But there were consequences. I was a few weeks pregnant and hormonal to the absolute max. For whatever reason, I decided to dig a hole and bury his ass in the side yard. We had a lot of gardening tools in the garage from when the lawn and gardens were put in, so I picked a spot in the side yard by the fence and started digging."

"That's hard work."

"That's an understatement. You have to move a LOT of dirt to get deep enough to bury a body, and that sandy, damp soil was really heavy. I was practically dead myself by the time I got down a couple or three feet, and even that wasn't nearly deep enough. The hole was too short as well. I had already dragged his body out of the kitchen. I had undressed him, wrapped him in garbage bags, and laid him in the garage next to that goddamn red car that mocked me every time I laid eyes on it. I worked for hours on end, still wearing all that hair and makeup that I'd had done for him that Friday. I'd even re-done everything early Sunday in the faint hope that something could be salvaged from the relationship. Add to that I would throw up once in a while, and I couldn't stop crying."

She paused and took a breath, then another sip of water. "I had lost track of time until I realized how cold it was out there beside the house. I'd spent hours digging, crying, puking, hurting, digging some more. I was sweaty and filthy, and at one point, I was in the garage, resting. I caught my reflection in the side window of my car —it was awful—and it all struck me. I just sank to the floor and...I don't know, Street, I just passed out or fell asleep or something. I woke up at three the next morning, cold and filthy on the rubber mat on the garage floor between our two cars. I went in, put on a jacket and some sweatpants, and dragged him out. I rolled him into the hole and covered him with some of the dirt. Of course, by now, I was also worried about being caught for killing him. Homicide did not come naturally to me."

I said, "Understandable. Your timing would be important in your cover story. Arnie was in the ground wrapped in the trash bag by now, right?"

"Sure. I'd read a screenplay a long time ago that gave me the idea for that. I went in and cleaned up, covered up with some heavier clothes, then drove his car to Huntington Beach. I parked in the lot across from the pier and sat on the beach as it got darker. The clouds were rolling in. It was easy."

"Let me guess. You planted his shoe in the surf and brought his clothes to the area later."

"Yeah." Weakly, she asked, "You want something to eat, Street?"

"I'm good."

Sylvia called to Alma, who walked onto the patio and responded, "Yes, Sylvia?"

"Hon, would you warm up some of that chicken soup that Street brought yesterday? That's one of the easiest things for me to keep down." Alma nodded and walked back into the kitchen. She turned back to me. "Sorry, Street. Where was I?"

"You were working on your cover story."

"Yeah. I called in sick to work that Monday, and once in a while, in that next week, if I wasn't working, I'd go all the way down to Huntington Beach or Seal Beach and plant something that I could say was his. We reported him missing and got that process rolling, and eventually, everything smoothed out."

"What happened to your pregnancy?"

"Oh...I lost that a few weeks in. I'd been cautioned that stress was a major negative in first pregnancies for older women. I guess I qualified for that, I was about to turn thirty-five. I was coming home from work, and I could feel it start to happen. I drove straight to my doctor's office, and she fixed me up. I was in the clinic for a day while I stabilized, and I called in sick two days at work." She frowned. "That also helped me keep the whole thing secret. Every once in a while, at home, ol' Arnie would *pop up*, and I'd have to plant his ass again. One of my studio techs kept me up to speed on *decomposition management*. She probably thought I was preparing for the role I was playing."

I grinned at that comment. "Well, in a way, she was right, wasn't she?"

She pursed her lips, frowned a little, then said quietly, "I suppose so."

I looked at her. "So, Syl. What are we looking at here? What do you want me to do with all of this?"

"I've thought about that a lot since I got sick. First, Arnie's remains are in the bag that's in his car. The red one. I would appreciate it if you'd give his raggedy cheating ass a decent burial. My first impulse was to drop him off at Lizzie Totts's house, but she probably wouldn't even remember him, so that'd be pointless." She paused, coughed twice, then joked, "Wait. Here's an idea. Grind him up and drop him off at her place. Some of her friends would probably smoke him."

"There's that." I laughed, squinted a bit, and looked at her. "Gee, Syl, good thing you're not bitter or anything." I had varying thoughts about Lizzie. Having met her, I thought of her as something of a victim of her own fame and the system that *made* her.

Sylvia laughed and coughed at the same time. "Hey, what choice do I have? I have to work with the material I'm given. My options of late are limited."

Alma walked onto the patio, pushing a rolling tray. "Here's your soup, Sylvia. Mr. Street, I fixed you a tray as well. I know you like that cheese we brought from Las Vegas."

"Thank you, Alma." I took the plate stacked with square, thin onion-flavored crackers and a small pile of sliced smoked cheese, paired with a bottle of Sam Adams beer. The woman could read my mind.

As Sylvia slowly downed her soup, I stood and took a short walk, taking my bottle of Sam Adams with me. In the garage, I lifted the cover from the side of the Shelby Mustang and looked inside. Sure enough, perched on the passenger side floor of the car was a lengthy, black plastic Hefty trash bag stuffed with maybe fifty pounds of dried skeletal remains. One of Arnie Lankershim's femurs poked through the hole at the top end of the bags. From the shape of the ball at the end of that bone, it looked as though he would've had arthritis in a few years. No, I didn't care.

My mind was primarily busy considering my options. According to California licensing statutes, I was required to promptly report my knowledge of any and all crime/s of which I had just been made aware. An awkward disposal of Arnie Lankershim's remains, such as they were, might be a separate legal issue. The fewer people knew about either situation, the better. I stood and looked at the car, magnificent despite its cargo, and wondered what I'd do next.

Back on the patio, Sylvia was reclining in her chair as I returned to my seat. Her soup bowl was about half-full and had gone cold. I sipped some more beer and ate a few stacks of cheese and crackers. Soon she stirred and smiled at me.

"So, Street, where were we?"

"We were talking about the skeleton in the Shelby and the issues it creates. Tell me, Syl, what is your prognosis?"

In a tone just above a whisper, she said, "The doctor just left an hour ago. They tell me that this, today, is the best I'm ever going to be. I'm a couple of weeks at the most from going into a coma, and from there, it's lights out. I have a great Hollywood funeral planned and a nice plot at Forest Lawn on the other side of the hill. Wanna be a pallbearer?"

"I'll give it some thought. I can't tell you how sorry I am that you're going through this. I know it's tough. How about this. Let me take care of Arnie's remains. Don't concern yourself with that at all. Who's handling the legal matters?"

"I hired your friend Lynn to update the will. There are lots of donations, and the *Old Actors* Home can get their walls painted or something. There's plenty to go around."

"Sounds good." I reached for the digital recorder and turned it off. "I'll see what I can do about this information, too. I have legal and licensing restrictions that I have to deal with, but I will make certain that it won't affect you." I could tell that she was tired, so as I ate the last of the cheese and finished the bottle of Sam, I decided to leave. "You need anything at all, call me."

She struggled to her feet, and we hugged. Sadly, I could feel her skeleton through her robe. She was down to about eighty pounds by that point. "I'll take the bag with me as I leave."

At whisper level, I heard her say, "Thank you, buddy."

———

One evening the next week, I drove to Marina Del Rey and borrowed a friend's powerboat, a veteran TV prop that had once seen duty on the original *Miami Vice* back in the '80s. I took it out on the ocean a few miles, powered down for a few minutes, and dropped the bag of bones into the water. The ocean was still at that point, maybe out of reverence for the moment, maybe not.

Sylvia lapsed into a coma three days after our meeting at her home while I was still trying to fathom a resolution to the situation that she had provided me. She had confessed to the murder of Arnie Lankershim over five years prior, and as a licensed private investigator in California, it was my responsibility to share the knowledge of that confession with law enforcement. Failure to do so, if discovered, would result in the cancelation of my license. Fair enough.

Over the next week, as I dealt with other clients' business, I gathered my thoughts, combined them with the legalities to which I was to be held, and formulated a statement that I sent to one of my contacts at the LAPD. Another week passed before I got a call from Lt. Jeff Ramsey, a homicide detective with the Wilshire Division and a sometime opponent across a pool table at a cop bar that I visited occasionally. He was curious.

He opened with, "Hey, Street. How's tricks?"

"Hangin' in, J-man. What's up?"

"Well, you tell me. I'm looking at this crime report that you sent in. Interesting material. Jersey. I'm just wondering what the hell I'm supposed to do with it."

"Well, Jeff, that's up to you. I know it was an open case and an old one, at that. Once I learned who did what to whom, I knew it was on me to make it known to the proper authorities. That's you. I did so. You're welcome."

He didn't say anything for about thirty seconds. "Yeah. Tell ya what, Street. I'm gonna have to give this some thought. Celebrity perp, prominent victim...where's the body? What's the evidence that this is legit?"

"Jeff, all I know is what I was told. Sylvia Tate was a client who had become a friend. This was a deathbed confession. There's no telling where the corpse is. That's all I have for you, and I know it's not much for you to work with. Do with it as you wish, but I'd ask that it not be treated as a headline. She was a nice lady, and her family put her through a lot in recent years."

"Yeah, I remember that thing in Georgia that you were involved in." Another short pause. "Okay, Street, tell ya what. For now, as far as I'm concerned, it's a cold case that is closed with your kind assistance and generosity. If there are questions upline, we know where you're at. Will that work?"

"Sure thing, Jeffrey. Stay in touch."

"You too."

EPILOGUE

Sylvia Tate's funeral was a quiet, dignified affair, held at the chapel at the Forest Lawn Cemetery in Burbank. A friend of hers, a retired Baptist pastor from Orange County with whom she had consulted for a role in a TV movie years before, performed the funeral. He spoke of her generosity and kind spirit. He told of her sharing her home with his family when theirs was damaged years before by a coastal wildfire. One of her younger co-stars spoke eloquently of her talent for patiently working through multiple takes of lengthy, poignant scenes with less-skilled actors, then defending them to demanding directors while *smiling*. "That *never* happens!" The actors in attendance laughed at that. The directors probably didn't.

The sincerity of the assembled friends, coworkers, and acquaintances was a bit of a surprise to me. Many of the people I was introduced to were *the elite*, either her fellow actors or in the TV production industry, and I would hear from a couple of them for professional reasons within the next two years. Hey, it's Hollywood. It's all about *who you know*.

One day in the next week, I got a call from Alma, Syl's friend and assistant, asking that I come to the LA house. It had sold within hours of being listed for sale, and she was starting the cleanout process. Most of the furnishings had been sold to one of the celebrity home decorators in the San Fernando Valley, and that firm's truck filled the driveway as I arrived. Alma smiled as I drove up, and she walked to the car as I exited.

"Hey, Mr. Street, thank you for coming up. Sylvia left something for you. I have it in the house if you'll follow me."

Workers passed us as they brought an elaborately carved wooden dresser down the steps from the bedroom.

In the living room, Alma offered me a seat and passed a glossy white stationery-sized box. "Syl was really fond of you, Mr. Street. She told me once that she wished she'd met you earlier, under different circumstances, and that you made her happy. She understood what you had done on her behalf. The note explains it all."

I opened the box and looked inside it as I withdrew and opened the accompanying envelope. *The Fugitive* DVD box set that I had loaned her was inside the box, with a handwritten letter on her personal stationery:

Hey, buddy, so the time has come.

Thanks for your patience and your work on my behalf. Sorry the family was such a mess. I know Beth would've loved you. Anyway, I saw how you looked at Arnie's old Mustang every time you visited, so I thought maybe you would give it a good home. All the paperwork is included with the signed title.

Wish I could be there to take a ride in it with you, that'd be fun.

Love, Syl

IF YOU LIKED THIS, YOU MAY ALSO ENJOY: WICHITA PAYBACK

WICHITA DETECTIVE BOOK ONE BY PATRICK ANDREWS

1940s Wichita, Kansas

Dwayne Wheeler, a slightly felonious private detective, plies his trade in the city's sub-culture of bookmakers, bootleggers and hookers. When he is hired to solve the murder of a local bookie and dear friend, the case is quickly linked to the arrival of a Kansas City mobster on the scene.

Sensing a takeover of local bookmaking and criminal activity in the works, Dwayne's investigation leads him into the upper echelons of Wichita society and into the arms of corrupt police. And it isn't long before some very powerful people decide it would be advantageous if he turned up face down in the Arkansas River.

Will Dwayne be able to use all his highly developed skills of self-protection to stay alive as he gathers the evidence he desperately needs to solve a murder and prevent K.C. gangsters from invading his beloved city?

Wichita Payback is book one in a historical private eye series that follows Dwayne Wheeler—a tough and hardboiled detective.

AVAILABLE NOW